ROYAL ELITE BOOK TWO

STEEL PRINCESS

ROYAL ELITE
SCHOOL

RINA KENT

To the lost souls,
You are not alone.

AUTHOR NOTE

Hello reader friend,

If you haven't read my books before, you might not know this, but I write darker stories that can be upsetting and disturbing. My books and main characters aren't for the faint of heart.

Steel Princess is a dark high school bully romance, mature new adult, and contains dubious situations that some readers might find offensive.
If you're looking for a hero, Aiden is NOT it. If you, however, have been itching for a villain, then by all means, welcome to Aiden King's world

To remain true to the characters, the vocabulary, grammar, and spelling of *Steel Princess* is written in British English.

This book is part of a trilogy and is NOT standalone.

Royal Elite Series:
#0 Cruel King
#1 Deviant King
#2 Steel Princess
#3 Twisted Kingdom
#4 Black Knight
#5 Vicious Prince
#6 Ruthless Empire
#7 Royal Elite Epilogue

Don't forget to Sign up to Rina Kent's Newsletter for news about future releases and an exclusive gift.

The princess isn't supposed to dethrone the king.

Elsa

He said he'll destroy me, and he did.
I might have lost the battle, but the war is far from over.
They say it starts with one move to dethrone the king.
No one mentioned he'll yank me with him on the way down.

Aiden

If Steel's little princess wants a war, then war it is.
There's only one rule: my rules or none at all.
By all means, show me what you got, sweetheart.

PLAYLIST

Let It Burn—Red
Up in Flames—Coldplay
Death and All His Friends—Coldplay
Up with the Birds—Coldplay
Fun—Coldplay & Tove Lo
Heroin—Badflower
Kill Somebody—YUNGBLUD
Anarchist (Unplugged)—YUNGBLUD
Break In—Halestorm
Unstoppable—Red
Hymn for the Missing—Red
If I Break—Red
Gone—Red
Not Alone—Red
Yours Again—Red
Obsession—Joywave
Teeth—5 Seconds of Summer
Youngblood—5 Seconds of Summer
Rush—The Score
The Descent—Bastille
Bury Me Face Down—Grandson
Burning Alive—8 Graves
My Friends—Bohnes
Guns and Roses—Bohnes
Dead—Normandie
I Don't Care—Our Last Night
Hollow—Barns Courtney
You Should See Me in a Crown—Billie Eilish

You can find the playlist on Spotify

ROYAL ELITE BOOK TWO

STEEL PRINCESS

ONE

Aiden

Intuition is interesting.

It's like turbulent energy slamming into a hard object.

Intuition can predict that you'll lose the battle before it starts.

I don't lose battles.

As soon as the coach's usual pep talk ends, I grab my messenger bag and stride out of the locker room without speaking to anyone.

Nash calls my name, but I zone him and everyone else out.

I get lost in my head more often than not, and they know better than to barge between me and my own mind.

Besides, they spent almost two decades with me, they should be used to it by now.

I pull out my phone and dial Elsa.

It's turned off.

Elsa doesn't turn off her phone.

Ever.

She won't admit it, but she's always conscious about not answering if either of her guardians calls her.

I stop outside the locker room and try again.

Still nothing.

I usually put the negative before the positive because the positive fucks you up.

But at the moment, I wish there's an exception to my perception.

I wish there's some positive before the negative.

I wish Elsa's fucking phone isn't turned off.

And I don't even do the wishing thing.

"Yo, King!" Astor crashes into me from behind and wraps an arm around my shoulder.

His uniform is tucked all wrong and there's still some shampoo in his damp hair like he couldn't bother to rinse properly.

He's an anomaly to his last name. If the great earl Astor sees him this way, he'll probably lock him up and teach him manners all over again.

If I weren't so preoccupied, I would've sent him a photo just to watch Astor's reaction.

He's entertaining sometimes.

Despite his appearance, the girls passing us by bat their eyelashes at him. He winks at one and motions for the other to call him.

This school needs to up its standards.

"You look like shit," I deadpan. "And remove your arm before I break it."

"Aaaand there's my mate." He grins at me. "I thought I lost you for a moment there. Now, where was I? Why did I come to your grumpy arse again…?" He snaps his fingers. "Right! Was Jonathan meeting the principal for the Premier League's scouts? Put a word for me, eh?"

"Jonathan was here?"

"*Bah alors,* mate. Everyone in the school knows your father was here, but you don't? What the fuck, seriously?"

Jonathan was in RES.

Elsa's phone is turned off.

I want to chuck it up to coincidence, but there's no such thing as a coincidence.

Coincidence is an excuse weak people use when reality hits them in the face.

It wasn't a coincidence when I met her again.

And it's not a coincidence that she disappeared now.

I told her not to talk to Jonathan. I made it clear that she's to stay the fuck away from him.

The sound of an ambulance cuts through the air.

And it's not an ambulance passing by.

No. It's coming straight for the school's back entrance.

"Ooh," Astor tiptoes to look through the window. "Drama. Let's go watch."

Jonathan came to RES.

Elsa's phone is turned off.

An ambulance is in RES.

The thing about intuition? It's always right.

At least in my case.

"Hey, King." Knight runs towards us, his brows drawn together. "You might want to see this."

"That's what I've been telling him," Astor says. "It's drama and we should always take part in drama —"

"It's Elsa." Knight cuts him off. "She was found drowning in the pool."

TWO

Elsa

Past,

"You can't be mine if you're weak."

The haunting voice becomes a buzz. A long, forgotten buzz.

Water fills my mouth, my nose, and my ears.

"Fight!" The voice shouts on top of me. "Fight, Elsa!"

My limbs flail in the water. My chest constricts with the pent up energy.

I can't breathe.

Please let me breathe.

That familiar dizziness lures me into its clutches. My limbs barely move anymore.

I'm hauled from the water. I gasp for air, choking and spluttering saliva. My heart almost beats out of my chest.

My vision is still blurry even after I blink several times.

The gloomy, cloudy air coats my skin with a sheen of stickiness. My clothes are glued to my body like paste as I shake. My teeth clatter, but them monsters wouldn't leave me alone.

I want to say a name, but if I do, if I say it, I won't only be thrown in the water, I'll also have to be the one who shall not be named.

So I call the other.

The only name I have left.

"Ma—"

I'm thrown into the water again.

I don't even get to take my fill of air this time.

I don't get to fight.

What's the use of fighting if them monsters won't let me fight?

Soon, I'll be like the one who shall not be named.

Soon, Ma will be hugging someone else because she won't be able to hug me.

Them monsters took everything from her and me.

Them monsters killed me. Not once, not even twice, but all the time.

Maybe I should've never come back to life.

If I didn't, them monsters wouldn't have killed me again.

If I didn't, I would've been like the one who shall not be named and the ones who came after him.

That's what happens to those who can't escape monsters, right?

Them monsters take everything they want.

A hand pulls me by the arm, hauling me out of the water. My lips curl into a smile.

He's here for me.

He'll always be here for me.

My limbs and my lungs fail me. I can't even open my mouth and breathe.

I can't do anything except for closing my eyes and drifting.

Present,

My eyes crack open, and the smell of antiseptic assaults my nostrils.

For what seems like forever, I stare at the white ceiling, letting the smell of antiseptic seep all around and inside me.

This must be a hospital.

Why am I in a hospital?

I'm too disoriented to recall what happened before I was admitted here.

Something about —

Could this be...?

I slap a hand over my chest, but I find no bandage.

Okay, so this isn't about the heart surgery.

I probe my brain for answers, but it feels dizzy. Everything is like a giant black puzzle with no pieces to put together.

"Oh, hon. You're awake." Aunt's brittle voice reaches me from the doorway before she appears by my bed.

Her red hair is held in a bun and she's wearing a black trousers-suit. The paleness of her face is more alarming than usual.

"Aunt..." I trail off at the grogginess in my voice and clear my throat. "What happened?"

I try to sit up, and Aunt helps me by adjusting the hospital bed and putting a pillow behind my back. I stare at the needle lodged in my veins and a deep-seated itch starts underneath my skin.

I rip my gaze from it to focus on Aunt.

She sits on the edge of the bed, a frown etching between her brows. "You don't remember?"

"I was going to the car park and then —"

Her parents killed his mother. The only reason Aiden approached that monster is to make her pay for her parents' sin.

I blink a few times at the onslaught of Jonathan King's words.

It's a dream.

It can't be true.

The more I deny it, the harder the memories hit me. They're like the crashing water that swallowed me and suffocated my breathing.

I gasp for breath.

But there's nothing. No air.

I can't breathe.

"One of your classmates found you in the pool. You stopped breathing and the school called an ambulance..."

Aunt continues speaking, but I'm struggling to breathe. Something heavy smashes my ribcage and my lungs.

I curl a fist in the hospital robe and hit my chest over and over.

Hit.

Hit.

Hit.

Breathe.

Breathe, you stupid thing.

"Elsa!" Aunt yells, her voice crackling. "W-what's wrong?"

Hit.

Hit.

Hit.

The stronger I hit, the harder I can't breathe. No air comes in or out. I'm going to suffocate.

Just like in the water, I'm going to stop breathing.

This is the end.

"Elsa!"

Aunt's voice turns shaky and brittle. She tries to grip my wrist, but she can't. Nothing stops me from hitting over and over again.

Steel blood runs in your veins.

You're my masterpiece, Elsa.

My pride.

My legacy.

The room fills with noise. I barely register Uncle's voice. Aunt's cries. The doctors. The nurses.

Someone is talking to me. A blinding light is shoved in front of my pupils.

Hit.

Hit.

Hit.

Get *out*.

Strong hands restrain me, but I can't stop hitting. They strap my hands and the material slashes into my wrists.

They tell me something, but I don't hear it above the buzz in my ears.

It's all over now.

Everything is over.

I scream above all the sounds in the room.

Get out!

Get out of me!

A needle pricks my skin.

Ow.

My hands fall on either side of me and my movements slow down.

My eyes roll to the back of my head.

It's over.

All of it.

Happy now, monster?

THREE

Elsa

When I wake up next, Aunt and Uncle sit by either side of me.

Aunt's eyes are puffy as if she's been crying while she wipes my hand with a soft, damp cloth. It's soothing, lulling even.

I'm tempted to close my eyes and go back to the void I just came from.

It's quiet in there. So quiet that I see nothing, smell nothing, and feel nothing.

Here, antiseptic and detergent surround me from every side.

I hate this smell. It's a reminder of my surgery and how utterly abnormal I am.

I'm about to chase sleep when I notice something on Aunt's hands. The sleeves of her jacket ride up, revealing scratch marks on her wrist.

My frantic gaze bounces to Uncle. He's leaning both elbows on his knees and watching me with furrowed brows and a stiff upper lip.

No.

I didn't.

… right?

The scene is like a flashback from those times I used to have nightmares.

And episodes.

I had an episode in the hospital. I think I hit my aunt again. Those scratch marks are because of me.

I *hurt* her.

"I'm sorry," I whisper, slowly sitting up.

"Honey." Aunt stops wiping my arm and lunges at me in a bear hug. "I'm so glad you're back."

"I'm sorry for hurting you, Aunt. I'm s-so sorry." I sob into her neck. "I didn't mean to. I-I don't know what's wrong with me."

"There's nothing wrong with you, okay?" She pulls back and brushes my hair behind my ears, her expression stern. "You're just stressed. Right, Jaxon?"

"Yes, pumpkin." Uncle inches closer and forces a smile as he takes my hand in his. "You just had a panic attack. The doctor said it looked worse than what it actually was."

"But…" I motion at the scratch marks on Aunt's wrist, lips trembling. "I h-hurt Aunt and…"

"The doctor said I shouldn't have stopped you in the middle of a panic attack." She smiles, stroking my hair like I'm such a good daughter. "So it wasn't your fault, hon."

How can she be so easy-going about this? I hurt her.

I did it before, too.

If Uncle didn't get her out, I don't know what I would've done.

If the doctors didn't inject me with something just now, I could've done much worse than scratches.

Aunt is the only mother figure I've ever known. It can't be normal that I'm hurting her.

"Tell me about what happened at school," Aunt probes and Uncle inches a little closer.

My lips tighten in a line.

That familiar itch starts under my skin.

The reason I had the panic attack is about to grip me again.

The room starts spinning and my free hand fists in the sheets until my knuckles turn white.

Aiden approached me for revenge. He approached me to hurt me.

To *destroy* me as he promised.

It was all a lie.

A game.

I was a pawn on his chessboard since the beginning, and I was too naive to notice it.

No. I did notice.

I was just too stupid to take it seriously.

"Pumpkin." Uncle's voice hardens. "Stay with us."

I shake my head, focusing back on their faces. The haze almost disappears as I take in their worried expressions.

Aunt's face is all flushed as if she's expecting me to hit her again. Uncle's body is angled forward as if to stop me if I do.

I can't put them through the hell that happened earlier again. They abandoned their work to be here. I can't just burden them more than I already am.

Aunt takes my hand in hers. "The surveillance cameras weren't working in the pool area for reparation reasons. Do you remember what happened?"

A full-body shudder zaps through my spine and my limbs stiffen.

I was floating and floating and *floating*.

I couldn't breathe.

All I sucked were gulps of water and more water.

I can still taste the chlorine on my tongue.

It was cold. So *so* cold as I floated in there.

For a moment, I thought it was the end. Because that's how the end feels like, right? It's endless.

And lonely.

And cold.

Hell isn't only scorching fire. That water was my special type of hell.

A cold hell.

Someone pushed me.

I think a hand pushed me straight into the pool.

But I can't be sure if it's true or a work of my imagination. After all, I was out of it from the car park to the pool. I shouldn't have gone to the pool in the first place.

If I lost time on the way to the pool and can't remember the faces I saw, why couldn't my mind play a trick on me? By thinking that I was pushed, my mind can protect itself from believing that I jumped in there of my own volition.

That's… a scary thought.

I have nothing to prove that I was pushed and there's no way I'll worry Aunt and Uncle when I'm not sure myself.

Sniffling, I smile. "I think I tripped."

"What were you even doing near a pool?" Aunt asks. "You avoid them like the plague."

"Blair," Uncle gives her a knowing look.

"What? She wouldn't go near a pool out of her own will." She narrows her eyes. "Did Aiden make you do it?"

My heart squeezes into itself at the mention of his name, but I shake my head.

"He was in practice…" I trail off as a crazy thought barges into my mind.

Was he in practice?

He's the ace striker and can ditch anytime. He could've been at the pool.

My lips tremble.

He couldn't have been the one who pushed me, right?

I inwardly hit myself. I need to stop making him the saint he'll never be.

The facts are: Aiden King is capable of drowning me.

After all, he's the only one at RES who wants to destroy me.

"Stop jumping to conclusions, Blair," Uncle tells Aunt.

"I'm just trying to find out what happened. She wouldn't just go to the pool willingly."

She's right. I wouldn't.

But I found myself in the pool area, anyway. No one took me by the hand and led me there, I went by my own feet.

What the hell was my subconscious trying to tell me at the time?

A knock sounds on the door and the three of us perk up.

"Come in," Uncle says.

I wipe my eyes as a boy dressed in RES's uniform walks into the hospital room. He appears old enough to be a senior, but I've never seen him before.

He's not the forgettable type either.

He's tall with broad shoulders and piercing hazel eyes that appear a bit familiar.

His light hair is cut short, almost like a military cut.

It's as if we've met before, but not quite.

"Oh, Knox." Aunt stands with a bright smile. "Come over."

Knox? Come over?

I throw a questioning glance between them.

"Hon." Aunt's gaze slides from me to the new boy. "Knox is the one who got you out of the pool and called an ambulance. If he didn't do first aid, you might've not been able to breathe."

"I'm glad you're okay." He smiles and his eyes close with the motion.

That's surprisingly charming.

"Oh," I say. "I don't have the appropriate words to thank you."

"You just did." He smiles again. "What a way to start in Royal Elite, right?"

"Start?" I ask.

"I just transferred to RES. Today was my first day."

That explains why I've never seen him before.

The door opens again and my breathing catches in my throat.

Aiden strides inside followed by Kim.

My lips tremble as I take him from head to toe. His uniform appears meticulous—aside from the missing tie, as usual. His inky black hair is tousled and the metal of his eyes appears neutral like he's out for a stroll.

But then again, that's Aiden; Irresistible as a god and dangerous as a monster.

And the sad part is that I knew it all along.

Just because I refused to hear common sense or to look behind the façade doesn't mean I was tricked.

Scratch that. I tricked myself into believing that Aiden can be redeemed.

Devils can't be redeemed.

Devils can only crash and burn.

He said he'll destroy me, and he did.

It's time I destroy him back.

I smile at everyone. "Can I talk to Aiden alone?"

Once I'm done, there won't be anything left of him just like nothing is left of me.

There's always been darkness inside me.

I fought it.

I denied it.

The time has come to embrace it.

After all, it takes a monster to destroy a monster.

FOUR

Aiden

On her way out, Reed's quizzical gaze bounces between me and Elsa like a ping pong ball.

I tune her out.

I tune everyone out except for Elsa.

And the new boy. Elsa's saviour.

Her knight in shining fucking armour.

What's the easiest way to break a knight and crush him to pieces?

Actually, I'll use the hardest way to burn him and watch as he turns to ashes.

He gives Elsa one last sickeningly sweet smile on his way to the door.

My head tilts to the side, studying his body language and searching for a tell—or a weakness.

He's too put together, but I'll find something.

I always do.

When I face Elsa, my left eye twitches.

Elsa is called Frozen for a reason. She's not sociable—at all. Even when people talk to her, her smiles are awkward at best. Inside, she's wishing for them to vanish and stop disturbing her introverted bubble.

But now, she's smiling.

No.

She's not only smiling, but she also has that slight twitch in her nose and dreamy fucking eyes.

The smile she gives me after sex.

Or when she sleeps tangled all around me.

That smile is exclusive to *me*.

Why the fuck is she offering it to the new boy?

I continue staring at his back even after the door closes.

Did I say I'll watch him burn?

Change of plans. That's too lenient.

After schooling my expression, I fall on the chair opposite Elsa's hospital bed.

Her light blonde hair has lost its shining streak and falls on either side of her pale face. It's even paler than the natural complexion of her skin.

The hospital robe appears three sizes too big, giving nothing away.

She still looks edible.

It's not about her physical appearance, it's about her entire aura.

Like a lighthouse in the middle of a dark sea.

A needle punctures her porcelain skin and lodges in her veins. The reddening flesh is like a bloody red rose.

I stare at it longer than needed.

It's almost similar to the hickeys I left around her scar.

Imperfection in little things.

My gaze slides back to hers.

She's watching my hands which are hanging nonchalantly over my knees.

I'm tempted to start shit about the new boy, but that's not for today.

She almost drowned.

She was floating in the pool, and I wasn't there.

The thought that I could've lost her after I've finally had her brings a gloomy feeling.

Like the one I felt when Alicia was gone.

If it weren't for the new boy, Elsa wouldn't be sitting here.

Hmm. Maybe I won't torture the new boy for long before crushing him to pieces.

Elsa's electric blue eyes focus back on my face. Only there's nothing electric about them.

They're dark and dead like the bottom of the ocean.

She's looking at me, but she's not seeing me. It's like she's lost in a world of her own making and no one is allowed inside.

Fuck that.

She doesn't get to hide from me. Not now.

"What happened?" I ask.

"It was cold," she says with a detached tone, her face emotionless. "Do you know how cold it gets when you're drowning? When you're suffocating? When you're gasping for air but all you get is water?"

"No."

She scoffs without humour. "Of course. You don't feel."

"Do you have a purpose behind this?"

She stares at me for a beat. Silent.

I stare back, keeping up with her silence game.

This is one of the methods Jonathan taught me and Lev. Silence can be used to your benefit.

People are usually burdened by long, awkward silence, and would be compelled to fill it or give you the answer you need.

Elsa better not be using that tactic on me because it takes more than the silent treatment to crack me.

I try studying her for a tell, but she remains as blank as a board.

Hmm. Interesting.

Since when did she become unreadable?

When I learnt about the drowning, I called Jonathan. He said he never spoke with Elsa at RES. Besides, the whole thing is supposed to be in my hands. Jonathan wouldn't interfere.

However, the intuition I had since practice refuses to disappear.

"Has it been fun all this time?" she finally asks.

"What?"

"The whole deal about destroying me for what my parents did."

My head tilts to the side.

She's not supposed to know that.

Jonathan doesn't lie. If he said he didn't talk to her, then he didn't. Besides, he likes taking his victims by surprise. It's not in his best interest if she learns that piece of information.

"How did you know that?" I keep my voice light.

"I have my ways."

I narrow my eyes at the tone she said it with. She's challenging me, and the beast inside me is clawing to rise up to it.

Easy, boy. Not now.

"I asked you a question," she continues.

"What question?"

"You know, I didn't want to believe it, but it makes complete sense now. After all, you said you'll destroy me upon first meeting. Did you know my background since then?"

Silence.

"You won't answer that? How about this one?" She pauses. "Didn't your mother commit suicide or something? How could my parents kill her from Birmingham?"

Just how much does she know?

How far?

Wait.

Did she get her memories back?

"Are you going to keep your promise?" I ask.

Her brows furrow. "What promise?"

So she doesn't remember. Makes sense. After all, Alicia shouldn't belong in her memories.

"I want to break up." She shakes her head with a bitter laugh. "Actually, no. We were never dating in the first place, so I want to end whatever we have right now."

My left eye twitches, but I remain silent. If I talk, I'll go straight to action. I'll pin her against the bed and fuck that idea out of her head.

But that'll alert her guardians who could or could not be eavesdropping as we speak.

Besides, she needs to rest.

Instead, I force a smile. "Try again, sweetheart."

She crosses those pale arms over her chest.

It's stupid, really.

She should've learnt by now that nothing—absolutely *nothing*—will keep me away from her.

Elsa can wear armour, and I'll stab straight through it. Hell, she can hide behind a fort, and I'll bring the whole fucking thing down.

"If you don't let me go," she deadpans. "I'll tell everyone you pushed me into the pool."

"What's your proof?"

"I don't need one. It's a victim's testimony."

"Hmmm. It'll be your word against mine, sweetheart, and I happen to have the entire football team and the coaches as my alibi."

She lifts a shoulder. "Doesn't matter. The entire school will think I'm not going out with someone I accused of pushing me."

"You think I give a fuck about what everyone thinks?"

"You will." Her emotionless tone grates at my fucking nerves. "Because this time, it'll be a fight to the death, King."

King.

She's calling me *King*.

I told her to call me that when I was on the mission to destroy her, but now it feels like a stab straight to the back.

"You think you can take me, sweetheart?" I stand up and stalk towards her with slow predatory steps.

Pity, she doesn't smell of that coconut shit today. Instead, she's all covered with the hospital smell.

The old Elsa would've watched me with a wild gaze. She

would've had a battle in those electric blue eyes about whether to fight or to save her energy.

Not this Elsa.

She doesn't flinch. She just remains as immovable as a statue.

A cold, frigid statue.

This isn't my Elsa.

And if I have to break the statue to bring her out, then so be it.

She stares up at me with dim eyes. "We're enemies, aren't we?"

"Maybe."

"Then we're over," she says with more strength than needed.

I push a stray blonde strand behind her ear, taking my time to feel the warmth of her skin against mine.

"That's where you're wrong, sweetheart," I murmur near her mouth, "Being enemies doesn't change the fact that you're fucking mine."

FIVE

Elsa

K im interlaces her arm with mine as we walk through the school's hallways.

It's bleak today.

Dim energy comes off the old walls as if they're filled with ghosts.

Even though none of the students throw any bullying remarks our way, it feels like those days where I had to walk through this hall as if I were walking through a war zone.

No.

This time is much worse.

It's stupid, but I would rather take the bullying from before than walk with the dead weight perching on my chest.

Back then, none of them could barge through my icy exterior.

None of them could reach me.

In a way, I was untouchable.

Now, I'm drowning and I can't come up for air.

"Are you sure you don't need to rest?" Kim watches me intently as if I'm thin ice about to break. "School isn't going anywhere."

She, Aunt, and Uncle have been watching me a lot since I was discharged from the hospital yesterday.

Since there was no injury, I was only admitted for twenty-four hours observation.

Aunt, Uncle, and Kim never left my side. Even when I went to the bathroom, either Aunt or Kim accompanied me.

It's normal that they're worried.

But there's more to it. The three of them aren't voicing the suspicions running rampant in their heads.

Since I never go near a pool out of my own accord, they don't buy the whole 'I tripped and fell'.

They probably think that I... what? That I tried to kill myself? That I'm suicidal?

I release a long sigh. Seeing that I'm not even sure about what happened that day, I can't appease their worries without appearing like the lunatic during the hospital episode.

"I'm totally cool." I smile at Kim. "Besides, there's no way I'm leaving you alone."

She side-hugs me. "Do you want to hang out with me and Kir later?"

"Sure."

It's her way to keep me in her sights and not leave me alone with my thoughts.

She's right.

I'm better off when I'm not stuck inside my head.

It's becoming a dark place way too fast.

"Morning, ladies."

Both of us come to a halt at Knox's voice. He stands with a hand in his trouser's pocket and an easy-going smile on his face.

"Oh, hey, Knox."

His eyes skim over me. "Do you feel better?"

I nod. "Again, I have no words to thank you."

"Me, too. Thanks so much." Kim shakes his hand, her eyes shining with tears. "If something happened to her, I don't know what I would've done."

"Kim..."

God. What a mess.

Aunt and Uncle must feel the same as her—if not worse—but they've done their best not to show it.

"I'm happy I was there." He smiles at me again. "You owe me one."

"Anything," I say.

"How about taking me on a tour?" He leans in to whisper. "Not going to lie. I feel a bit lost around here."

"I know the feeling." I laugh, shaking my head. "How about after school? I don't have practice today."

Or more like, Aunt called Coach Nessrine and ordered ever so politely that I take a break.

"See you then." He gives one more smile before he disappears around the corner.

Kim's gaze bounces between me and where Knox disappeared to. "I can take him on the tour."

"Why?" I nudge her with a mischievous grin. "Do you like him?"

"He's hot and all, but not my type of hot."

"Then why do you want to take him on the tour?"

"Uh… Ellie. It's true that Knox saved your life and you should be thankful, but you know that King will flip if he sees you with him, right?"

"Fuck, King."

"Wait. What?" Her eyes almost bulge out of their sockets. "I mean, WHAT?"

"He and I are over. Don't speak his name in front of me again."

"But… but… why?"

"Because I finally woke up and saw him for what he truly is."

A monster.

My blood still boils from the nonchalant way he spoke at the hospital.

He didn't apologise or try to explain.

He didn't tell me that all I heard were lies. He didn't even try to defend himself.

He was just his usual jerk self.

Even if he didn't change, I did.

This time, there's no way in hell I'm letting him step on me.

As soon as Kim and I go into class, I'm assaulted by Ronan and Xander. Cole follows close behind them.

"Ellie," Ronan takes my hand in his. "I couldn't sleep last night thinking about you."

"He was smoking weed," Xander says.

"*Fait chier, connard!* That's because I couldn't sleep." Ronan pushes Xander away before he meets my gaze with a pitiful one. "I didn't even throw a party, *chérie.*"

"Thanks, I guess?" I say.

"Are you okay?" Cole asks.

I smile and say in a loud voice for the entire class to hear. "Things like that can't kill me."

"Party at my place to celebrate Ellie coming back to life!" Ronan announces and many in the class cheer.

"That's not a good idea." Kim smiles awkwardly. "Ellie doesn't like parties."

"I'm in," I tell them.

Everyone, Ronan included, stare at me open-mouthed.

"You'll really show up without extortion?" Ronan eyes me suspiciously. "I was about to rob Knight and Nash's money and give it to you as a bribe."

I smile despite myself. Ronan always has that effect on people. "I'll really show up without extortion."

"I'm robbing Knight and Nash's money and keeping it to myself." He points a finger at me jokingly. "You can't change your mind."

"Be my guest."

"As if I'd let you." Xander glances at him with a challenging gleam.

"Oh, you're on, Knight!"

Arguments break between the two, and Cole tries to meditate

as usual. Half the class—Kim, included—watch in fascination. The other half is already making plans for tonight's party.

I could've declined, but I purposefully didn't.

I'm done running away and hiding.

It's all part of the plan, because the more I see Aiden, the more I'm reminded of his monster nature and the harder I'll hate him.

He shouldn't have let me that close to him because now? Now, I'll take everything I learnt and slam it back in his face.

Aiden doesn't show weakness, but I already caught one.

I had to have my heartbroken to have this bit of information, but I'll make great use of it.

My gaze strays around the classroom. It's useless to search for him. If he were here, that damn awareness would've gripped me by the gut and my eyes would've automatically found his stormy ones.

I flop to a seat and take out my notebook. Knox walks into the classroom with a nonchalant swagger, headphones on.

It's like he couldn't care less whether he's at school or not.

He smiles at me and winks at Kim. She waves back with a huge grin, momentarily distracted from eavesdropping on Ronan and Xander's conversation.

Knox lets the headphones fall around his neck and speaks in a voice that calls for the entire class's attention. "Hey everyone. I'm Knox Van Doren and I'm new here. Looking forward to seeing what Royal Elite is all about."

Everyone gapes at him. He has an easy confidence for a transfer student, and I guess that makes my classmates mesmerised by him.

Everyone except for the three horsemen.

Cole doesn't break eye contact from his history book.

Ronan continues arguing, but it's one-sided. Xander isn't listening to him or even pretending to.

He stares at Knox with contemplation that's rare for him to show.

"I'll show you around," a girl shouts from the back of the class at Knox.

"Sorry, love. I already have my guide." He grins at me again.

Another girl offers to give him her notes.

In no time, he's lost between a few girls.

"I knew he'd be the popular type." Kim sighs while taking her seat. "You think he'll remember that we're the first who talked to him. He doesn't look like the conceited type."

"I'm sure he's not. After all —"

Words die in my throat.

I can't continue talking even if I want to.

My skin prickles with that usual awareness, and I can feel him approaching even before he appears at the class's threshold.

This level of awareness isn't funny anymore.

It's downright irritating.

Aiden strides through the door. As usual, his uniform misses the tie, but he still appears like a magazine model with the tall frame and the tousled hair.

I wish I poured acid on his features when I had the chance.

His expression is casual. Bored even.

As if nothing happened.

As if my world wasn't flipped upside down two days ago.

Aiden doesn't even pretend to focus on anyone else and makes a beeline in my direction.

I ignore him and pull out my notebook.

He stops by my desk, looming in front of me like suffocating smoke. "My place or your place later?"

"Ronan's place," I continue retrieving my history book. "He's throwing a party for me."

He narrows his eyes on Ronan who pretends to whistle before grabbing Xander by the shoulder.

Aiden's gaze slides back to me with a predatory streak. "Careful there, sweetheart. You're starting to push me. I don't have to remind you that I'm not so nice when I push back, do I?"

I lean my elbows on the desk and meet his metal gaze with my hard one. "I don't have to remind you that we're over, do I?"

His left eye twitches, but he remains as immovable as a rock. "Hmmm. Is that so?"

"Yes, King. It's time you accept it."

"Or what?"

"We have to wait and see." I smile. "But I promise that you won't like it."

He reaches a hand for me and it takes everything in me not to flinch back.

Aiden is Aiden no matter how courageous I am or what I think I know about him.

His calm mode is scary.

No. It's terrifying.

I just have to learn how to ignore that fear.

He grips a stray blonde strand between his fingers and takes his sweet time to tuck it behind my ear.

It's never good when he offers this deceptive type of softness.

Bending over, he whispers in dark words to my ear, "By all means, show me what you got sweetheart."

SIX

Elsa

After school, I find Knox in front of the seventh tower. Headphones cover his ears and he types away at his phone. His expression is easy, but he appears lost somewhere out of the physical world.

Heavy metal music thrums louder from his headphones as I approach him. Upon seeing me, he drops the headphones around his neck and smiles. With a click, the music comes to a halt.

"I see you're into metal," I tell him.

"What can I say? Heavy things speak to me."

Interesting.

We walk down the uncovered hall separating the seventh and the eighth tower. "Not sure if you know this, but RES has ten towers. From one to three are for the first year. From four to six are for the second year. Senior year students get the four remaining towers."

"Why?"

"What do you mean?"

"Why do senior year students get four towers?"

I lift a shoulder. "To reflect well on the school since they'll be the ones admitted to colleges."

"You sure it's not because of their rich parents?"

Laughing, I shake my head. "That's exactly the reason. You're going to fit in here just fine if you learn the hierarchy of things."

"Is that important?" He fingers his headphones.

I stop at the threshold of the eighth tower. "What is?"

"Hierarchy. You can switch it up if you don't like it."

I resume walking and he joins me. "It's been this way for centuries. It can't be just switched up."

"You never know until you try." He searches our surroundings. "Where is your friend with the green hair?"

"Ah. Kim. She has to pick up her brother so we can go to a party."

"Did you just say a party?"

I look Knox up and down, and a crazy idea comes to mind.

An idea that might end the ill-fate between me and Aiden once and for all.

I promised him that he'll regret it and I meant it.

The more he tries to smother me, the harder I will fight.

The more he suffocates me, the stronger I'll search for air.

This time, he'll be the one hurt, not me.

"Do you want to come?" I ask Knox.

"To a party?" He grins. "Hell yeah."

"Kim and I will pick you up."

"Can I do that?" He runs his hand through his hair. "I don't like it when someone drives me."

"Sounds good." I laugh.

"What?"

"We're the complete opposite. I don't like driving. I didn't even apply for a licence."

"Why not?"

"It makes me nervous, I guess."

"Well, if you need a ride, I'm here."

"Aww, thanks."

"It's me who should thank you, Elsa." His eyes soften at the corners. "It sucks to be the transfer student, but you're making it easier."

"I'm happy to. You kind of saved my life, remember?"

"You certainly aren't going to let me forget that."

"Hell no. I'm indebted to you for life."

He bends over, grinning. "I'll hold you to that."

We resume walking and I show him the best places to find calm and peace, which aren't much.

I glance up at him. "Can I ask you something?"

"Sure."

"When you found me in the pool, did you notice anything strange? Or anyone?"

He hums. "Not really. I was lost and found myself in the pool area and then I noticed a body floating upside down. Imagine my shock."

"Sorry."

"Don't be. It wasn't your fault." He pauses. "Did you really trip and fall?"

"Yes." *No. I don't know.*

According to my nightmares and my episodes, the hand that pushed me could be a figment of my imagination.

That scenario means I'm hallucinating and have a worse mental state than I thought.

It scares the shit out of me.

I opt to change the subject. "Where did you use to study?"

"In another private school."

"Really? Students in private schools rarely transfer, especially during the senior year."

"We had to move because of my father's work."

That makes sense.

As we step outdoors, I lock gazes with Xander. He narrows his eyes on Knox like he's trying to see past his skull.

Before he can make a move towards us, I tell Knox, "Let's go."

He lets me lead him to the garden.

I have no doubt that Xander will tell Aiden all about this.

Doesn't matter.

Aiden will see the present himself tonight.

"You look hot. Like I'd totally do you, girl." Kim stares me up and down as we stand in front of the mirror in my bedroom. "Why haven't you been dressing up before, again?"

I add another clip to my hair, letting the ponytail fall to my back and straighten.

I wore a sleeveless little black dress that hugs my breasts and waist and falls to a little above my knees. I also put on mascara, lip gloss, and Aunt's Nina Ricci's perfume.

"Are you sure it's a good idea, though?" Kim meets my gaze in the mirror. "You never dressed like this even when you were with King."

My lower lip trembles and I thin my mouth in a line.

With Aiden, I always felt the need to be myself. I loved being myself and how much Aiden liked it.

Or that's what he made me believe. It could be a game like everything he played thus far.

"King doesn't matter," I say.

"Then who does?"

"No one."

She takes my hands in hers, making me face her.

Kim opted for skinny black jeans and a white top that drops off her shoulders. Her hair falls on either side of her face, the green highlights shining under the light.

"Ellie, talk to me. What's going on?"

"I'm changing, Kim. Just like you changed in the summer."

"What's your excuse?"

"My excuse?"

"I had an excuse to change. I was done being an outcast and decided to do something about it. What's yours?"

"I was hurt." I laugh with a bitterness that slices straight through my chest. "My heart was stomped upon, Kim. All this time, I've been a bloody joke. A plot. A game. I feel like if I don't blow off steam, I'll explode."

Her bright green eyes soften. "Is it because of King?"

"You know, people react differently when someone breaks their heart. Some would lick their wounds and run. Others would keep their distance and hide."

"What camp are you?"

"Neither. I choose to fight for my freedom. I owe myself that much, don't you think?"

"You do. I understand that more than anyone." She hugs me from the side. "But be careful. King doesn't lose."

"He will now." I wrap my arm around her. "I promise."

Because I don't have any more chances to lose.

As agreed, Knox picks me and Kim up.

During the ride, he jokes with us about the number of times he got lost in RES in one day.

Kim, who's not big on making conversation with strangers, engages him and laughs at his easy humour.

"So she took the wrong sign?" Kim asks him.

"Imagine this." Knox doesn't take his eyes off the road. "I'm lost between those towers shit and there's no human in sight. Even the cats look at me funny as if they want to exorcise me. Then, I spot a blondie and I run up to her, but she thinks I'm asking her out. She readjusts her glasses in a smart way and tells me, *I'm sorry, Mr Van Doren, but I'm married to math. Thank you for your interest, though. It made me happy even though it doesn't show right now.*"

Kim laughs from the back seat. I wince, pretending to scroll through my phone.

The girl sounds so much like me once upon a time.

"And did you correct her?" Kim asks.

"Nah, I just followed her from afar to find my way back to civilisation." He pauses. "Now that I think about it, that probably hurt my case, didn't it?"

"Oh, man." Kim giggles. "She'll probably tell her friends that she turned you down and you still stalked her."

"Bloody hell."

I smile at his comically shocked expression.

We step into Ronan's house together. After exchanging all types of social media and contact information, Kim and Knox continue joking about his day in RES.

As expected, most of the school's student body is here. Some Spanish music thumps from the speakers, but it's not loud enough to drown out the dozen conversations floating through the air.

Ronan's lounge area smells of alcohol and a mixture of expensive perfumes—but mostly alcohol.

A butler passes us by, wearing a black suit and white gloves.

This is the upper class.

Ronan's father is an earl. He's not only loaded like the upper middle class, Kim, Aiden, and Xander, but he's also a nobility.

I always forget that part because Ronan doesn't act like an aristocrat at all. He's more vulgar and spontaneous than commoners.

Kim perks up and grins at me mischievously. "I'm not driving today."

"Not that it stopped you before."

She stands between me and Knox and interlaces her arms through ours. "You should drink, too."

"Pass." Not only is drinking not good for my heart condition, but I also don't like the taste.

It's bitter and burns. No idea why people like alcohol so much.

"Come on!" Kim urges. "This party is in your honour, remember?"

"I'm sure that's just an excuse Ronan used to throw another party."

The three of us push through the bodies grinding to the music.

"Isn't it Ellie and Kimmy?" Ronan cuts in front of us, a sloppy smile painted on his lips. "You can't be late to your own party, Ellie."

A strong whiff of alcohol and expensive women perfume comes off his Elites jacket. Is that lipstick on his T-shirt?

"And who are you?" Ronan's smile drops like a bad habit as he watches Knox quizzically. Almost in the same way Xander did earlier.

Like he's a threat.

"I'm Knox," he offers with his signature easy smile. Either he doesn't feel the threat or he doesn't care.

I'd be impressed if it's the latter.

"Thanks for having me," Knox says.

"I didn't." Ronan deadpans. "I don't remember inviting you."

"Hey." I elbow Ronan. "I invited him. Isn't this my party? I have the right to invite whoever I like."

Ronan's gaze slides from Knox to me as if he's calculating something, then he murmurs to me, "You're playing with fire, Ellie. You might burn."

I'm already burning.

Aiden has set fire to my life since the first day I walked into RES.

Now I have to do what I should've done back then.

Stop the fire from spreading.

Stop the mortal disease from eating me from the inside.

"Come on, Knox." I pull at his sleeves. "Let's find something to eat."

Kim gives me a discreet nod and takes Ronan in the opposite direction. As soon as they disappear, I let Knox go and motion at the reception table. "You'll find anything you want here."

He goes straight to the scones and scoops two of them before taking a bite.

My gaze strays in the hall even when I don't feel *him* there.

I'm not naive to think that Aiden will let all this slide.

I straighten.

So what if he doesn't?

Why the hell am I acting like I'm doing something wrong? I properly ended whatever we have. It's not my fault that he thinks otherwise.

"Did I land in a weird situation?"

My attention snaps back to Knox. "What?"

"I seem to have made an enemy out of your friends." Still chewing on the scone, he motions behind him without looking. I follow the direction and find Cole and Xander glaring at Knox's back.

Or more like Xander is glaring. Cole just stands there, nonchalantly leaning against the doorframe, ankles crossed.

Both of them wear Elites jackets like Ronan as if they dropped here right after practice.

Neither of them meets my eyes. Instead, their entire attention is on Knox.

Despite Cole's nonchalant expression, they appear kind of intimidating.

I ignore them and face Knox. "They're not my friends."

They're Aiden's friends. When it comes to choosing sides, the knight and rook always protect their king.

The thought of having the three of them turn on me makes my chest hurt more than I like to admit.

"I don't mind making enemies." Knox takes another bite and chews leisurely. "Let me know if you have any trouble with them."

"No, Knox. You don't want to make enemies with the four horsemen in RES. They're kings here."

I'm sounding just like Kim on my first day in RES.

If I ran away at that time, would I still end up like this?

I inwardly shake my head. It's worthless to think about what-ifs when all is said and done.

Besides, Aiden would've found me sooner or later no matter how much I hid or ran.

"It's cool," Knox says.

"What do you mean?"

"I didn't come to this school in search of glory."

"Could've fooled me with this morning's introduction."

"Well, it doesn't hurt to be accepted." He grins. "But seriously, it's fine if I don't. RES is only a stop on my way to Cambridge."

My jaw nearly drops to the floor. "Mine, too."

"You're going to Cambridge?"

I nod several times.

He offers me a scone and takes a bite of his own. "I knew we had things in common."

It feels kind of warm to meet someone who's using RES as much as I am to get to our dream university.

"There you are."

My smile drops and a tremor shoots down my spine and straight to my chest.

No matter how much I try to erase his voice from my memory, it's still engraved deep within like a curse.

I can recognise that slight huskiness at the end and the deep tenor even with the music.

Aiden wraps an arm around my waist from behind and pulls me to his side.

He might as well have wrapped a noose around my throat.

My lower lip trembles with frustration as I stare up at him. Just like in the classroom, he appears calm. Nonchalant, even.

He's wearing dark jeans and a grey T-shirt that brings out the colour of his eyes. Like the other horsemen, he's also wearing Elites royal blue jacket with the Lion-Shield-Crown logo on the pocket.

It's almost like he's making a statement.

No. Not 'almost' like. He's certainly making a statement. Aiden's moves are always calculated to a T.

That doesn't mean he gets to touch me so casually as if nothing happened.

I bite my lower lip to stop the profanities from spilling. Instead, I elbow his side. He doesn't even budge. It's as if he doesn't feel—or if he does, then he doesn't care.

"Van Doren, right?" Aiden smiles and offers his hand. "Aiden King. It's nice to meet you."

What the…?

Is Aiden shaking hands with Knox right now? I think I heard him say that it's nice to meet Knox.

No. He couldn't have figured out my plan.

I meant to throw him off by coming with Knox. Instead, I'm the one thrown completely out of my element.

Knox shakes Aiden's hand with a smile. "Same. It's kind of hard not to hear about you around here."

"Hmm." Aiden's smile doesn't falter, if anything, it widens. "Then you must've heard that Elsa is mine."

My eyes widen. "I'm not —"

"I don't react well to anyone who threatens what's mine." Aiden cuts me off. "If you understand that, welcome to RES."

"I told you that I'm not —" Words die in my throat when Aiden's lips slam to mine.

He grabs my jaw with harsh fingers and squeezes hard. He's trying to make me open my mouth.

I keep my lips in a thin line and claw at his chest with my nails.

It's like he feels nothing. Not even when I scratch his collarbone.

His other hand wraps around my nape, imprisoning me. He brings me flush against his hard chest, crushing my hands and my resistance.

It's his way to tell me that I can't resist him. That, if he wants, he can kill any of my attempts.

I'm like a wave, no matter how high or wild I get, I'll always crush against the unmovable rock at the shore.

Because that rock?

That rock is where waves like me go to die.

When I still don't open, Aiden bites my lower lip so hard, I'm surprised no blood comes out.

A whimper escapes my throat, but I keep my mouth sealed shut.

A part of my body melts, wishing for friction. For something. Anything.

But that part is a fucking idiot.

That part is why I'm in a losing battle against the damn rock.

I attempt pushing him away, but he has me under his perfect control as he ravages my mouth.

The kiss is a punishment as much as it's a claim.

It's a brute force and bruising without an ounce of tenderness.

Not that Aiden does tenderness, but he used to at least deceive me before.

He used to try being gentle.

The mask dropped and he's showing his true colours now.

He's playing the real game.

But it takes two armies to go to battle.

I bite his lip back the hardest I can. A metallic taste explodes on my tongue.

Aiden stops for a moment as if he's taken aback. I seize the chance and shove him away.

Blood oozes on the side of his mouth, and I try not to get caught in the sight.

I made him bleed.

I made Aiden King bleed.

I can still feel the metallic taste on my tongue and stuck between my lips and teeth.

That itch to wash my hands overwhelms me out of nowhere. It takes everything in me not to bolt out of here.

If I do, Aiden would think I'm running away from him and I promised I'd never do that anymore.

He wipes the slight injury with his thumb slowly then stares at it as if it's a wonder.

Or a curse.

"You and I are over, King," I announce loud enough for everyone in our surroundings to hear. "Stop being a clingy, annoying ex."

A few gasps erupt around us.

While he's still watching the blood on his thumb, I hit my shoulder against his and walk out with my head held high.

SEVEN

Elsa

Kim and Knox find me outside running down the street from Ronan's house. They decide to call it a night, too.

I'm thankful Kim doesn't ask questions and just stays by my side in the back seat as Knox drives us home.

Once I'm in front of my house, Kim switches places to the passenger seat and rolls the window down. "Are you sure you don't want me to stay the night? We can watch some cheesy rom-com?"

"Kir needs you more than me."

She winces, then smothers it with a smile. "Text me?"

"You bet." I bend to meet Knox's gaze. "Thanks for everything, Knox, and I'm sorry."

"You did nothing wrong." He winks and the car revs to life.

I stand at the threshold, crossing the coat over my chest until Knox's Range Rover disappears down the road.

"I'm back," I say to no one as I step into the door.

The house is empty and… cold.

As usual when Aunt and Uncle aren't here.

Maybe I should've been selfish and asked Kim to stay the night.

For some reason, I don't want to be alone tonight.

Once in my room, I remove my coat and throw it on the desk's chair, open the balcony, then drop on my bed headfirst.

Since I left the party, there's been this crushing weight on my chest. It's suffocating my air and making me feel claustrophobic in my own skin.

I won tonight.

Not only did I stop Aiden, but I also humiliated him in front of the entire school like no one did before.

He's the king after all. No one would dare to look him in the eye for more than five seconds, let alone disrespect him while the entire student body is in earshot.

But I did.

I *won.*

Then how come I feel no sense of victory? If anything, it's a bit emptier inside.

Rolling on my back, I stare through the balcony at the rain.

It's barely a drizzle, but I feel it in my bones. The scent of the earth after rain fills my nostrils and a sigh rips from me.

I pull my phone and type in Google's search bar, *Alicia King's death.*

Several articles come by. All of them state that Alicia died in a car accident. Her crashed car was found at the bottom of a cliff. The coroner's report says that it took her several hours to die. Since the place is desolate and it was raining that day, it took people some time to find her.

I swallow, my fingers hovering on the screen of the phone.

How did she feel during those hours as she slowly and painfully died in her car?

It hurts to even imagine it.

Some reporters speculate that she had suicidal tendencies and King Enterprises is just camouflaging it as an accident.

They also speculate that James King, Jonathan's eldest brother and Levi's father, who was reported to have died from an accident four years ago, actually died from an overdose.

If that's true, then Jonathan does a lot of media play to make his family appear so mighty and without weaknesses.

I flip back to Alicia's articles and stare at her pictures. She was petite with dark brown hair and pitch-black eyes. Even her features are so tiny, they're distinguishable.

She's like those maidens in period films. Sophisticated, elegant, and with a mysterious smile.

"What exactly happened to you, Alicia?" I whisper to her image. "How did you end up with a man like Jonathan?"

Except for the small beauty mole at the side of her right eye, Aiden looks nothing like her. He's definitely a carbon copy of his father.

Even after seeing her images, it brings nothing to memory.

My eyes skim over the article, and I pause. The date of Alicia's accident was one day before the fire that took my parents' lives.

No.

It must be a coincidence.

Alicia died in London. We were in Birmingham.

There's no way my parents killed her as Jonathan told Silver.

I type my mother and my father's names in the search bar, John Steel and Abigail Steel.

No photos or articles come out. Even the article I read a few weeks ago about the domestic fire has completely disappeared.

That's… weird.

Well, my parents weren't as important as Alicia King or James King.

I scroll through my phone's gallery and find a picture I took of an old polaroid of Mum and Aunt.

The fire destroyed everything I had of my parents. This old picture is the only thing I have left of her. I stole the shot from Aunt a few years ago.

Aunt doesn't like to talk about my parents or anything in the past, basically. She always says that I'm better off saving my energy for my future.

In the picture, Aunt Blair grins wide at the camera, her arm surrounding Mum's shoulder. Mum has a small smile that barely reaches her eyes.

Even though Aunt is the eldest, she was wearing fashionable denim shorts and a tank top. Mum, on the other hand, wore a straight knee-length dress and her golden hair was pulled into a conservative bun.

They were about my age at the time the picture was taken, or maybe a year older, but Mum appeared like she was thirty.

It's uncanny how much I resemble her. The eye colour. The shade of hair colour. And even the facial form. It's like I'm staring at myself from a different time.

"What happened, Ma?" My voice is brittle. "I wish you were here to tell me."

I hug the phone to my chest and close my eyes, fighting the tears trying to escape.

I must've fallen asleep because when I open my eyes next, the soft lamp I always keep on is off.

Disoriented, I search around me and freeze.

My hands.

A rope surrounds both my hands and is tied to the bedpost. I'm lying on my back with my hands stretching above my head on the bed.

And they're tied.

What in the…?

I pull at the ropes, but they don't loosen. If anything, they tighten around my wrists until it's painful.

Before I can clearly focus on that, something else cuts into the black.

A shadow looms over me.

A dark, familiar shadow.

For a second, I'm too stunned to react. A thousand shivers break over my skin and terror explodes in my spine.

Is this… another nightmare? Are the monsters finally coming for me?

I scream.

A strong hand wraps around my mouth, suffocating the shriek and my breathing.

Goosebumps form over goosebumps as I stare up with wide eyes.

"You fucked up, sweetheart," a cruel voice whispers near the hand blocking my mouth.

A-Aiden?

I take a long breath through my nose. The male shower gel and his unique scent underneath assaults me.

It is Aiden.

His arm is taut as his free hand slams on the side of my face. His knees straddle my thighs.

He tied me.

Why the hell would he tie me? He never did that before.

Is this another sick game?

Game or not, he won't get his way anymore.

Renowned energy pushes through my haze. I pull at the ropes and buck off the bed.

He tightens his knees against my thighs, pinning me down. I wince, but I don't stop.

I pull at the ropes and try to get my knee up to hit him in the balls.

He leaves no moving space as if he knew what I was planning.

I scream again, but like the first time, it's muted by his hand like I'm a victim in a horror film.

I'm *not* a victim.

I won't let Aiden reduce me to a victim.

Adrenaline shoots through my veins, tightening my muscles.

Pulling at the ropes only tightens them around my wrists. I release a muffled groan as I attempt bucking off the bed again.

"Stop," he grunts. "Or I will make you."

"Fuck you!" I yell but it comes out like a madwoman's muffled screaming.

Still blocking my mouth, he wraps his other hand around my neck. His thumb latches on my pulse point as all his fingers squeeze.

My lungs burn, and I stop moving.

Oh. God.

I can't breathe.

I can't fucking breathe.

"You know…" His hot breaths tickle my cheek as he speaks in a dark, chilling tone. "If it were anyone else, I would've finished you. Is that what you want, Elsa? Hmm?"

I try to squirm free with the remaining energy I have left.

He tsks and squeezes harder, stopping all my movements. "What did I say about acting smarter? Are you choosing to be a pawn?"

"Uh… ungh…" Unintelligible sounds escape my throat as my energy fades away.

"I can still destroy you." He licks the side of my cheek, leaving goosebumps in his wake. "So don't fucking tempt me."

The shadows cast an eerie cloak on his face. He's like an unmovable stone. Nothing will stop him.

No one.

The fear I ignored all this time crashes into me. I'm like that wave hitting the rock and dying a slow, excruciating death.

How could I ignore this side of Aiden?

He'll break me. If he chooses to, he'll crush me and watch as I disintegrate into pieces.

I thought of him as a cliff before, and cliffs are unmovable.

Cliffs are where people go to die.

Tears fill my eyes as I stare at his shadowed face with no breath coming in and out of my lungs. I'm so lightheaded that I think I'll faint, but I swallow my tears.

I promised myself that he won't see me cry again.

Not now.

Not ever.

Aiden removes his hand from around my neck, easing the pressure. But he doesn't release my mouth.

I suck in greedy breaths through my nose, and it comes in like wheezes as if I'm breathing from another place.

"You dolled up tonight."

His words are razor-sharp, meant to cut.

I knew his caveman side wouldn't like that and I did it on purpose.

Because the best way to win against Aiden is to play his games. I thought I was above them before, but that only kept me as a pawn that he can use and kill off whichever way he chooses to.

Steel blood runs in my veins. I wasn't born to be trampled on.

My brows furrow. Where did that thought come from?

While I'm lost in my mind, Aiden traces a finger over my breasts and down my belly. He's not teasing. No. His touch is downright sinister.

"What were you trying to prove, sweetheart?"

Obviously, he's not expecting an answer since he keeps his hand firmly locked over my mouth.

It's almost as if he doesn't want to hear my voice.

My nails dig into my palms the lower his hand travels. My lungs burn, and I realise it's because I've been holding my breath.

Without a warning, Aiden yanks my dress up my waist and thrusts a harsh hand between my legs.

I close my thighs together, but he slaps them apart, making me whimper.

"Did you dress up for him, hmm?"

I meet his stare in the dark with my own. He's a shadow and it'd be a lie if I said he doesn't scare me, but there's no way in hell I'm letting him walk all over me.

Strength would never work with him, but I have another weapon.

I slowly nod. Several times. He didn't ask that question to get an answer, but I'm giving it to him, anyway.

Yes, I dressed up for him.

I never dolled up for Aiden, but I dolled up for Knox.

It's a fuck you to Aiden.

He can force me.

He can show me his worst, but he can't control my feelings.

Or at least the feelings I show.

Because deep down, that damned part that got me into this whole freaking mess still yearns for his touch.

For his wild possessiveness.

For his uncontrollable madness.

His fingers tighten around my sex.

I wince, trying my hardest not to fall for the sensation.

Not to fall for his dark deep hole.

Because the thing about Aiden?

He draws you in and before you know it, there's no way out.

Before you know it, you feel like a joke.

Like the pawn that's out of the game.

He yanks down my boy shorts and I cry out against his hand, kicking my feet in a helpless attempt to push him away.

He thrusts a finger inside me, and I close my eyes against the intrusive sensation.

"Hmm, you're not soaking today." He thrusts another finger as if punishing me. "Why aren't you as wet as usual, sweetheart? Do you feel wronged?"

I glare up at him with all the maliciousness I have inside.

"I told you," he whispers in a chilling tone. "You wronged me first."

He works his thumb on my clit, and a needy sound claws its way out.

"Maybe I need to remind you who you belong to, huh? You look like you need a reminder."

He scissors his fingers inside me and flicks my clit over and over. And *over*.

My eyes roll to the back of my head. My back arches against the bed, causing the ropes to dig deeper into my wrists.

I want to run, hide, and never return.

But my body doesn't recognise the need for survival.

It doesn't even try to see the danger Aiden represents. It's still enchanted to his touch, to the way he knows all the buttons to push in my body. To the way he works me up like I'm a marionette.

Because that's all that I've ever been to him.

While I was falling and being an idiot, he was playing me like a marionette.

A pawn on his board.

A little insignificant pawn.

He thrusts his fingers inside me harder and faster. The brutality and my chaotic feelings draw a sob from my throat.

It's like he's punishing me. He's making me fall to his will by using my body.

And I do fall.

It doesn't even take long for the wave to hit me.

My lower abdomen contracts. My back pushes off the bed, only to be pulled down by the ropes.

My nails dig into my palms so hard that I'm sure I'll draw blood.

I come with a sob, my chest heaving like I'm about to have a heart attack.

I don't even notice when he removes his hand from my mouth.

"That's it," he murmurs near the corner of my lips. "Break for me, sweetheart."

I do.

I just do.

Tears fall on my cheeks and my heart aches so much that I can't breathe or speak.

Aiden leans over and like that first day at senior year, he flicks his tongue on my cheek and licks my tears.

He takes his sweet time tasting them before he licks my bottom lip and bites it into his mouth.

"Good girl."

EIGHT

Aiden

I knock the white queen with the black king.

Hmm.

It feels good to knock down queens.

I lift her up, let her stand proudly in the middle of the board, then I knock her down again.

It doesn't feel as good as the first time.

This is how addicts feel. It's almost impossible to recreate the first high, but they keep chasing it anyway.

I should've known better than to run after an imaginary high.

The light goes on in the lounge area, and I blink.

Jonathan stops at the entrance. He's wearing black trousers and a button-down. A mug of coffee hangs from his hand. He's probably pulling an all-nighter. I'm surprised he didn't stay at his company's office.

His eyes narrow on me.

He doesn't like it when I stay in the dark. Usually, I'd avoid triggering his red alarms.

But I don't give a fuck today.

I just left Elsa in her bed after I wrenched an orgasm out of her.

I unbound her hands and left without fucking some sense into her.

Not because I wanted to stop. Fuck no. But because I knew I would freak her out more than I already did.

I would push her to the road of no return.

She was right there, bound, and spread for me. She glanced up at me with tears, anger and fear in her eyes, and it took all my self-restraint to leave.

Because at that moment? I was tempted to make her cry more.

Hurt more.

Break more.

I tell myself that I don't really want to hurt her. That, deep down, Elsa is special.

But the harder she engraves herself under my skin, the more persistent I become about ruining her.

Since I left her room, I've been 'blowing off steam'—Jonathan's words, not mine—by working out and playing chess. I had to stop myself from climbing back into her room and showing her the true blackness inside me.

She thinks she knows.

She thinks she has an idea of who I am.

Truth is, she's so fucking clueless I'd pity her if I knew how to pity people.

Elsa Steel won't truly see me until the truth hits her in the face.

"Do you want to play?" Jonathan motions at the board.

It's four in the morning.

Jonathan tries to blame his lack of sleep on being a workaholic.

Lifting a shoulder, I rearrange the board so the black glass pieces are in front of me. Jonathan always plays in white because he's a control freak who likes to make the first move.

He pushes his first pawn forward. "Why aren't you asleep?"

"I've been thinking about Alicia," I say with fake care.

"Cut it, Aiden." He pinches the bridge of his nose.

"Cut what?"

"You haven't been thinking about Alicia."

"I was trying to remember what Alicia looked like. She's becoming a blur."

"That's because she's been dead for a decade." He pushes another pawn forward.

He lives by the belief that a king can't rule without sacrificing a few pawns—or all of them.

I watch him closely. He's speaking about his dead wife, but he shows no emotions whatsoever.

Not that he does most days.

I don't remember the last time I saw Jonathan smile. The showtime laughs for business don't count.

He doesn't show emotions either. Not even when he talks about Alicia.

It's like she's an inconvenience.

A nothingness.

But would he have started all of this if he really didn't care?

I tilt my head to the side. It's still impossible to figure out his exact angle.

The challenge of going against Jonathan used to excite me.

Now, it's a nuisance.

Now, it's dangerous.

"Where were you tonight?" he asks with a low tenor.

I push my knight forward. "Out."

"With Elsa?"

My left eye twitches at the sound of her name out of his mouth, but I quickly school my expression. "Not exactly."

"I don't care what you do with her as long as you keep your eyes on the endgame."

"Yes, Sir," I say with boredom.

"Silver mentioned that you're getting a little too cosy?"

"Queens mentions a lot of shit." I stare at him with eyes so similar to his, it's kind of creepy. "Do you want me to remind you that your little chat with her the other day when Elsa was within hearing distance is ruining my plan?"

He knocks my knight and raises an eyebrow. "You mean *our* plan?"

"It's ruining every plan. She won't trust me anymore."

"If anyone can convince her, then it's you." He holds the queen piece between his index and middle finger. "You did it the first time, no?"

"Elsa isn't a simple pawn."

"A pawn is a pawn." Using the queen, he knocks my bishop down and threatens both my rook and king. "If you can't handle it, I will."

On the outside, I'm half-leaning against my palm, appearing bored. On the inside, a fire erupts out of nowhere.

It takes everything not to let the flames climb to the surface and ruin fucking everything.

Jonathan didn't push Elsa into the pool. I know because he doesn't want her dead.

Not yet.

According to the car park's surveillance camera, Queens left without going back to the school that day, so she's out, too.

Not that she'd do something so stupid.

My chat with the janitor produced shit.

He only saw a girl go into the pool area; Elsa. Which leaves the whole incident with two possible theories.

A- The culprit was already waiting for her by the pool.

B- She fell on her own.

I hope to fuck it's not the second one.

"You gave me your word to let me handle it," I tell Jonathan with a neutral tone.

He's big on his words, and I hit him where he doesn't want to be criticised.

"Only if I see results. If not, it'll be my way." He pulls his queen again and this time, he corners me with no way out. "You're distracted, King. Checkmate."

Fuck.

"I don't give second chances." He stands up and glares down at me. "Try to sleep."

The moment he disappears down the hall, I knock all the chess pieces on the board.

My way or Jonathan's way.

Elsa is well and truly fucked now.

Being mine isn't a choice or a push and pull game anymore.

It's her only hope of survival.

NINE

Elsa

"Are you sure about this?"

I suck in a breath through my teeth and release it out of my nose.

No. I'm not sure.

Truth is, I feel like hiding in a corner and never coming out.

But this is the only way to dig into my past and find anything of value. The only chance I have to find myself.

And hopefully, escape Aiden.

Maybe if I know what happened, I'll hate him enough to stop reacting to him the way I do.

The memories from last night still haunt me. They still move underneath my skin like a living being.

How could I orgasm that hard? How could I react to his brutality the way I did?

Am I becoming sick like him or was it in me the entire time and he's just awakening it?

Nope.

I didn't come here to think about Aiden.

I meet Dr Khan's gaze from my position, lying on the recliner chair, and force out a smile. "Yes. Please help me."

He smiles, but there's no warmth behind it. If anything, Dr Khan seems more unsure about this than I am.

"I need you to close your eyes and relax."

Crossing my hands on my stomach, I try to get comfy on the leather recliner chair.

"Inhale through your nose. Hold it. Then exhale through your mouth."

I do as he says.

In.

Out.

We spent what seems like minutes in an inhale-exhale exercise.

"Try to imagine that you're going down a staircase," he says with a soothing tone.

"A staircase?"

"Yes. Every step down is like leaving your consciousness to reach your subconscious. Can you imagine a staircase?"

"I think?" My brows furrow as I try to concentrate on the image.

"Relax, Elsa." Dr Khan's voice comes from opposite me. "It'll never work if you're tense. How about you take deep breaths again?"

I can do that.

Inhale.

Exhale.

In.

Out.

The staircase comes into sight. It's black and grim, appearing straight out of medieval times. Mould and something grey covers the walls.

"Am I supposed to see a dark staircase?" A tremor interlaces my voice.

"It's your subconscious," he says. "Don't fight it, embrace it."

I thin my lips into a line to stop them from trembling.

"Now, take a step down."

With a shaky foot, I take one step, but I don't follow with the other foot. I'm scared the old staircase will disappear and I'll end up falling into a dark hole.

"Take another," Dr Khan urges with a calm voice.

I clutch the wall for balance as I follow his instructions.

One at a time.

One black step after the other. It's dark as long as the vision goes. I can't see what's beyond me no matter how much I squint.

I can do this.

I *need* to do this.

"Slowing down and shutting down," Dr Khan's voice comes low as if from another room. It keeps getting distant with every word he says. "Slowing down and shutting down... slowing down and shutting down... Shutting down completely."

Dr Khan's voice disappears.

Or that's what I think? I believe he's speaking to me and asking me things, and I could be answering him, but I don't register that.

I find myself in front of a wooden door that appears straight out of those World War documentaries. I push it with shaky hands.

Strong, white light blinds my eyes.

No. It's not white. It's... red.

I squint, trying to see past it. The atmosphere is like a thick sheen of blood red. Like those red rooms used in photography.

Only it isn't a red room. No.

It's... my home.

My Birmingham home.

I stand in the middle of a vast lounge area with elegant floral wallpaper.

It's so large that I seem like an ant in comparison. The chesterfield sofas and the tall paintings hint at a refined taste.

It's almost like a rich person's taste.

Lion statues are everywhere; beside the sweeping stairs. On the way to the entrance. Near the tall French windows.

Everywhere.

I shudder at the image.

No matter how much I blink, the red doesn't disappear. With careful steps, I approach one of the tall windows from which the red light comes inside.

I freeze in front of it. It smells of something... burning? Flesh burning?

When I glimpse through the window, a large garden with unkempt trees and withering flowers comes into view.

It's also red—if not redder than the inside of the house. Even the sun is projecting red light.

A lake glints in the distance. It's dark and inky. Even the red light doesn't reduce from its pitch-black darkness.

A shudder goes through my spine and I avert my gaze elsewhere.

I don't want to look at that lake.

Across from me, a blonde-haired woman sits on a swing. Her frail pale arms are wrapped around a child who's sitting on her lap as she rocks back and forth. The child is giving me its back and is completely hidden in the woman's lap, so I can't make them out.

The woman, however, is in complete view. She's wearing a white dress that stops under her knees. Her pale skin and white-blonde hair make her appear like an angel.

A heartbreakingly beautiful angel.

She stares in the distance with a vacant expression. It's like she isn't seeing anything at all.

A sob catches in my throat and I block the sound with a hand to my mouth.

Ma.

It's my ma.

I resemble her so much, it's haunting.

"M-ma..." My voice catches no matter how much I want to call her name.

But that's not all of it.

I also want her to call my name back.

My eyes stray to the child sitting on her lap, carefully tucked into her chest.

Her polka-dot dress reaches her knees. Her blonde hair is gathered in neat braids that fall down her back.

My heart beats louder as Ma strokes her hair and says something I can't hear.

Is that... me?

Am I seeing a memory?

I open the window with trembling fingers. My heart beats so fast, it's threatening to cripple me.

Thump.

T-thump.

Thump...

The moment the outside air hits me, I fight the urge to throw up.

The air is asphyxiating with something rotten.

I block my nose with both my hands as I stare at Ma. She doesn't seem bothered by the smell as if she's not detecting it.

How could she not? The rotten air is so potent like a fucking morgue.

Wait.

A morgue?

"Hush little baby don't you cry..."

No.

Ma continues stroking the little child's hair. "Everything is going to be alright."

No. Shut up, Ma.

I block both my ears with my hands.

It's useless.

The sound continues barging through my head like a symphony gone wrong.

The scratching of nails against a chalkboard.

The monsters' slow haunting murmurs.

"Hush little baby... hush little baby..."

Her voice grows in volume and intensity. It's the only thing I hear.

It possesses me and flows under my skin.

I can't even make out my own breathing.

I can't even hear my own heartbeat.

"Hush…"

"Hush…"

"Shut up!" I scream, but no words come out. "Shut up, Ma!"

The little girl raises her head.

I freeze.

Slowly, too slowly, her head turns in my direction. My heartbeat nearly stops when I meet those blue eyes.

The same eyes as mine.

Me.

The girl is me.

I looked like a little monster at that time, too. I was a monster just like them.

Tears run down her cheeks. Black, inky tears.

A chill crawls down my abdomen and straight to my ribcage as she mouths something.

I squint, trying to make out what she's saying.

"Help. Me." She mouths over and over again.

My heart jolts in its cavity, but before I can do anything, a dark figure snatches her from Ma's arms.

Ma shrieks and I shriek, too, when the dark figure throws little Elsa in the lake's water.

The dark, murky water swallows her whole.

"Help me!" The voice screams in my head.

I wake up with a hoarse cry, tears streaming down my cheeks.

For a second, I'm screaming so loud, I can't recognise what's in my surroundings. For a second, I feel like I'm in that water, hauled in its inky depth.

I'm floating. My lungs burn with the need for air, but the hand won't let me be up.

I can't breathe.

My name will be forgotten, too.

It takes me some time for other voices to filter back into my consciousness.

A soothing calming voice.

A familiar non-threatening voice.

I blink twice and Dr Khan's blurry image comes into view.

I swallow past the ball in my throat and my choked breaths.

"I'm not in the lake," I say, searching my surroundings.

"No, you're not." He offers me a glass of water.

I gulp it down in one go letting it soothe my scratchy throat.

However, I'm still searching for the lake.

For the little girl who asked me for help.

Dr Khan sits opposite me, watching me intently the way I imagine a researcher would watch his lab rats. "How do you feel?"

"I don't know," I choke out.

"Do you feel like you got anything out of your subconsciousness?"

"Yes." I meet his gaze through blurry eyes. "I think I'm not normal."

"Not normal how?"

"I'm just abnormal, Dr Khan."

"How did you come to that conclusion?"

"I want to go back again." I bite down the fear and terror clawing at my chest. "I need to know why I'm not normal."

TEN

Elsa

Kim and I walk through the hall as she tells me about her latest Korean soap opera.

I nod along, but I'm not hearing a word she's saying. Since my appointment with Dr Khan yesterday, I've been in this haze of my own making.

Last night, I relived the same memory. When I woke up, I found myself still trapped in the nightmare. It took me a few fake wake-up cycles to come back to the world of the living.

I had to watch that dark figure drowning the child version of me over and over again.

I had to listen to her gurgles and cries for help.

I drowned with her, too.

Black water swallowed me whole and I couldn't scream or come out, no matter how much I tried to.

It was like my own custom hell.

For some reason, I didn't scream when I finally opened my eyes to find myself sweating in my bed.

I didn't wake Aunt and Uncle. I just washed my hands over and over. At that moment, when I looked in the mirror, I contemplated breaking it to pieces.

It took everything in me not to confront Aunt and Uncle and ask them what the hell they're hiding from me.

This is my life. *Mine.* How can they keep me in the dark about it?

I stopped myself because if I raise any red flags with them and they figure out my secret therapy plan with Dr Khan, they'd put an end to it. He's sworn to patient confidentiality, but I'm still seventeen. As my guardians, Aunt and Uncle could—and would—ruin the progress I've been making in my therapy.

Maybe it's because of the endless nightmares, or what I've seen in said nightmares, but today, I'm exhausted, lethargic and... numb.

"It's going to be *so* much fun."

My attention snaps back to Kim. "What?"

"A party at Ronan's."

I groan. "Not again."

"Yes, again! We're totally breaking some records this year."

"I'm in no mood to break any records."

"Ellie?" Kim stops and makes me stop, too. We're standing near our class as she watches me too intently, it's almost creepy. "Are you okay?"

"Huh?"

"You're not, are you?" She asks slowly, appearing on the verge of panicking.

Shit. I forgot that Kim, Aunt, and Uncle have been keeping a close watch on me since the pool incident.

Aunt and Uncle think I don't know, but I heard them talking to the principal on the phone.

Their exact words were: *Please contact us if anything out of the ordinary happens to Elsa at school.*

"I'm okay, Kim, really."

She rubs the side of my arm. "You know I'm here if you need someone to talk to, right?"

I nod once.

One day, I'll tell her everything, but not until I figure it out myself.

It's a blur now.

The images in my subconscious are even more complicated than the nightmares. I feel like I need to gather the pieces one by each bloody one before I can begin to put them back together again.

That's why I'm willing to do the painful sessions with Dr Khan. I don't care if I wake up screaming or crying.

My cowardice left me in the dark for years. It's because of my cowardice that Aiden is in the know and I'm not.

Although indirectly, it's my cowardice that allowed him to lure and trap me.

"Morning, ladies." Knox joins us on the way to class.

"Morning." Kim and I greet back.

"You're so unlucky, Knox," Kim tells him. "You transferred when we have a math test."

"I don't mind. I love math."

I grin. "Me, too."

He lifts a brow. "I bet you can't get a perfect score like me."

"You're on."

"Ugh. You shouldn't challenge her like that." Kim rolls her eyes. "Now her nerdy mode is on."

Knox laughs, the sound easy and contagious. "How about a bet?"

"What do you have in mind?" I ask.

"If you win, I owe you one and vice versa."

I shake his hand. "Deal."

At that exact moment, Cole and Aiden appear down the hall, heading to our class from the opposite direction.

My throat dries and my lungs burn with the lack of air.

I can't breathe properly.

Breathe, you idiot. Breathe.

The uniform glues to his tall frame like a second skin. It's like he was born to wear RES's uniform. The jacket is thrown over his shoulder like he couldn't bother to wear it.

As I watch him, my mind crowds with images from the other night.

The way he tied me up, leaving me helpless at his mercy—or the lack thereof.

His shadowed face in the dark as he wrenched that orgasm out of me.

His touch as he licked my tears.

Those images won't leave me the hell alone.

Aiden stops at the classroom's entrance, forcing Cole to slow down, too.

He spares a fleeting glance at Knox then at his hand shaking mine. Aiden's attention slides back to my face slowly.

Too slowly.

I stop breathing at the crazed look in his metal eyes.

It's like demons possessed him.

It's so reminiscent of the time he used to glare at me from afar like he wants to kill me with his bare hands.

He wants revenge, doesn't he? So, of course, he thought about killing me. He must've been thinking about it for two years.

But why?

I just can't understand why he stayed away for two years and decided to screw me over now.

Is it all a part of a grand plan?

A psychological mindfuck?

Aiden glares at me for a few seconds, but it seems like years and decades.

The air crackles with stifling tension that flows in my blood.

I can fight it all I like, but when he looks at me, everything and everyone disappears.

It's only him and I in the middle of the hallway.

The world surrounding us is merely an accessory to our battlefield.

He glares and I glare back. He's challenging me and I'm pushing his buttons in return.

True, he scared me that night, but he also pulled out a part of me I thought didn't exist.

Yes, he terrified me, but he also pleased me like he never did before.

He made me feel defective for liking it the way I did.

But if he thinks that will break me then he has a long way to go. It takes more than that to bring me to my knees.

Besides, it's his time to burn, not mine.

"Ellie!" Ronan slams into Kim and I from behind, breaking the tension. I release Knox's hand and inwardly shake myself.

"Repeat it."

I cut eye contact with Aiden and meet Ronan's playful stare. "Repeat what?"

He pulls quotation marks. "*Stop acting like an annoying, clingy ex.* Say it again. I need to catch it on camera and show it to King's grandkids."

I smile despite myself and throw a glance at Aiden to gauge his reaction.

The place where he used to stand is empty.

How could he disappear so fast?

Not that I care.

Nope. Not one bit.

Kim and Knox go into class, chatting amongst each other.

I'm left with Ronan punching the air and telling me that it's the quote of the century.

"Be quiet for a second, Astor," Cole cuts off his animated speech.

"Seriously, Captain. Stop killing my vibe."

Cole ignores him and meets my gaze with eyes so icy, they're more chilling than the outside air. "I'll tell you something to think very carefully about."

I swallow and nod. Cole was never threatening. Hell, he was always the one I felt more comfortable around.

The change of attitude is disturbing, to say the least.

"King's silence is worse than his words." He pauses. "You don't want him silent."

"I second that," Ronan says in a semi-serious tone. "If King's silent then it means he's trapped in that fucked up head of his."

My spine jerks upright as if someone tugged on it.

I kind of knew that, but hearing it from Aiden's closest friends makes it an immediate reality.

Ronan and Cole walk with me towards the class. I pause at the entrance and search for Aiden.

He's sitting by the window, staring into the distance, appearing to have cut connection with his immediate environment.

Lost in his own world.

What's on your mind?

Why is no one allowed in there?

"Isn't it Frozen?" An annoying voice smashes through my thoughts.

"Cut it out, Silver," Cole grits out at his bitchy step-sister.

She doesn't even spare him a glance and levels me with a haughty glare. "I heard you almost drowned. Who was your knight in shining armour?"

I meet her with maliciousness of my own. "Was it you?"

"Was I what?"

I narrow my eyes on her. She was talking with Jonathan at the time, so she couldn't have pushed me, but I lost sense of time from the car park to the pool. It could've been minutes. It could've been more. She could've had the perfect time to push me into the pool.

She leans in to whisper, "The whole show at the party was pathetic, by the way. King was never yours to dump."

"Screw you, Silver."

"Oh, I'll be doing more than screwing now that you're out of the picture." She straightens and flips her golden locks of hair over her shoulder. "Thanks but no thanks."

She pushes past Cole and waltzes to her seat like a queen to her throne.

My blood boils and my fists clench on either side of me.

The thought of Silver having Aiden all to herself shouldn't bother me.

After all, I'm the one who pushed him away.

Still, a green monster rears his head out.

It's like a compulsion under my skin.

A prisoner that needs to be set free.

I want to pull Silver by that perfect hair and bash her head to the ground as she kicks and screams—before she finally grows silent.

That's... a scary thought.

A compelling awareness snaps my eyes to the side.

Aiden was watching the window a second ago. Now, his grey clouds bore into me, watching my heating face and my clenching fist.

Then, slowly, too slowly, a smirk tilts his lips.

Oh, fuck.

ELEVEN

Elsa

I should've known better.

I really, *really* should've known better.

My skin prickles as I approach the car park and see them. Aiden and Silver.

She opens the door and slides into his Ferrari. Silver sits in the passenger seat that used to belong to me.

The urge to go in there and smash her face to the metal overwhelms me. I want—no, I *need*—to wipe that smug expression off her face for good.

It's strange how I have all these violent thoughts about Silver when I'm not a violent person.

Aiden wears the usual poker face as he takes the driver's seat. It doesn't take long for the car's engine to rev to life.

Does Silver feel the same excitement I felt at the roar of the engine? Is he taking her hand in his and placing it on his lap?

My feet itch to go after them, open the car's door, and pull Silver out kicking and screaming.

I bite the knife with its blood, but I don't move.

Aiden is doing this on purpose after seeing my reaction to Silver this morning.

He knows she gets under my skin and like the usual arsehole, he's using it in his favour.

It's a mindfuck. A way to pull a reaction out of me.

But he won't get what he wants.

"Ugh. That *bitch*," Kim groans from beside me. "Are you okay?"

"Why wouldn't I be?" I force a smile. "I'm the one who dumped him, remember?"

Even as I say the words, I can't stop the tiny needles from prickling my heart repeatedly.

Death by a thousand needles.

That would be a tragic way to die.

Cole strides inside the car park and stops beside me as Aiden's car squeals out of the school.

He's silent for a moment, watching the Ferrari disappear in the distance with an emotionless face.

"Are you okay?" he asks me.

Why is everyone asking that? I *am* okay.

In fact, I couldn't feel better.

If Aiden is with Silver then he'll leave me the hell alone.

That's exactly what I want.

I don't trust myself to speak, so I nod once.

Cole nods back, "I'm here if you need anything."

I'm about to shake my head when I spot Knox coming out of the school. His headphones are on as he scrolls through his phone.

A vindictive idea comes into mind.

An idea that will probably get me into trouble.

But you know what?

Staying out of trouble did me no good, so I might as well crash into it headfirst.

I smile, meeting Cole's forest-coloured eyes. "Actually, you might. I have a brilliant idea."

"This is a shitty idea," Ronan whines. "*Quel idiot* is behind this?"

"That would be me." I smile.

Ronan, Cole, Kim, and I are at Ronan's mansion in one of his usual parties. I swear he throws them every other day.

Today is different. Instead of drowning in alcohol competitions, Ronan is putting his glory on pause to stay with us peasants.

We stand in the spacious kitchen from where butlers shuffle in and out with drinks and snacks.

Rock music thumps from down the hall where the rest of the students are dancing, drinking, and smoking pot.

Aiden and Silver haven't shown up yet. Actually, unlike the cliché of mean girls, Silver isn't big on parties. She'd usually sit on a sofa like a queen with her minions surrounding her. Even with her passive participation, she manages to attract the party's attention and several of her admirers fall at her feet in worship.

The fact that I haven't spotted her outside means she's with Aiden. They've been together since the ending of school.

I try not to think of what they've been doing all this time.

I'll be doing more than screwing now that you're out of the picture.

Silver's words from earlier assault me.

Nope. Not going there.

"Ellie, *je t'aime.*" Ronan taps the back of his neck. "But I still need my head."

Cole sighs. "Stop being such a pussy, Astor."

The three of us gawk at him. It's the first time I've heard Cole say something like that.

"A pussy?" Ronan scoffs, appearing dramatically offended. "I'll show you what a pussy can do, Captain."

Cole hums as if he doesn't believe him and Ronan elbows his captain in the ribs.

"Let's go, Ellie." Ronan grins, flinging an arm around my shoulder. "I'll be your white knight."

"I don't need that."

He feigns sadness. "Yeah, you kind of got yourself a king."

My lips purse, but I try not to let it get to me.

"Are you sure about this?" Kim asks, her eyes filled with worry.

She's game for partying, drinking, and the whole teenage scene, but she's chicken shit when it comes to plotting.

Leaning in so no one can hear her, she whispers, "You know King isn't the type to be manipulated."

"I'm not manipulating him. I'm giving him back what he deserves."

"True that," Cole offers me a high five that I return.

"Okay, bitches." Ronan pauses. "Aside from Kimmy and Ellie… so that only leaves Nash and Knight. Wait." He searches around as if just realising something. "Where the fuck is the devil X?"

True. I didn't see him for the entire day.

I'm surprised Ronan is just noticing that, though.

"He's on a family trip for his father's work," Kim says with a low tone before she meets my gaze as if she's caught off guard. "What? He lives across the street, remember? Besides, our parents are friends and the little shit Kir wouldn't shut up about him. It's not like I have a choice in any of this."

"How come I don't know about that?" Ronan taps his chest. "This shit is bad for my abandonment issues."

"Do you even check our group chat?" Cole asks.

"Group chat?" Ronan furrows his brows. "Oh, that. *Mais, bien sure.* I totally know about it."

"Right." Cole faces me. "You can go now."

"Thanks for helping out," I tell him and Ronan.

"Hey, anything to get a reaction out of King." Ronan waggles his eyebrows.

"And to teach him a lesson," Cole adds.

"Now, drink." Ronan shoves a tequila shot between my fingers. "Ahh, I love ruining the youth."

With one last deep breath, I chug it in one go. Then another one.

The burning taste brings nausea. I shake my head at the strength of it. Ronan's phone flashes as he takes pictures from the side.

If I could help it, I wouldn't have drank, but it's the only way to make the act believable.

I wave at the guys and leave, weaving through the bodies. Silver's minions, Veronica and Summer laugh at my face as I pass them by.

"Ex whore," Veronica snarls.

I flip her the middle finger and continue on my way. They won't get to me. Not them and not their bitch queen.

But you're doing all of this because she's getting to you.

I shut that small voice up as the night's fresh air hits me. The wind whips my ponytail in front of my face.

I inhale deeply and open the passenger door of Knox's black Range before slipping inside.

"You okay?" he asks.

"Yeah," I smile. "Thanks for being my ride. I had a bit of a drink and Kim doesn't want to leave yet."

"I'm happy to." He shakes his head, suppressing a smile.

"What?"

He motions at my face.

I cradle my cheeks, massaging the skin. "There's something on my face?"

Knox reaches over and plucks a hair from my mouth and tucks it behind my ear. "There."

"Thanks." My head hits the back of the seat as nausea threatens to take me over again. "Sorry. I'm not used to drinking."

"You don't have to apologise to me." He weaves through the streets with an easy-grip on the steering wheel. "You know, you can call me even if you don't need a ride. You're not with King anymore, right?"

"I was never with him."

I groan inwardly at the slight slur at the end of my speech.

Good job in being a mess, Elsa.

"That's... smart."

My attention snaps back to Knox. Was that a smirk in his words or am I imagining things?

It's probably the alcohol.

The taste of nausea lingers at the back of my throat, threatening me with vomit.

It's definitely the alcohol.

Knox and I talk about Cambridge. Like me, his father has great expectations for him.

The more Knox talks about his father, the more it reminds me of Aunt and Uncle.

"Thanks again," I tell him as he stops in front of my house. "You keep showing up for me when I need you since we met."

"I'm happy to be of service, my lady," he says in a Shakespearian tone and even kisses the back of my hand.

I giggle as I stand in front of his car and fake a curtsy. "Night, good sir."

It takes me two tries to tap in the code of our house.

This is totally the last time I drink.

I freeze at the entrance.

Aunt stands there as if she's been waiting for me.

Shit. I need to leave before she smells the alcohol on me.

If I knew she'd be here, I would've never taken the damn shot.

"A-Aunt? Weren't you supposed to work tonight?"

"I can't leave you alone all the time or I'll die from concern." She takes my backpack. "Was that Knox just now?"

"Uh, yeah. He picked me up because Kim couldn't."

Contemplation covers her features. "Does that mean King is no more?"

"Knox and I aren't like that."

"Well, if you have to choose, my vote goes for him."

I study her for a bit. "Why have you never liked Aiden, Aunt?"

She freezes with the backpack in her hand before she forces a smile, and I know, I just know that there's something she's not telling me. "I feel like he's taking you away. You haven't been the same since he came into your life."

She can say that again.

"Wait a minute." She sniffs the air and my breathing stops when she gets closer to inhale me.

"Is that... were you drinking?" She all but shrieks.

"It was only a glass, I promise."

Her eyes blur with unshed tears and I feel as if someone jammed a knife into my heart. I don't like making Aunt upset. What the hell is wrong with me?

"It won't happen again," I offer in a small voice. "I'm not even drunk."

"What if your heart condition relapses? You know how hard we've worked to get you stabilised."

"I-I'm sorry." God. I feel like the most horrible person ever.

Aunt clutches me by the shoulders and pulls me inside to sit me on the sofa. "A few days ago, you were found drowning in a pool. Then you had an episode in the hospital and now you're drinking? This isn't you, Elsie. Tell me what's going on."

I want to know the truth. Tell me the truth, Aunt.

But I can't say that, so I apologise one more time and promise her that it won't happen again.

We eat dinner together and I try to ignore how she watches me as if I'll have an episode any second now.

It's at times like these that I wish Uncle Jaxon was around.

After helping out with the dishes—and Aunt making me drink some soup to chase away the alcohol—I go to my room.

I sit at my desk to work on some homework, but I end up slouching in my seat with a pen in my mouth.

Did the plan work?

Cole or Ronan are supposed to send a picture to Aiden that I ditched the party to go with Knox.

Would that ruin his mood or is he too busy with Silver to care?

Maybe he's fucking her in his indoor pool as he did to me the other time. Maybe he has her spread-eagle as he eats her the way he devoured me.

My hold on the pen turns painful.

How could he move on with Silver when it's barely been two days since we ended it?

Since *I* ended it.

The time frame doesn't matter. I don't have the right to question him anymore.

I groan and run a hand through my hair in frustration. I don't care who he fucks.

Not one bit.

Giving up on homework, I snuggle in bed and pull out my phone.

My heart surges in its cavity at the two texts waiting.

Aiden: Let's play that game you love so much, sweetheart.

Aiden: Be mine again or...

I refresh the page, searching for his next text, but there's nothing.

He always offers two options. Where's the other facet of the coin?

Then it hits me.

He sent those texts after school when he was leaving with Silver.

He wants me to be his again or he'd... what? Fuck Silver?

Is he going to send me a pornographic text of how he fucked her now?

Disgusted, I open Instagram. I unfollowed him the other day, but I search for him anyway.

His last post was after the night he attacked me in the middle of the night.

It's a black and white picture of a chessboard with all the glass pieces scattered. There's no caption and he posted the picture around five in the morning.

I scroll in the comments. There's one from SilverQueens a few hours ago.

Can't wait for 2nite. Xo.

I click on her profile and something in my heart dies.

Since they left together, I knew it was for this, but I kept telling myself that he wouldn't do it.

Not after he promised he'd stay away from Silver.

On the picture Silver posted half an hour ago, there's enough evidence to shut off my delusions.

There's a selfie of Silver sitting at the edge of the pool, still in her uniform's skirt. At first glance, she appears alone, but at the bottom corner of the picture, there's a hand gripping her thigh.

Even if the hand isn't clear, the pool is.

The same pool in which I felt special.

The same pool in which Aiden made me think that I could live past my fears and my traumas.

And now, he tainted it with Silver.

I throw the phone away and hide my face in the pillow as tears barge into my eyes.

I guess it's really over now.

TWELVE

Aiden

I twirl a pawn chess piece between my index and middle finger as I stare out of the locker room's window.

Both the football team and the girls' track team are inside the changing rooms.

Elsa lingers back with their coach. She discreetly keeps herself the last to shower so none of her teammates sees her scar.

She spent her entire life hiding. And for what?

Finding her was never an option. It was always bound to happen.

I waited eight years to find her and if she thinks I'm letting her go now then she really doesn't know me.

And here I thought she was beginning to understand me.

Until Jonathan and Queens screwed up everything.

I continue following her with my gaze even after she disappears inside the building with her coach.

Two years.

I've been watching her for two years, biding my time and waiting for the moment to strike.

I got close—so close—before everything blew up in smoke.

But I'll fix it. I always do.

The battle is still the same. I just need different tactics.

Still clutching the pawn's chess piece, I retrieve my phone and pull up the pictures Astor attached to the group chat a few days ago.

In one picture, Elsa is taking one shot—when she never drinks.

In the second, she's climbing into the new boy's car.

If Nash sent those pictures, I would've had a different theory. Nash becomes a little bitch when it comes to Queens. I knew he wouldn't like me taking off with her, but I ignored his opinion.

However, this is Astor. He's the most neutral person in our group. During parties, he'd be so busy with pussy, alcohol, and weed to plot anything like this.

He even asked me to spare his head when we met for practice the following day.

I scroll through the photos to a shot where the new boy was caressing Elsa's face.

My left eye twitches as I strangle the pawn between my fingers.

He had his hand on her.

He had his fucking hands on what's mine.

I warned him. He didn't listen.

Now, he'll pay.

But first, my gaze zeroes in on Elsa's face. Her easy smile. Her flushed cheeks. Her glistening lips.

My clutch tightens on the phone, I'm surprised it doesn't break to pieces.

I gave her a choice. I gave her the right to make the first move, but I should've known better.

Elsa doesn't work that way.

She acts better when her will is taken and ripped to pieces.

The track team's coach comes out from the building with her pad in hand. I stand up and tuck the phone in my pocket.

"Where to?" Knight asks from in front of his locker.

I don't answer him.

Nash throws a T-shirt over his head and steps in front of me, his damp hair still dripping water down his chest. "We need to talk."

"Not today."

"Party at my house!" Astor calls, abandoning his conversation with the goalkeeper. "It's our off week. Let's party until the morning!"

I meet their gazes and tilt my head to the side. "Get out of my way."

Nash's shoulders tense, but he doesn't move.

I'm a few inches taller so I glare down at him with my best 'Back the fuck off' look. If he wants payback for what happened with Queens, I'll give him that.

Just not today.

Knight claps Nash's shoulder and pulls him back. He's smarter sometimes.

I sidestep them and stride out of the door.

"Later, King!" Astor calls after me. "Try not to commit a crime."

Hmm. Maybe that's exactly what I'll do.

THIRTEEN

Elsa

My head hangs against the wall as the water beats down on me.

I let it rinse me, cleanse me, but it can't reach the itch beneath my skin.

It's slowly but surely ripping me apart.

Yesterday was my second session with Dr Khan. I found myself in the same vision from last time. However, my younger self's screaming was much louder to the point my ears popped.

When I asked Dr Khan why I ended up in the same vision, he said that I could be blocking my subconscious.

The cause is probably stress.

A heavy sigh rips from me as I stare at the white tiles.

I need to get myself together. If I don't, then I'll be trapped as I've been for ten whole years.

Problem is, whenever I close my eyes, all I could think about is Aiden and Silver.

Or more accurately, Aiden fucking Silver.

My temper flares at the thought.

I want to hit something.

Scream at someone.

Because deep down? I'm bleeding.

It doesn't help that Aiden's been ignoring my existence for the past few days. When he walks by me, he doesn't even spare me a glance as if I don't exist.

Since the first day we met, I've always been visible to him. Even from afar, Aiden always had his attention on me. His metallic eyes followed me everywhere.

Being invisible hurts more than I'd like to admit.

Nope. I'm not going there.

This is for the best.

It's the weekend so I'll go home and do some homework. I was supposed to sleepover at Kim's but they're having a family dinner, so my weekend plans changed to me and my empty home.

Yay.

I'm about to shut off the water when a rustle comes from outside the door.

Coach Nessrine is out for the day and asked me to close up after I'm done. Maybe one of the girls forgot something.

I remain in the stall, biding my time until whoever they are leaves.

The handle to the stall's door moves.

I gasp, my eyes widening. "W-Who is it? Tara? Coach?"

No answer.

I gulp, my heartbeat escalating.

The handle doesn't move anymore. It's locked. No one can come in here.

I remain rooted in place for long seconds even when no other sound comes out.

Pounding water is the only thing that cuts through the silence.

Ten seconds pass.

Twenty.

I release a breath. It's nothing after all.

Something jams against the handle and the door flies open, hitting the wall.

I shriek, but a strong hand wraps around my mouth, muffling the sound.

My eyes widen as I stare up into Aiden's dark metallic gaze.

It's bottomless.

It's a void.

Tremors jolt through my limbs and goosebumps cover my skin despite the warm water.

"You can run but you can never escape me, sweetheart."

"Mmm," I mumble against his hand.

That's when I take the rest of him.

He's naked.

The water soaks him in a second. Like an exotic model, his jet black hair sticks to his forehead.

The droplets of water travel down the ridges of his muscled chest and his abs.

His strong thigh barges between mine and that's when I recall that I'm also naked.

My hands fly up, clawing at his arms so he'll release me. Aiden pushes me with ease. My back hits the tiled wall.

I gasp at the violent impact.

It's like that night in my room all over again.

This is the scary side of Aiden. The side that takes without boundaries.

The side that only leaves havoc in his wake.

"Did you mistake my silence for approval, Frozen?" His chilling tone tickles my skin like a dark promise.

If he's calling me Frozen, then I should be scared.

This isn't the Aiden who sometimes tries to restrain himself.

No. This is Aiden at his worst unhinged self.

The bully. The devil.

My spine jerks upright against the cold tiles and my lips tremble under his hand.

"Is it fun to defy me, hmm?" He thrusts his hips forward. An unmistakable erection slides between my legs and against my folds.

I whimper, shaking my head.

He doesn't stop.

I'm starting to think that Aiden doesn't know how to stop.

His chest crushes my breasts as if he can't get close enough or torment me hard enough.

"Being mine isn't a choice," he says in that scarily calm tone. "It's a fucking reality."

He reaches his free hand between us and wraps two fingers around my throbbing nipple. He squeezes so hard, I nearly topple over with pain.

I cry out, but the sound is muffled by his hand.

He presses his fingers harder as if engraving his words into my body.

My body isn't the only thing he's interested in.

He's also trying to reach into my soul and write those words in black, permanent ink.

Tears barge into my eyes, but I swallow them inside.

"You can fight me on anything, but you don't get to fight me on the fact that you're mine." He runs his tongue along the shell of my ear and bites down. "Is that clear?"

A whimper claws its way out, but I gather the strength to glare up at him.

"You think you have a choice, but you don't. Not this time." He meets my glare with his stormy eyes. "I won't stop. Not now. Not fucking ever. Your fate has already been sealed, sweetheart."

Those words draw a shudder from deep inside me. The need to fight pumps through my blood, but his steel hold shackles me in place.

The pad of his forefinger runs up and down my assaulted nipple. It takes all my self-restraint to hold in a moan.

What is he doing to me?

A voice in my head screams at me to run, hide and never return.

Aiden is batshit crazy. And apparently, I'm crazier if I feel this way in his arms.

My reaction to him scares the living bejesus out of me.

I'm not this girl. I won't be a stop in his endless stops.

I try to push him away. He pinches my nipple again. A mixture of a whimper-moan leaves my lips.

Oh. God.

I mumble against his hand and fight.

I fight everything.

The tears.

The overwhelming sensations.

The tightening at the bottom of my stomach.

But most of all, I fight the part inside me that craves surrendering to Aiden's touch.

That's the hardest thing to fight. How can I fight myself and not lose?

How the hell did I let Aiden engrave himself into me this deep?

"If you scream." He licks the water off my ear as he murmurs in a chilling low range, "You won't like what they see when they come to find us."

I gulp against his hand, my heartbeat skyrocketing.

"Be smart, sweetheart. You've been stupid enough this past week."

He slowly removes his hand, but he doesn't step back. If anything, he pushes me further into the wall so my back and arse are glued to the tiles.

I gasp for air, breathing through my nose and then my mouth.

I stare at his punishing dark eyes.

At the cruelty.

At the determination.

At the water forming rivulets down the hard lines of his face.

A wave of sadness and injustice flares through me. Soon, all those emotions turn into boiling rage.

How dare he?

How fucking dare he?

"What part of 'we're over' do you not understand?" I ask with the calmest tone I can manage.

If I scream then I'll start crying and I promised to never show this dickhead my tears again.

He narrows his eyes. "What did I just say about being smart?"

"We're over." I breathe so hard, it's almost like I'm choking on air. "We're fucking *over*, Aiden."

"I never agreed to that."

"*You never agreed to that?*" I repeat, incredulous. "So in your mind, we're still together?"

"We are." He doesn't even miss a beat.

"If we're still together and you took Silver to your pool, do you know what that means?" I hit his chest with a closed fist, feeling my walls cracking. "It means you *cheated* on me. I told you it's over when you cheat on me."

"But you said we aren't together." His infuriating poker face is on. "It's not cheating when you dumped me in front of the entire school."

"Fuck you, Aiden!" I pound both my palms on his chest. "Fuck. You!"

He grabs both my wrists in his strong hand and slams them on the tiles atop my head.

His shoulders strain with tension even as his face remains a calm façade. "Nothing happened with Queens."

"Don't lie to me! I saw —"

His mouth slams to mine, cutting off my outburst.

He sucks my lower lip into his mouth and then plunges his tongue inside, taking claim of mine. His hard muscles mould to my softer curves as he ravages my mouth.

It's one of his animalistic, out-of-control kisses. I can only stand there in full stupefaction as he sucks the life out of me.

A part of me wants to let go.

A part of me wants that pleasure he always wrenches out of my body.

A part of me yearns for the intensity. The freedom of letting go.

But that part is a fucking idiot.

That part forgot that Aiden has a revenge plot against me. That he took Silver to his pool when it should've been our place.

That part needs to be eradicated.

I bite down on his lower lip so hard, a metallic taste explodes on my tongue.

I thought that would stop him. Just like at the party.

I thought wrong.

After all, the same trick doesn't work twice. At least not on someone like Aiden.

If I've taken him by surprise once, he'll make sure it never happens again.

He grinds his hips against mine and continues kissing me savagely. His hand cradles my face to pin me in place as he smears his blood all over my lips and tongue.

He makes me taste him. Taste what I did to him. This time, he doesn't let me go. He makes me feel it over and over again as he twirls his tongue against mine.

The water washes away the blood, but not the lingering taste he leaves behind.

When he pulls away, I forget to breathe as I stare at his cut lower lip. At his rogue, exotic features.

"I never lie to you."

I stare, not sure what he means.

"I don't lie to you, so when I say nothing happened with Queens. It means nothing fucking happened with Queens." He drags his thumb down my lower lip as if he's still kissing me. "But if you continue acting this way, I don't know what I'll do."

My lips tremble. "I told you. If you touch Silver, I swear to God, we're fucking over no matter what you do."

"No matter what I do, huh?" His fingers wrap around my throat as he pushes his hard cock against the bottom of my stomach. "Do you think you'll ever get rid of me?"

"If you touch Silver or anyone else, you better be ready to rape me, then." I deadpan.

The corner of his lip tilts in a cruel smirk. "Are you sure you want to throw that word around when you know I have no boundaries when it comes to you, sweetheart?"

I meet his gaze through blurry eyes. "I'm curious if you'll still want the shell I'll become."

His left eye twitches.

"Do you know what a shell means, Aiden?" My voice raises with confidence. "It means that I'll be your fucktoy. I'll do everything you want without thinking about it. I'll have no thoughts of my own and I'll fade into nothing."

"Shut up."

"I'll be good. I'll be so good to you, Aiden. You'll find no resistance," I taunt. "I'll be yours and you won't even have to remind me of it anymore."

"Shut the fuck up, Elsa." He pulls my hands from the wall and slams them against it again.

"Why?" I breathe harshly. "Isn't that what you want? Isn't that what you've been trying to do since the beginning? Destroy me? So do it. Rape doesn't scare you, right? So do it now and ruin me once and for all."

He watches me intently with his left eye twitching like crazy.

I just hit a button.

Aiden loves the challenge I bring to his life. He said it himself that I break the endless vicious cycle. I figured he'd be pissed off if I threaten to take all the challenge away, but I didn't think it'd hit his buttons this hard.

It takes him longer than usual to strap his reaction behind the infuriating poker face.

His mouth hovers inches away from mine. His intoxicating scent is all I can smell. His harsh breathing mingles with mine, almost muting the water beating down on us.

"Nice try, sweetheart." He tilts his head, a smirk tugging on his lips. "You almost got me there."

Shit. Fuck.

Still, I jut my chin. "You think I'm bluffing?"

"No. But I figured out your angle."

"My angle?"

"You want me to rape you so that you can hate me."

My breathing hitches. Is that what I really wanted?

Nope. He's not dragging me into another one of his mind games.

"But guess what, sweetheart?" He licks the shell of my ear, causing a shiver to crackle down my spine. "When I fuck you, you'll only be screaming in pleasure. With every thrust into your pussy, you'll be chanting my name and begging for more."

My chest heaves causing my throbbing, sensitive nipples to brush against his hard muscles.

It only makes me more aware of him and his presence. It makes me feel him straight to my bones.

He's not right.

He *can't* be right.

I didn't say that because I wanted to hate him. I only said that to piss him off.

How the hell did the tables turn on me?

"You know. You should've never chosen to be a pawn." His fingers leave my throat and trail down to my stomach. He hovers on the path leading to my folds.

I suck in a breath and fruitlessly try to get him off me. He pumps his hips against mine, killing my resistance.

He glides his erection up and down my pussy. I clench my thighs, but he slaps them apart and rubs his thumb on my clit agonisingly slow.

My stomach tightens into itself.

A pleasure so harsh and twisted shoots through my veins no matter how much I try to ward it off.

My nails dig into my palms, but I can't do anything with him pinning me to the wall.

"Aiden... stop," I grit out.

"Why?" He slides his cock up and down my hypersensitive folds.

Up.

Down.

I'm breathing in unison with his moves. I try to tune myself out, but I can't. I just can't stay still when he touches me.

I'm always craving more.

Needing more.

"I hate you, that's why," I pant.

"I think you're lying, sweetheart. I think you don't hate me, but you hate how much you can't hate this." He pushes the tip of his erection at my entrance.

I tense, expecting him to thrust inside, but he goes back to running his cock up and down.

My stomach dips.

And no, it's not because of disappointment.

"Do you feel your walls inviting me? Do you feel how fucking soaked you are for me?"

I shake my head frantically.

"Stop fighting what we have," he growls at my ear. "Stop fighting us."

Aiden increases his tempo. Shivers cover my skin, and it's not because of the water. It's due to the torturous slide of his cock. The way he has me at his mercy—or the lack thereof.

The moment he slaps my clit, I scream.

I don't even know what's come over me. I don't know how in the ever-loving hell he made me come this fast.

The waves roll over me and I scream louder. Then, I recall we're in school, and anyone could hear me. That's supposed to kill the orgasm, but it's the exact opposite.

A different type of wave slams into me. I bite my lower lip to contain the shriek.

Just like that time in my room, I'm about to die with self-mortification. I want to dig a grave and just bury myself alive.

Aiden continues pumping his cock up and down. His muscles turn rigid. I can't help watching as his handsome features contort and he grunts. I feel his cum coating the inside of my thighs, and I close my eyes.

Not out of mortification. No.

It's because the sensation is about to throw me over the edge again.

He releases my hands, letting them fall on either side of me. It takes everything in me not to wrap them around my midsection.

"There," he whispers before biting down on my ear. "Good girl."

"I hate you," I murmur. "I hate you."

"If you say that one more time, I'm going to fuck you in a more public place. I'll make the entire world see how much you hate me while you're bouncing on my cock and screaming my fucking name."

My eyes fly open and I gasp through the sob. I know, I just know that Aiden's threats aren't empty ones.

The crazy psycho would do it.

"Now." He drops a quick kiss on my mouth before he nibbles on my bottom lip with his teeth.

I stop breathing, expecting him to draw blood.

He's not that vindictive, right?

Scratch that. He is.

Shit. I really should've thought of that before drawing his blood. Not once, but twice.

"Are you going to be mine?"

I want to cry.

God. I want to cry and smash his head to the ground at the same time.

For a few seconds, I remain silent, glaring up at him.

He tilts his head to the side, a slight smirk tilting his lips. The cut only makes it appear more monstrous. "The only way to stop me from going near Queens is if you're mine."

Screw him.

Screw the fucking bastard and his mind games.

And screw that bitch queen.

"I ha—" I cut off when I notice the gleaming look in his eyes.

"Go on," he challenges. "Say it."

I clamp my lips shut.

He releases my hands and pulls at my cheek. "See. You can be adorable."

I swat his hand away.

"Hmm. And here I was contemplating telling you what you want to know."

I blink through the water. "What I want to know?"

"The story behind what you heard from Jonathan and Queens' conversation."

My heartbeat escalates. He's willing to tell me that?

Aside from Aunt and Uncle, Aiden is the only one who can shine a light on my past.

He said it before, didn't he? That he knows a lot more than I think I do.

This is my golden opportunity.

Wait.

Aiden is a fucking psycho and he's probably playing a mind game.

"What do I have to do in return?" I ask.

"You're learning." He smiles, and it's more proud rather than sadistic. "You should've done this from the beginning, you know."

"As if you'd tell me."

"I would've. For the right price." He strokes my bottom lip and for some reason, it feels intimate. Too intimate, it's scary.

I step back from his touch. The tenderness in his eyes is creeping me out. What is that supposed to mean? Another mindfuck?

Don't you dare fall for it, Elsa. Don't you fucking dare.

I need to deal with this opportunity logically.

I stare up at him. "What's the price?"

"Not so fast." He grabs me by the waist and pulls me to him as he shuts off the water. "First, you have to pay."

FOURTEEN

Elsa

When Aiden said he'll make me pay, I didn't know what the hell he meant.

I had to fight him off so I could dry myself and wear my clothes.

He sits on the bench, elbows resting on his thighs and fingers interlacing at his chin. He watches me with darkened heat as if I'm putting on an erotic show for him.

Oh, and he's doing that while stark naked.

I couldn't escape his gaze even if I wanted to. It penetrates my skin and flows into my blood.

It takes everything in me not to watch him.

My cheeks heat.

The fact that he watches me as I change my clothes is a different level of intimacy. For Aiden, it seems as if mundane things like buttoning my skirt or my bra is the show of the day.

My gaze falls on my scar, and I step behind a row of the lockers to finish dressing without combusting.

A light chuckle reaches me from the other side before a rustling of clothes follows.

Finally.

It should be a crime that he walks around naked like that.

It isn't until he drags me to the car park that I start thinking about the meaning behind his words in the shower.

No way in hell am I going to let him take me in the car. I barely escaped his caveman clutches in the school—a place full of people. Who knows what he'll do if he takes me somewhere no one can find me?

I come to a screeching halt in front of his Ferrari and yank my arm from his.

He stops, too, and looks between me and his car. "I thought you wanted to know the story."

I fold my arms over my chest. "You can tell me here. I don't have to get into your car."

"Tough shit, sweetheart. You have to get into my car to know the story."

I bite my lower lip and my hands ball into fists. He knows I'm desperate for answers, and he's using it against me in the most brutal way possible.

If I go with him, I don't know what the hell he'll do. But am I ready to throw away my only chance to know about my past?

Even my therapy sessions with Dr Khan will become useless if I keep blocking myself.

"I'm almost sure you don't mean to seduce me." Aiden tilts his head to the side, eyes darkening. "But you are."

I follow his gaze. With my hands folded, my breasts push against my shirt in which there's an undone button. My bra and the line of my breast show through.

"Perv." I turn away from him and button the shirt. "It's because of you that I dressed in a rush."

His grin widens. "Hmm. Do I unsettle you that much, sweetheart?"

Yes, dickhead.

But I don't tell him that and huff instead.

"Get in the car." He points at his Ferrari. "We don't have all day."

An idea comes to mind. I lift my head. "I won't get into the same seat Silver used. Who knows what she left in there?"

"Your jealousy is showing."

"What? No." It was meant as a jab so he'd give up trying to get me into his car. It wasn't meant to show that I care about whoever he let ride in my seat.

"I know you're possessive of me." He steps closer like a predator. "Not as much as I'm possessive of you, but it's close. The only difference is that you're ashamed about showing it."

"Stop putting words into my mouth." I glare at him. "I'm not getting in the car and that's it."

He stares at me for one second.

Two.

Three —

He lifts a shoulder and stalks to the driver's side.

Wait. He's leaving?

Of course, he is.

What did I expect from someone with his level of conniving evil?

I run to the passenger side and flop inside with a groan. I don't need to look up to see his smirk. I feel it in my bones.

Dickhead.

The car revs in the streets and I clench my thighs. I'm still sensitive—and stimulated—from the shower. The engine's vibrations are making it worse.

Or better—depends on how you see it.

"So?" I bite the unease down.

"So what?"

"I'm in the stupid car. What's the story?"

"I told you." He glances in my direction. "You have to pay first."

"Pay for what?"

"Think about it." He grabs my thigh at the small space where my skirt meets my stocking.

I try to push him away, but he only grips me harder.

After a while of futile struggling, I give up and stare out of the window.

I try not to think of his skin on mine. I try not to feel how his fingers draw maddening circles on my inner thighs.

It's impossible.

For the entire ride, he appears nonchalant while driving and teasing me.

Someone is good at multi-tasking.

His fingers draw paths over the sensitive flesh of my inner thigh. I squirm in my seat.

Every time I tell him to stop, he just inches his fingers up under my skirt, teasing the edge of my underwear.

I try to remain still and he takes it as approval, letting his finger roam at my folds.

There's no winning with him.

"Hmm, someone is wet."

I clamp my lips in a line and try to clench my thighs. He grips me harsher.

The intrusiveness forces a yelp out of me.

His eyes are on the road, but he still wreaks havoc in me.

"Do you want me to finger you, sweetheart?"

I don't reply.

"I can hit that spot that drives you crazy and make you scream for the entire road to hear."

"Stop, damn it!" I groan, my face heating with exertion.

His dirty words have always been the death of me.

"Hmm. You should know that the more you say that…" He plunges two fingers inside me in one go. "The harder I will push."

I cry out, almost toppling over in my seat.

Oh. God.

I don't know if it's the position or the way he thrust into me. A wave comes so close, it's impossible to fight its intensity.

"I missed your tight pussy, sweetheart." He pounds into me, hitting that hypersensitive spot over and over again.

How the hell does he know my body more than I do?

"See, your pussy knows it belongs to me." He keeps his eyes on the road as he works me towards the edge of a high cliff.

"Your pussy knows that no one else will give it what I do, but you keep fighting it."

He presses his thumb against my clit. I gasp and clutch the seatbelt for balance.

I'm close. I'm so, so close, I can taste it in the air.

"Oh... Aiden... oh, please."

"Hmm. Do you want me to let you come, Elsa?"

I hate myself instantly as I nod. He's had me under his spell whether I like to admit it or not.

"Then maybe you shouldn't have pissed me off, huh?"

Before I can make meaning of his words, he withdraws his hand, leaving me empty and aching.

I stare at him with widened eyes.

Did the arsehole just abandon me on the verge of an orgasm?

"I told you." He sucks his fingers—the same fingers that were just inside me—into his mouth. "Payment first."

FIFTEEN

Elsa

I'm so frustrated and angry that I don't pay attention to where we're going.

Yes, I want him to tell me everything. Yes, the dickhead knows my body more than anyone should.

But is that an excuse for my strong reaction to him?

I'm supposed to push him away not pull him in, damn it.

I only come out of my stupor when the car slows to halt in the middle of nowhere.

And I mean the middle of freaking nowhere.

My limbs stiffen.

This isn't the King's mansion or somewhere in civilisation.

No.

The place appears deserted without any houses or people in sight. The only sign of human intervention is a dirt road that we must've taken to get here.

Countless pine trees stand in the distance, nearly colliding with the cloudy sky.

The only building in sight is a cottage-like house with a wooden structure and a small garden at the front.

My shoulder blades stiffen and I frantically watch my surroundings as if I'm searching for help.

And maybe I do need help.

Why the hell would Aiden bring me here if he didn't plan to hurt me in some way?

He steps out and closes the door. I flinch at the sound.

What the hell is wrong with me? If Aiden saw that, he would've used it against me.

When I don't get out of the car, he rounds to my side and opens the door. His forearm rests on the hood of the Ferrari as he peers down at me like I'm a wonder.

From this angle, he's so otherworldly, it's unfair.

"Are you planning to stay there all day?" he asks.

"No way in hell am I leaving this car."

His poker face is on as he speaks in a detached tone, "Don't worry. I don't bury them here."

My eyes almost bulge out of their sockets as I gawk up at him.

He bursts into laughter, the sound echoing around us like an instrument.

A dark as hell instrument.

But for some reason, I'm caught in that laughter.

In the ease behind it.

In the honesty of it.

Aiden rarely laughs, and when he does, it's usually a part of his mask. But right now? He appears genuinely happy. Something swells at the thought that I'm the reason behind it.

"Jesus." He pulls at my cheek. "You should see your adorable face."

I swat his hand away, trying to feign offence. "That's not funny."

"It isn't. But you are." He motions to the house-cottage. "Come on."

I shake my head. "We can talk in here."

I don't get a warning.

One second I'm sitting in the car and the next, Aiden is releasing the seatbelt and pulling me out. He places an arm under my legs, the other at my back, and effortlessly throws me over his shoulder.

I'm so impressed by his strength and the confident ease he carries me with that I spend a few seconds speechless. All I can do is watch the ground moving under our feet.

It's like I weigh nothing.

My head bumps against his back, pulling me out from my stupefaction. Blood rushes to my face from the upside-down position.

I hit his back with closed fists. "Put me down!"

It doesn't faze him. Not one bit.

So I do it again.

I hit him with everything I have, screaming profanities at him.

He doesn't get to act like an actual caveman after everything that's happened. He doesn't get to take me to his cave as if I always belonged there.

"Let me go!"

Smack.

I freeze, the sting heating my arse.

Did he just... spank me?

My cheeks heat in humiliation and something else I can't put my finger on.

I try to squirm free. He smacks me again—harder this time.

I jolt, crying out in something a lot more different than pain.

What the...?

"Stay still or we can do this all day." His hand caresses the flesh he just smacked, slowly, too slowly.

Tingles erupt on my skin, and an unintelligible sound escapes my lips.

"Hmm. Or would you like that, sweetheart?"

I clamp my lips shut because whatever I'll say will only make my situation worse.

He doesn't remove his hand from my arse as if it's some sort of a threat. I remain still, not ready to experience those strange sensations again.

Once in front of the house, Aiden enters the combination—which means that this place belongs to him or his father.

Automatic light goes on as we walk down the hall.

He puts me to my feet in the middle of a medium-sized lounge area with grey sofas and a kitchen bar in sight.

Designer lamps hang from the ceiling giving the cottage a modern look that I didn't notice from the outside. There's a billiard table at the corner and a chessboard with an unfinished game on the coffee table.

It seems so much cosier than the King mansion. Homier, too.

When my gaze strays back to Aiden. He's watching me watch the space with those drawn brows as if he's trying to crack a code.

"Is this your place?" I ask in a light tone, trying to dissipate the tension.

"It's the Meet Up."

Oh.

So this is the Meet Up I heard so much about.

It's basically a secret hideout for the four horsemen and Elites' startup players.

Everyone at RES speaks about it like a secret society or something, but that's probably because only selective players are allowed access.

"Why did you bring me here?"

"So no one interrupts us."

I gulp, staring at him to read his mood. However, that damn poker face doesn't slip.

If only he were a bit more accessible. He's like a stone. Unchanging and unmovable.

I'm afraid of the answer, but I ask the question anyway. "Interrupt us from what?"

He sits on the sofa, legs wide apart, and props his elbow on the armrest. He leans against his fist and continues watching me.

The way his metal eyes bore into mine promises trouble.

Lots of it.

"Did you figure out what you have to pay for?" he asks in a neutral, low tone.

I instinctively take a step back so I'm not within arm's reach.

Cole and Ronan were right. Aiden's calm side is much more terrifying than his enraged one.

His calm side is a facade that he's perfected so well to make you feel safe before he pounces and devours you alive.

"I don't know what you're talking about," I speak in my most confident tone.

"Here's what I think, sweetheart. I think you know exactly what I'm talking about, but you're playing the ignorance card."

"I really don't."

He narrows his eyes before going back to his poker face. "How about a certain new boy that you've been shoving in my face?"

Oh. Shit.

He pulls his fingers up and counts, starting with his thumb. "You wore pretty dresses for him. Put on makeup. Perfume. You got into his car." He pauses with only his pinky up and his eyes darkening to a frightening colour. "Oh, and you let him touch you."

I take another step back.

It's true that I want to be strong and stand up for myself, but I'm not an idiot.

This side of Aiden terrifies me. I don't want to be on the receiving end of whatever his demons are planning right now.

I need to be smart about picking my battles.

And this isn't one I'd win.

"You let him fucking touch what's mine." His voice raises a notch with every word.

His features sharpen. It's like I hit a switch and shed a light on Aiden's demons.

I brought them out from the shadows. They stare at me with deranged anger and possessive obsessiveness.

And I know. I just know that I need to run.

Call it intuition or self-perseverance, but I feel it in my bones.

I need to escape him.

Whatever he has to tell me can wait until he's no longer surrounded by a murderous gloom.

I whirl around and run, my breath catching in my throat.

I don't make it three steps before an arm yanks me back. I cry out as I fall on the sofa head first. A suffocating weight slams on my back, covering me completely from behind.

Tremors jolt in my veins and my face nearly explodes from the heat.

"A-Aiden… w-what are you doing?"

He removes a stray strand of hair from my cheek with a gentleness that frightens me. "Do you remember what I said when you asked me what would I do if you cheat?"

I suck in shaky breaths. It's like I'm asphyxiating.

He bites the shell of my ear, "Answer me."

"That you won't leave me." My lips tremble.

"I changed my mind."

"Y-you changed your mind? You'll leave me?"

Why the hell is my heart shrinking into itself at the thought?

"I'll never leave you, sweetheart."

"But…" I breathe in the leather scent of the sofa. "You said you changed your mind."

"I won't leave you, but I'll make you pay for every time I stopped myself from ripping his heart out."

"Aiden…"

"Did you mistake my silence for approval?" he whispers in hot words. "Did you think you could provoke me and just walk away?"

My breathing deepens with each of his words.

I'm so fucked.

"I gave you a chance to be smart and get back in the game. I gave you the chance to make the right move, but you don't want that, sweetheart, do you? You want me to make the move for you."

"I wasn't cheating. It's not cheating if we were over."

"Wrong answer. I guess we have to do it my way." He yanks my skirt up.

"I didn't cheat!" I cry out. "I never let him touch me."

"But you did." He licks the shell of my ear before he bites down.

"Get off me," I shriek.

"Be smart, Elsa. If you pay like a good girl, you get what you want."

I remain motionless for a while. I didn't do anything wrong to pay, but if I say that, if I provoke him right now, then I have no idea what his demons will do.

Fine. If he wants sex then I'll consider it a charity.

Or at least that's what I tell myself as I nod.

He gets off me and cold air causes goosebumps to rise on my naked thighs.

I swallow, fingers clenching on the sofa as I wait for the inevitable.

Five seconds pass.

Ten.

Twenty.

I glance behind me through my tangled blonde strands.

Aiden sits on the chair, leaning on his elbow and watching me intently.

I stumble to a sitting position, smoothing my skirt down. "Now what?"

"Now." He tilts his head. "I'll fuck that mouth, sweetheart."

SIXTEEN

Elsa

I*'ll fuck that mouth, sweetheart.*

My lips part in stupefaction as Aiden stands up. He rolls the cuffs of his shirt to his elbows, revealing a hint of his arrow tattoos. They ripple with the strong veins of his forearms.

He motions in front of him. "Kneel."

No way in hell.

"Do you want me to make you?" He raises an eyebrow. "Is that it?"

One second passes.

Two.

Three.

"Last chance, sweetheart."

If I bow to his command, he'll have me at his mercy all over again. He'll step on me just like before.

I promised myself that I'll no longer take what he offers while I'm lying on the ground.

I'll give back what he takes.

"Tell me something about you," I blurt.

"Something about me," he repeats still wearing that poker face.

"If you want to fuck my mouth, then you'll tell me something no one else knows. I want the real Aiden, not the one hiding behind a facade."

"You seem under the misconception that this is a negotiation." He approaches me. "I don't remember giving you a choice."

It takes everything in me not to scramble back on the sofa and hide. That's equal to admitting defeat before even starting. If I want to be equal to Aiden, then I need to have his level of confidence.

Or as close to that as possible.

I lift my chin. "I'm the one giving you a choice, Aiden. Either tell me or force me and fuck the mouth of a shell."

His left eye twitches.

Aiden doesn't like to be threatened, but it's the only way I can think of to get to him.

The real him.

I expect him to force me and push me to the road of no return. Since I already don't trust him, if he does this, I'll really start disintegrating from him.

And for some reason, my chest aches at the thought.

"I've had insomnia since I was a kid," he says in a quiet voice I can barely hear. "I spend my nights playing chess, swimming, or working out in the gym."

I process the information.

Now that I think about it, every time Aiden and I spent the night together, I always wake up to find him either watching me or running a bath for me.

I figured it was because he always woke up first. Does that mean he never slept on those nights?

Wait.

"You were deep asleep the first time you spent the night in my room."

"That was one of the times I collapsed."

"Collapsed?"

"If I spend two or three days without a wink of sleep while

working out, swimming, and practising football, my body shuts down and I collapse. That's the only way I get to sleep."

I watch him intently. He never appears tired. Hell, he doesn't even have dark circles like most insomniacs. If he didn't tell me he had insomnia, I would've never guessed it.

I wonder why he can't sleep.

Then I recall a text he sent me that night.

Something about...

My head snaps up. "You said you see a ghost when you close your eyes. Is that why you can't sleep?"

Something flashes in his gaze before he completely seals it behind the poker face.

"You said to tell you one thing no one knows, and I did."

"Cole, Xander, and Ronan don't know?"

"They suspect it, but they don't know for sure." He points at the ground in front of him. "Now, your turn."

When I don't move, he says, "A deal is a deal, sweetheart."

I wish I could extract more from him, but I already cornered myself. If I don't respect my part of the deal, he'll never open up again.

With one last deep breath, I scramble to my knees in front of him.

I want to think that he's making me. That even if I struck a deal, this is a form of a violation. At least those thoughts will make me hate him.

But is it a violation if I'm impatiently waiting for his next move?

Maybe, just maybe, it's impossible for me to hate Aiden.

That thought terrifies me more than any I've had before.

"Good girl."

Aiden's eyes soften at the corners.

My heart jumps, beating so loud, I can hear the thump, thump, thump...

It's so rare to see him softening. He usually fakes it before he strikes. Aiden's softening is the frightening type, not this heartwarming, almost reassuring type.

Am I imagining things?

He unbuckles his belt and frees his hard cock. Keeping eye contact, he grips himself and strokes up and down, not so gently.

My thighs clench.

There's something so utterly masculine about the rough way he touches himself.

He points his dick at my mouth. "Open."

"If I do this." I meet his gaze. "You'll tell me what I want to know."

"Hmm." He glides the tip of his cock on my mouth, smearing the pre-cum on my lips.

My breathing catches the more he does that. My lips part and I take the first taste of him.

I shouldn't have done that. Now, I want more.

He nudges my mouth open and I take him in, slowly.

I've only given Aiden a blowjob that one time at Ronan's party. Since then, he's been exclusively the one who gives oral.

It's because of the control.

Aiden is the type who lives for control even during sex—especially during sex.

Maybe I like control, too. Maybe this time, I want him to feel what it's like to have him at my mercy.

I lick him at a slow pace and lift my hands to cup his balls. I take my time in working him up.

Aiden throws his head back with a grunt. "Fuck, sweetheart."

He yanks the band free from my hair, letting the blonde strands fall to my shoulders, and tangles his fingers in my scalp.

I quicken my pace and take him as far as I can without gagging. I become bolder with each stroke of his fingers in my hair and groan out of his lips.

So this is how it feels like to have control. No wonder he loves it so much.

"You're so adorable." He smirks down at me. "Look at your proud expression."

My pace slows a little, but I don't stop as I get trapped in his cloudy gaze.

"You're only at that pace because I'm letting you, sweetheart." He gathers my hair around his fist, making me wince. "But this is a punishment, remember? You don't get to enjoy it."

My eyes widen when he thrusts his hips forward and his cock hits the back of my throat.

My gag reflex shoots up, and I cease to breathe. I slap both my hands on his thighs trying to push him away.

Using his fist in my hair, he pulls almost completely out. I barely get a breath before he slams in again.

"You're so fucking beautiful." *Thrust.* "And breakable." *Thrust.* "And *mine.*"

I try to keep up with his pace, but it's impossible.

He literally fucks my mouth like he promised he would.

In and out. Deep and hard.

He buries himself inside my mouth, and then he's out. I splatter and gasp for air before he does it again and again.

And *again.*

With every thrust, my body burns. Every time he pulls out, I keep my lips open as if I'm begging for more.

I can't get enough of him and his taste.

Or maybe I can't get enough of the intense way he stares down at me.

It's like he really wants to break me, but at the same time, he wants to keep me.

For the first time since I met Aiden, I see a different side of him. One that I've never seen before.

I had to kneel at his feet while he fucks my mouth so I could notice it.

The conflict.

The doubt.

Aiden has always been assertive to the core, but right now? As he plunges in and out of my mouth, he appears on the fence.

About what? I don't know.

All I know is that I'm most likely the reason behind the conflict.

His grey eyes flick to affection for a second before they darken again. He watches me like he hates me.

This isn't the blind hate from two years ago. No. This time, he looks like he has no control over the hate.

It cuts me deep and hard. Like it wouldn't have hurt this much if I were punched in the gut.

What have I done to you?

Tears barge into my eyes. I'm not sure whether it's due to the lack of air, the way he brutalises my mouth, or the emotional pain slashing me open out of nowhere.

Aiden reaches down a finger and wipes under my eyes. "Shhh."

He pulls out of me completely without coming. If anything, his cock is harder, the veins throbbing with the need for release.

Aiden clutches me by the shoulders and lifts me in his strong arms. Still disoriented, I stare at the hint of his arrow tattoos. For some reason, the sight of them calms my breathing.

He carries me to the sofa and sits down, manoeuvring me so I'm sitting on his lap, facing him.

Tears still stream down my cheeks as I place both hands on his shoulders.

I couldn't stop them even if I wanted to.

Without breaking eye contact, he reaches between us and pulls my boy shorts down my legs.

He yanks my skirt up and positions his hard cock at my entrance. My inner muscles clench in raw, crippling anticipation.

"See what you do to me?" He buries himself deep inside me in one go.

I bite my lower lip, but the moan comes loud and clear.

He never fucked me this way. Face to face. At this angle, he reaches a place inside me he's never reached before.

I bounce on his lap, almost toppling over with each of his merciless thrusts.

He pounds inside me with a maddened urgency.

I'm breathless, mindless, and thirsty for more.

No matter how much I deny it, I'll always want more from Aiden.

And maybe that's why I'm in pain. Because maybe he'll never care about me the way I care about him.

Maybe I'll always be a game.

"Do you feel yourself clenching me, sweetheart?" His eyes bore into mine.

They're more intrusive and intimate than his cock inside me.

"Do you know what that means?" He grunts. "It means you're fucking mine, Elsa. Not only your body, but also your heart and your fucking soul."

More tears stream down my face because I know, I just know that I'm screwed.

The building intensifies at my abdomen, and with it, an arrow lodges straight to my heart. I'm falling off that edge with no landing in sight.

How could I let him get this deep under my skin? If I attempt to pluck him out now, I'll probably bleed to death.

"Don't cry." He leans over and darts his tongue out to lick my tears.

Unlike the other times, his eyes aren't filled with sadism. If anything, they're breaking and shredding apart.

Just like my damn soul.

He licks each of my cheeks and underneath my eyes with infinite care like he doesn't want to miss a drop.

His metallic eyes meet mine again. "I'll protect you."

Those words drive me over the edge. I come with a sob tearing from my throat.

He said he'll protect me.

But who will protect me from him?

SEVENTEEN

Aiden

Her eyes are fluttered closed as she snuggles in my embrace.

She fought it when I pulled her into me.

Of course, she did.

Elsa is the type who feels like she's failing herself if she doesn't fight.

But she should know by now that her fight is futile.

Eventually, her energy waned and she fell into a deep, exhausted sleep.

We're still on the sofa. The leather creaks as I manoeuvre her so she's half-lying atop of me. Her head rests on my chest and my leg wraps around hers.

I can't get close enough to Elsa.

Or touch her deep enough.

Not when a great part of her mind is numb to me.

I tilt my head to the side to get a better view of her.

Her uniform is in disarray, and the sorry excuse of a skirt barely hides her bare pussy. I'm tempted to finger her tight walls and make her come all over again and again.

The exhaustion on her brows stops me.

Dishevelled blonde strands fall on my chest. I run my fingers through her hair, stroking it back. She smells of coconut, sex, and *me*.

She smells of me and I'll do anything to make sure she always does.

Elsa moans and mumbles something in her sleep.

My dick hardens in an instant.

She can lie to me all she likes, but her subconscious is the truth.

The truth is in the way she wraps her leg around mine. Or how she keeps her hand at the small of my back as if she doesn't want to let me go.

Or maybe I'm being fucking delusional.

I become that way around this girl.

She had this effect on me long before she realised it herself.

For what seems like forever, she's been carefully tucked beneath my skin like an unreachable itch.

I knew there would be a day where I would have to cut that itch clean, but I never planned for it to go this way.

I never planned for this fucking girl to get to me the way she did.

Jonathan and Uncle James—when he was alive—taught me and Lev to plan our moves before making them.

I've been raised on strategic thinking. Every move and every piece has a purpose.

Jonathan used to say that a king isn't a king by title only, it's also because of the power he has to bring everyone to their knees in front of him.

For my entire life, when I plan to do something, the result is clear before I even take the first step.

Until her.

Elsa fucking Steel.

She was supposed to be another chess game with a known result, but she's turning out to be more unpredictable than any game I played before.

She barged on my board, shuffled my formation, and wreaked havoc in my court.

Everything changed when she refused to be a fucking pawn like she was supposed to.

I drag my thumb along her bottom lip and her mouth parts as if inviting me in.

Since I first saw her, she's been pulling me in with her seemingly innocent ways.

Truth is, her ways are more destructive than innocent. And the worst part is, I don't think she even recognises that.

She shifts again and her tits push against the shirt. I undo the first three buttons. My fingers freeze on the fourth button as the faded scar comes into view just above her pale left breast.

I run my fingers on the smooth, deep tissue. It's been a while since I left a mark on that scar.

Hmm. I need to change that soon.

This scar holds an entire story of its own that I doubt her guardians would ever tell her.

This scar was the beginning of the end.

Elsa just doesn't know it yet.

Since I saw this scar on the first day of senior year, I've been fucking everything up.

My thumb presses into the skin harder than I intended. Elsa mumbles something and I remove the pressure.

With careful fingers, I re-button the shirt. She doesn't need to catch me staring at her scar like the freak she already thinks I am.

Besides, she's too self-conscious about her scar. There's no need to dig that wound open.

Not today.

I wrap my hand around her neck and caress the pulse point in her throat.

It's curious how such a normal heartbeat can belong to her.

Frozen.

She really is.

She's so frozen, it pissed me off in the beginning.

It still pisses me off sometimes, but I have other things to worry about.

Such as Jonathan and her fucking last name.

What would it be like if she were someone else? If she really was Elsa Quinn, not Elsa Steel?

Fuck.

Why would I even think about something impossible?

This girl isn't only messing up my carefully-laid plans, but she's also screwing with my head.

I'm the one who's supposed to screw with heads, not the other way around.

Elsa shifts again, and this time, her eyes slowly peel open. She stares at her surroundings, appearing confused before she focuses back on me.

She freezes when her electric blue eyes meet mine.

Those damn blue eyes.

I don't know if I want to poke them out or stare at them all day long.

Elsa freezes like this sometimes. It's like she's putting two and two together.

She's trying to make sense of a situation that her politically correct mind isn't able to accept.

Usually, she fails, and that makes her frustrated.

Like right now.

She glares up at me.

Will there be a day where she wakes up in my arms and doesn't overthink everything?

In the beginning, I didn't give a fuck. Now, it's starting to piss me off like that unreachable itch.

Elsa shoves at my chest to sit up.

I let her go.

Picking battles is the surest way to win a war.

She's still pissed off—no thanks to Jonathan and Queens—so I can't push her too far.

Yet.

"How long have I been out?" She reaches for the elastic band on the floor.

I snatch it from her fingers before she ties her hair.

Elsa huffs while standing up and gathers her hair in a bun and ties it with itself.

"Some time." I plop on my elbow and tilt my head to the side to watch her.

She finds her bag on the chair and retrieves her phone.

Her simplest, most mundane gestures draw me in like nothing in this world ever did.

Like a distant memory from the past.

The way she bites her lower lip when concentrating. The way she sits with her legs tucked closely together like a good little girl.

"It's late." She groans. "I need to go back."

"No."

She lifts her head, chest-puffing. "What do you mean no?"

The spirit of this girl.

She's always ready for a fight.

It makes my dick hard.

"Aren't you here for the story?"

She bites her lower lip as if she's contemplating it. "Fine, tell me and then I'll go."

I shake my head.

Her brows scrunch. "I did my part of the deal. You promised, Aiden."

Those flushed cheeks are adorable when she's angry.

I can't get enough of being under her skin.

I doubt I ever will.

"Stay the night and I'll tell you."

"I can't. Aunt and Uncle expect me to be home."

"Tell them you're staying the night with Reed." I pause. "You were planning on it before she cancelled last second, no?"

"How the hell do you know that?" She narrows her eyes. "You manipulated Kim into telling you, didn't you?"

I lift a shoulder. "Stay the night or I won't say anything."

Her nose twitches as she mulls the proposition in her head. I can see that eagerness. The need to know, and it feels good to have her need me.

Even if I have to threaten her for it.

At least now, she won't be fucking around and telling me it's over. It'll never be over.

I might have to give up some of my bargaining chips to keep her close, but it's worth it as long as I have her in my space.

Even if she still can't trust me.

Elsa is smart and has more self-preservation than anyone I know. Good.

She shouldn't trust me. At least not yet.

Because when I tell her what I know, there'll be no going back.

It'll be the beginning of her decimation.

And mine.

EIGHTEEN

Elsa

I agreed to stay the night.

Okay, agreeing isn't the right word. I was *coerced* to stay the night.

Aiden knows how much I need the truth and like the psycho he is, he used my desperation to his benefit.

But then again, I'm well aware of his manipulations and I fell for them anyway, so I guess that makes me an accomplice.

I sit in the spacious round bathtub because Aiden ran another bubble bath for me.

It still baffles me how he has this level of care in him but still acts in an overbearing, almost oppressive kind of way.

It's confusing.

He's confusing.

He sits at my back like an overwhelming presence. I can feel his warmth without glancing back.

It's different from the water's coolness. Like a halo, it swallows me whole.

Goosebumps erupt on my skin with each passing second.

Aiden leans back against the bathtub with his legs stretched on either side of me as I sit in the middle.

I pull my knees to my chest and will my body to cool down for a freaking second.

If I give in to him one more time, I might start losing myself to him again.

That is if I didn't already.

Why the hell did he tell me about his insomnia? He should've deflected like always. And what's with the way he looked at me?

I'll protect you.

His words send a shiver down my spine.

Nope. I'm *not* going there.

I'm only here to hear what he has to say. Once he's done, I'm out.

A sponge comes in contact with my tense back. I purse my lips as he slowly lathers my skin with careful, gentle strokes.

The scent of coconut wafts in the air and fills my senses.

Stop.

Why can't he be mean? Why does he have to enchant my body more under his spell?

"So?" I snap harder than I mean.

I wanted to douse the tingles he's drawing out of my body, but it's not working at all.

"So what?" He continues his ministrations.

"I'm waiting for the truth."

"You sure you don't want to change your mind?" His voice is quiet in the dooming silence of the bathroom.

"No."

"Hmm. You might want to, sweetheart. I still don't think you're ready."

"Let me worry about that."

He's quiet for a bit, and I think he'll bail on me. He'll be unfair like all the other times and laugh in my face.

This time I'll only have myself to blame. I made a deal with the devil knowing exactly how conniving he can be.

"I'll tell you a story," he says.

"I don't want a story, I want —"

"There were two friends." He cuts me off, still sponging my back. "They were both ambitious and stopped at nothing to get what they wanted. They both had flowing businesses, but they decided against a partnership because they loved challenging each other more. The rivalry grew harsher and nastier over the years. They were both notorious businessmen and never cut each other any slack."

His movements slow like he's absent-minded. Instead of the sponge, his fingers draw down my back like he's scribbling something. "Their rivalry began to cross limits in ways that neither of them noticed. Or maybe they did notice but they never gave a fuck. The moment their families got pulled into their rivalry, things became ugly."

He stops talking and his fingers stop their caress. I turn around so my back leans against his bent leg.

Aiden watches me with darkened eyes. It's like he's surrounded by his black demons and all of them want to hurt me.

My breath hitches as my instinct screams at me to run. It's one of those times when looking at him is exhausting.

I swallow, but I don't move. "And?"

He's silent for a beat. "And what?"

"Where's the rest of the story?"

"Next time."

"Next time?" I all but snap.

"You've been through a lot today." His poker face is on. "You should sleep."

"I'm not tired." I push at his chest.

"Hmm. I thought you were sore. Maybe I shouldn't hold back, huh?"

My cheeks heat at the promise in his words. I quickly recover when I recognise his tactics. "You don't get to deflect your way out of this. You promised to tell me everything and now you're telling me to go to sleep?"

He clutches my wrist and manoeuvres me so I'm facing him. His legs cage my waist and I have no choice but to bend my legs on either side of his hips.

At this position, my legs are stretched open and even though our lower halves are covered by the bubbly water, I can almost feel his erection near my most intimate part.

He threads his fingers into my loose hair and his gaze travels to my flushed breasts. My nipples harden under his intense scrutinising.

I only release a breath after he slides his metal eyes back to mine. "I didn't say I'll tell you everything, I said I'll tell you a story which I just did."

Frustration bubbles in my veins. Damn him and his manipulations. Will there ever be a day when he won't pull me in hook, line, and sinker?

But that's how it is with Aiden. If I want to get anything out of him, then I need to play his stupid games. I need to try and think with a mind as deviant as his.

Taking a calming breath, I briefly close my eyes before opening them again. He's staring at my scar with that poker face.

If only I could read his mind and see what's behind that facade.

Having him fixate on me that way brings a strange sense of vulnerability. The itch under my skin blooms to the surface.

I don't know why he has an obsession with my scar.

Or with me, basically.

If what I heard from Jonathan and Silver's conversation is true, then Aiden is supposed to hate me, not be this obsessed with me.

But then again, isn't obsession just another form of extreme hate?

"Does the story you just told me have to do with what I overheard from Jonathan and Silver's conversation?"

His gaze reluctantly leaves my scar to meet mine. "Maybe."

"Ugh. Aiden! Give me something."

"I will." His lips tilt in a smirk. "If you're a good girl."

"Let me guess, that includes fucking you?"

His grin widens. "I'll be the one doing the fucking, but yes, sweetheart. That comes with the package."

I narrow my eyes on him.

It's all a ploy. A mindfuck. Something he uses in his push and pull. If I want to know the truth and somehow still come out intact, then I need to negotiate my way out of his rules.

He doesn't get everything.

Not anymore.

"No."

He raises an eyebrow, but his hands tighten in my hair. "No?"

"If I follow your conditions, you'll get whatever you want and you might never tell me anything anymore." I place a palm on his wet chest and trail my hand down his hard abs. "I have a condition."

"A condition," he repeats as if he needs to hear the words to believe them.

"Yes. Every time you tell me a tidbit, you get to touch me. That includes oral sex, by the way."

His left eye twitches. "What makes you think I'll agree to that? I can get you to spread your legs for me any time I want, sweetheart."

The arrogance of this fucking bastard.

Still, I keep my smile plastered in place as I run my fingertips on the hard ridges of his abs. "Sure you can, but do you remember what I said about being a shell? If you force your way with me more than this, then you'll get that shell to spread her legs for you."

He yanks my hand from his stomach and his left eye twitches.

I most definitely hit a nerve.

We stare at each other for long seconds. This time, I don't cower away.

This time, I'm not a mere soldier. I'm a general in the battle he's trying to win.

Tension crackles in the air and goosebumps cover the earlier goosebumps. All I can breathe is his intoxicating scent. All I can feel is the pulse of my wrist in his grip.

"So?" I break the lethal silence. "What will it be?"

His lips pull into a cruel smirk. "Well played, sweetheart. Well played, indeed."

A wave of pride hits me and it takes everything in me not to grin like an idiot.

I just got Aiden King at his own game.

Before I can gloat, he stands up, yanking me up with him by the wrist. Water splashes all around us.

The blackness in his eyes is the last thing I see.

He releases my wrist, grabs me by the hips and throws me over his shoulder like earlier.

I gasp as the world tilts upside down. "A-Aiden? What are you doing?"

He slaps my arse, the sting reverberating in the air.

I squeal.

It fucking hurts when my bottom is all wet.

"You said sex time after story time."

"We already had sex earlier."

"That was before the new arrangement. It doesn't count."

Oh. Dear God.

This bloody psycho will be the death of me.

He stops at the shelf to retrieves towels. I use the chance to try and wiggle free and push at his back.

He spanks me again. My thighs clench together.

"Ow. That hurts."

"Then stay fucking still."

He puts me to my feet in the middle of a bedroom with black wooden frames and a king-sized bed.

I'm still taking in my surroundings when he wraps the towel around my hair.

Aiden stands in front of me in all his naked glory, water dripping down his muscled chest and the defined V leading to —

Nope.

I snap my attention back to his face. His lips are curved into a smirk as if he can hear my thoughts.

Dickhead.

He dries my hair with masterful, gentle strokes. Then he does the same with my body; slowly and gently.

He takes his sweet time in rubbing the towel over my hardened nipples and around my breasts. He bends and glides the towel over my arse and between my legs.

Tingles start at the bottom of my stomach and spread all over my body the more he touches me.

It takes all my will not to moan aloud and melt in his arms.

He's not only drying me off. No. He's also awakening the monster inside. The monster that used to be dormant, but refuses to sleep since Aiden first touched me.

After finishing with my legs, he comes up again and flicks the towel against my throbbing nipples once more. His thumb and forefinger squeeze my other nipple. It's not harsh, but I'm so stimulated that the slightest touch feels like I'm being set on fire.

I bite my lower lip against a whimper and clench my thighs. "A-Aiden."

"Hmm, sweetheart?" He doesn't even look at me, still busy torturing my nipples.

Get it over with, arsehole.

I glance between him and the bed, silently communicating my point.

His poker face is on, but his left eye twitches.

My muscles lock together. Oh, shit. It's never good when he's pissed off.

"Do you want me to fuck you?" He runs the towel up and down my breasts, making me squirm and gravitate towards him. "How do you want me to do it?"

Any way will do.

"I can take you against the wall. You'll wrap your legs around my waist like a good girl, won't you, sweetheart?"

I bite down on my bottom lip. The double assault of his dirty words and his touch make me delirious.

"And then I'll pound inside you so hard, you'd scrape your back against the wall. Or I can take you on the floor on all fours until your knees bruise from how hard I'll thrust in and out of your tight pussy. Hmm. Choices."

His hand roams down my stomach, to the apex of my thighs and glides over my folds. "Hmm. You're soaked."

My eyes flutter closed briefly. I'm burning and his touch is like spilling gasoline on the fire.

More.

I need more.

He parts my folds with his finger. My head falls on his shoulder with a soft moan.

"You love it when I touch you here, don't you, sweetheart?"

I have no words to say so I let my whimper answer his question.

"You love it when I work you up until you scream, don't you?"

I grip his shoulder for balance as he runs his fingers up and down, touching me everywhere except for where I need him the most.

"You love when I make you come, don't you?" He turns me around and pushes me against the bed. I fall face down with a gasp, my cheek hitting the soft mattress.

He wraps a hand under my stomach and pulls me up so I'm on my hands and knees.

I'm shaking, sweating, and feeling stimulated more than I've ever been before.

I'm ready to beg when Aiden thrusts balls deep inside me in one go.

I cry out as his length fills me to the rim. With this position, it's like being stretched open all over again.

There's a sick type of pleasure that comes with the pain and the intensity that Aiden always brings.

It's crazy.

It's out of control.

And I crave it more than I like to admit.

He grabs a fist full of my hair as his other hand clutches me harshly by the hip. He pulls on my hair until I'm staring at the ceiling.

His thrusts start slow and moderated, making me moan. My fingers sink into the sheets, and my eyes roll to the back of my head with each roll of his hips. He alternates between clutching my hips and flicking, pinching, and twisting my nipple.

"Oh... A-Aiden..."

The building intensifies like a hurricane and pulls me to its centre.

"Ahhhh..." I come with a deep moan.

The orgasm takes me by surprise. I feel cherished. Almost... worshipped.

What the hell is he doing to me?

Aiden doesn't stop. He continues thrusting with that moderate rhythm that messes with both my body and head.

Another riot starts at the bottom of my stomach, slashing and clawing at its walls.

"Does that feel good, sweetheart?"

I nod, pushing against him for more.

"Then why the fuck are you putting a limit on it?"

My eyes widen as he picks up his pace.

Oh, shit.

Oh, fuck.

The earlier rhythm and orgasm were only a deflection method. I should've known he's pissed off. I should've known he'd make this a punishment.

His thrusts turn merciless and out of control. I almost topple over the bed with how hard he pounds into me.

While the earlier rhythm made me feel content, this one scratches a darker side inside me.

That side craves the pain Aiden offers.

That side feeds off Aiden's depravity.

That side *scares* me.

Wanting him in this unhinged way terrifies the shit out of me.

"Aiden..." I try to coax him. "Slow down."

His body covers mine from behind. "You don't get to put a limit on when and how much I get to touch you, then ask me to slow down. You're well and truly fucked, sweetheart."

He pulls at my nipple and I'm a goner. It's like I can't control my body when he touches me.

I barely come down from the orgasm, panting, and clawing at the sheets for dear life.

Aiden doesn't stop.

His merciless pace goes on and on and *on*.

I'm so sensitive and spent. My nerves endings shiver and beg for this to end.

But if I tell him that, he'll just do the opposite.

I have one option now.

Using all the strength I have left, I push back, wiggling my arse against his thighs and balls.

If he doesn't finish any time soon, he'll go at this all night long.

He hits a sensitive spot inside me. I moan, but I don't stop wiggling against him.

"What do you think you're doing, sweetheart? Hmm?" He growls.

"C-come inside me," I whimper, trying to keep up with his pace. "I want you to come inside me, Aiden."

"Fuck." A grunt spills from his lips as warmth coats my walls.

I collapse on my front as he pulls out of me. Hot liquid trickles down my thighs, but I couldn't care less right now.

I'm so exhausted and I could sleep for eternity.

Aiden flips me around and I let him, a soft mumble spilling from my lips.

He kneels at the foot of the bed as I lay stark naked in front of him, my eyes starting to flutter closed.

He pulls my legs apart, hands clutching both my thighs as he slowly watches me with darkened eyes. He sniffs the air as if he wants to engrave our scent into memory.

"Did you honestly think you could manipulate me, sweetheart?"

My eyes shoot open.

"Do you think it's over because I came?"

"I-I'm sensitive."

His devilish smirk greets me. "You should've thought of that before putting a limit on when I get to touch you."

"It's too much." But is it too much if my entire body is tingling for more?

Is it too much if I'm impatiently waiting for his next move?

"You know what's too much, sweetheart? Too much is craving you and not being able to touch you because you put a limit on it."

"Now." He tilts his head to the side. "You'll come for me one more time like a good girl."

And then he's feasting on me and I'm screaming his name.

NINETEEN

Elsa

Past,

I'm humming as I trot down the path in the middle of the garden. Ma said she'll read me a story today. She stopped reading me stories since the one who shall not be named disappeared.

A red rose is tucked carefully between my small fingers. My brows scrunch as I try to keep the rose pretty.

It's for Ma because she likes red.

Our house isn't in the city. Daddy has to drive for *sooo* long to arrive where he works. When I asked him why do we live where there aren't other people, he said he and Ma don't like to be bothered.

He's like the prince who took the princess to his faraway castle and is living happily ever after with her.

Or maybe it's not happily ever after.

When does forever end in them fairy tales?

Near the back garden, sounds of fighting rise in the air.

No. Not fighting.

I stop in my tracks, my heart beating loud and fast. My clutch tightens around the rose.

Them monsters are here again.

I hide behind the plum tree and hug the rose close to my chest.

My eyes screw shut, so hard, they hurt.

Them monsters won't take me.

Not anymore.

No other sound comes. I slowly open my eyes and search around me.

Movement catches at the top floor of our house.

Ma stands at the window of her room, staring at the distance and putting red lipstick on.

My mouth parts to call her name, but I close it again. Them monsters will find me before she does.

They always do.

I breathe as quietly as possible while hiding behind the tree. There are wires in the distance, surrounding the entire garden.

Daddy's friends who wear black and don't talk to us put those so no animals or people come inside.

But even the wires can't stop them monsters.

"I told you to back off."

My spine stiffens at the voice coming from around the corner. Daddy?

With snail movements, I place a hand on the stone and peek. Daddy sits at the garden table, his back facing me.

He's wearing his black suit. His chestnut hair is short at his nape but is long at the top.

The view of his back alone makes him appear far like I can't reach him anymore.

Maybe them monsters come after Daddy, too.

Uncle Reginald sits opposite Daddy and facing me. He has scrawny looks and bulging blue eyes that used to scare me when I was younger.

But not anymore.

Monsters escape when Uncle Reg is here.

He's like a superhero.

Ma and Dad don't like it when I speak like him and say 'them' instead of 'the'. They say that's not how educated people speak, but I like saying 'them'. I just have to not say it in front of Ma and Dad.

Now, Uncle Reg appears angry like Daddy when I don't stay in my room at night.

"It's your last chance, Steel." Uncle Reg spits on the ground—eww, gross. "If you don't give me what I want, I'll find someone who will."

Daddy stands to his full height and my heart shrinks. Daddy is scary when he speaks with so much calm. "You think a cockroach like you can cross me?"

Uncle Reg stands, too. "Try me, boss, and you'll see what a cockroach is capable of."

"Get off my property," Daddy grinds out. "Now."

I flinch at the tone, my nails digging into the rose.

Uncle Reg smiles and comes in my direction. I hide back against the tree, holding the rose close to my chest.

I'm so going to give Uncle Reg a scare.

"What do we have here?" Uncle Reg speaks from in front of the tree. "I can see your hair, princess."

Uh-Oh.

I step out, pouting. "Not fair, Uncle Reg. I was about to scare you!"

He places a hand at his heart. "Oh, I'm terrified, princess."

"It's okay, you can stop being scared now."

"Thank you, my lady." He straightens and points at the rose. "Where are you taking that?"

I grin, showing him my missing tooth. "To Ma! She said she'll read me a story today."

He lowers himself so he's crouching. "Your ma has been good, yeah?"

"Yeah! She's putting red lipstick."

Uncle Reg's expression falls.

But why?

Ma is totally cool when she's putting red lipstick and wearing red dresses. It means she'll read me stories and put me to sleep. She'll be there for me when them monsters voices start coming from the basement.

Ma is bad when she has no lipstick on and wears that white dress. That's when she makes me sit on her lap and sings me that haunting song. That's when them monsters come to take me away.

Uncle Reg motions at my rose. "Is that for her?"

"Yes!" I grin. "Ma loves red."

A heavy sigh leaves his lips as he stands to his full height and pats my head. "Careful, princess. Red also means blood."

Uncle Reg morphs into a shadow.

My heartbeat picks up.

No, no…

I shake my head.

It isn't real.

Not real.

I need to take the red rose to Ma. She'll read for me. She'll put me to bed when them monster voices come.

The rose's sharp thorn pierces my finger.

Ow.

The first droplet of blood hits the ground. Another follows.

Then another.

Before I know it, a pool of red surrounds me, its surface is like a mirror.

My breathing turns shallow when I look down.

Hollow black eyes stare back at me.

I shriek.

Present,

I startle awake, screaming and frantically studying my hands.

No blood.

There's no blood.

There are no dark hollow eyes gaping up at me.

No monsters.

"Hey... hey..."

A hand clutches my arm. I claw and hit them.

The monsters won't take me away again.

I escaped them. They can't find me anymore.

"Elsa!"

My breathing catches at the sound of my name. I blink twice and realise I'm in a bed in a familiar room.

Aiden is trying to hold me to his chest. A scratch mark runs down his left pectoral muscle.

My eyes widen.

Did... did I cause that?

Aiden grabs both my hands in his. The same hands that I just used to smack him with.

A deep frown etches between his eyebrows as he watches me intently as if preparing himself in case I have another episode.

Oh. God.

The nightmare. I had an episode after the nightmare.

I close my eyes and a tear slides down my cheek.

"Hey." Aiden brings my fingers to his mouth and kisses them one by one.

I slowly peel my lids open.

How can he kiss the same fingers that I just hurt him with?

No. He's not only kissing them. He slides his lips over each fingertip as if he's worshipping them.

"What are you doing?" I murmur through hiccoughs.

He offers an easy-going grin and speaks against my fingers. "Getting you back."

"Getting me back from where?"

"From whoever was trying to take you away from me just now."

A sob tears its way out of my throat and I let my head fall against his chest. My cheek rests to his hard muscles and I listen intently to his heartbeat.

His soothing, normal heartbeat.

I run the pad of my finger over the scratch mark on his chest. "I-I'm sorry... I'm s-so sorry. I didn't mean to do this... I... I..."

"Shh," Aiden's arms come around my back and he wraps us both in the sheet as I cry softly into his chest.

I can still feel the prick of the thorn and see the blood.

So much fucking blood.

It's on my hands, under my skin, and all around me.

Was that a memory or a nightmare? If it was real, how could there be that much blood and no one knew about it?

And who's Uncle Reg? Is he a real person or a play of my imagination?

Careful, princess. Red also means blood.

A shudder shoots through me at his words.

"Another nightmare?" Aiden asks calmly.

I nod against his skin but say nothing.

He draws small circles at my back. I'm all sweaty and dishevelled, but that doesn't stop Aiden from holding me close until his chest crushes my breasts and all I can smell is him.

And my scent on him.

And the scent of sex in the air.

He barely let me go to sleep and only after he wrenched two more orgasms out of me. I still feel sore and sensitive.

But right now? Right now, I feel something else.

I feel the familiarity of Aiden's embrace and how much I need it. How much it's just right to be in his arms.

No. It's wrong.

I can't fall for his games again.

I try to squirm away, but he only tightens his hold on my back as we both fall to the mattress facing each other.

He wraps his hand around my midsection and I place both palms on his chest. His heartbeat booms under my fingertips, and I instantly feel calmer.

It's like my own custom-made lullaby.

"Just sleep," he murmurs in that husky voice.

I shake my head.

"Why not?"

"What if they come back?" I sniff.

"I'll be here." He wraps a hand around my head and places it on his chest like that's where I've always belonged.

Like he can't have it any other way.

We remain like that for a few, and I'm too tired to fight anything at the moment.

"Remember when I told you that I'll protect you?"

I nod, my eyes starting to flutter closed.

"That includes the monsters from your nightmares, Elsa."

I make an unintelligible sound as sleep whisks me away.

Aiden will protect me from the monsters in my nightmares.

But how did he know they were monsters?

I never told him that.

Right?

TWENTY

Elsa

When I wake up in the morning, it's cold and empty. I slept cocooned in Aiden's embrace, but he's nowhere to be found now.

No sound comes from the bathroom either.

I sit up in bed and try to fight off the wave of disappointment that hits me out of nowhere.

Where did he go?

Did I scare him off with my nightmare yesterday?

I tell myself that Aiden isn't the type that can be scared off, but the doubts jam into my mind anyway.

My backpack rests on a chair and my uniform is neatly tucked beside it.

If he took the time to do that, it should mean that he didn't bail on me, right?

Tucking the sheet around my body, I stand up and glimpse out the window.

There's no trace of his Ferrari.

My chest squeezes so hard like it's on the verge of breaking.

Aiden stranded me in the middle of nowhere.

This feels so much like the first time we had sex; he just up and left without a word.

Back then, I gave him my virginity. Yesterday, I gave him my true, raw self.

He left after both times.

A wave of anger hits me—at myself, not him. Isn't this what I want? What am I so disappointed about?

With a huff, I take a quick shower and change into my uniform.

I'm leaving this place and never returning.

Pressure builds behind my eyes as I glance back at the bed.

The bed in which he made me feel both pleased and safe—even if he was a dick about the first one.

He couldn't have faked the care in his eyes. He couldn't have pretended to hold me and soothe my nightmares after I scratched him.

It takes a special person to do that.

But he left.

I swallow the tears and exit the room. He won't get to me. If he wants to consider this arrangement as a sex only type of thing, then so be it.

I can do that.

I can be as detached as he is.

Use then throw away.

Now, I just have to convince myself not to feel like a dirty whore.

Sounds reach me from downstairs.

Very distinctive sounds.

I stop at the top of the stairs, my cheeks heating.

Moans and grunts come from the lounge area.

My heart slams against my chest and I nearly fall to the ground.

It's not… Silver, right? Aiden wouldn't have brought Silver over to antagonise me.

He wouldn't rip my heart open that way.

Not after the connection we built last night.

"Fuck, princess. You taste like sin."

A harsh breath heaves out of me.

It's not Aiden's voice, but it's a familiar one.

The moans escalate and then the air is filled with rough slaps of flesh against flesh.

I remain rooted in place with my cheeks aflame. No idea if I should disappear inside or stay here to not make a sound.

"Fuck, fuck!" The man grunts as she whimpers.

"Oh, God. Harder!"

"Harder, huh?" *Slap. Slap. Slap.* "How about that?"

"Aaaah! Levi!"

Levi?

Levi King?

The sounds die down as they both appear to have reached their heights. I still don't know if I should go back inside or run out of here.

If I barge in on them now, they'd think that I've been hearing them all along and that would be super awkward.

And perverse.

"Oh, stop it." Astrid—or who I assume is Astrid—scolds.

Her voice is a bit husky, but I hope it's because she's breathy, and not because she's a different girl.

Please let it not be a different girl.

"You just came," she hisses.

"I can never get enough of you, princess. Besides, I have other ways," he grunts and soon after a giggle comes out.

Are they going at it again?

Maybe I should return to bed and pretend I'm asleep or something.

"Get a room."

My back snaps at the signature bored voice.

Aiden.

He's... back.

Something in my chest lifts. I don't know if it's joy or relief or anger.

Or all of them.

The anger at myself wins. How could I give him the remote control of my emotions this easily?

Astrid's gasp is followed by scrambling about and a rustle of clothes.

"What the fuck are you doing here, Aiden?" Levi growls.

"This is my mother's place."

Wait. The Meet Up was Alicia's place?

"Stop looking or I'll poke your fucking eyes out," Levi tells him.

"Looking at who?" I can almost imagine the smirk on Aiden's face.

He's taunting his cousin and he seems to enjoy it a bit too much.

The bastard can be so sadistic.

"Cover your arse, Lev. It's not exactly a good sight first thing in the morning."

"You little fucker, I'm going to —"

"I'm good," Astrid sounds flustered, and I'm sure she is Astrid now that she's speaking normally.

"Since when do you come over on the weekend?" Levi asks.

"Since now. Find yourself another place. Don't you have a flat?"

"Fuck you," Levi tells him. "I'll be here whenever I damn well please." A pause. "What's that?"

"I'm making breakfast," Aiden says. "And stop eating my groceries. Fill the fridge when you come over."

"Wait. *You* are making breakfast?" Levi asks in an incredulous tone.

"Yeah." Astrid laughs. "What gives?"

Aiden doesn't answer, then after a moment, he speaks. "Leave. Both of you."

"Nah." I can hear the grin in Levi's voice. "We're staying for that breakfast."

"In your dreams."

"Wait," Astrid says in a suspicious tone. "Is Elsa here?"

"No." Aiden doesn't miss a beat.

Why is he lying about that?

"She is, isn't she?" Levi laughs. "Princess, go search upstairs and I'll search the downstairs."

"Deal."

Aiden grunts.

Footsteps come closer.

I run back to the room and close the door. I quickly remove my jacket and pretend to put it back on.

A knock comes through before the door cracks open. Astrid's head peeks inside. When her sparkly green eyes meet mine, a huge grin breaks on her face.

"Found her!" She barges inside.

Her denim overalls are buttoned all wrong and her brown hair is dishevelled at best.

I try not to recall what I heard happen between her and Levi downstairs.

"Morning, Elsa."

"Morning."

She leans in, face scrunching as if she's about to tell me a top-secret. "I have huge news. Aiden is making breakfast."

I offer her an awkward smile. "Okay."

"*Okay?* What do you mean by okay? This should go in the Daily Mail or something. Hell. Jonathan should use it for marketing." She pauses, narrowing her eyes on me. "Wait. Your lack of reaction can't be because he made you breakfast before, right?"

I nod.

She stares at me with a parted mouth.

"Is it that strange?" I ask.

"Strange? Try miraculous. Aiden never makes breakfast. Not even when Levi forces him to help out."

"He's not the type who can be forced into doing anything."

Understanding covers her features. "True."

"Did you just come over?" I try to sound innocent like I didn't hear her and Levi fucking each other's brains out.

God. I'm so bad.

"Yeah. We wanted to spend the weekend at the place that started it all."

"Started it all?"

She beams. "Levi and I started at the Meet Up. Crazy, right?"

I shake my head. "You guys are so good together."

"Right? I agree. I need more people like you to say it to his fangirls." She laughs before a nostalgic expression covers her features. "We weren't always on good terms, you know, but I think the clashes in our personalities are what brought us together even more. Like yin and yang of sorts. We're not there to be each other, we're there to insert a piece of us in the other half."

I heard about their rocky relationship last year, but I never asked. It's understandable, though.

Levi might appear fun, but he has his own demons. Just like Aiden, he keeps them carefully tucked under the surface.

And this petite girl, only a year older than me, has managed to not only see his demons but to also make friends with them.

Hell. She fell in love with them.

Astrid seems like the type of girl who's all in. She took Levi the way he is and even loved him for being who he is.

Maybe that's why Levi watches her like she holds the world in the palm of her hands.

She doesn't have to worry about the fangirls. Levi never looked at anyone the way he looks at her.

The look of a king to his queen.

The look I thought Aiden was about to give me last night.

"I know how hot-headed those with the King last name can be." Astrid takes my hand in hers. "But they can have a big heart."

That only includes Levi.

Aiden doesn't have a heart.

I can be a naive fool and try to find it, but it's full of wires in there.

I've already wounded myself enough, I can't do it all over again.

"Well, Aiden is negotiable." She winks. "But he's been so different since you started to spend time with him."

"Different how?"

"He smiles more and he appears a tad more human. Not to mention that he's preparing freaking breakfast! You're a miracle maker."

We both laugh at that.

"Astrid, may I ask you something?"

"Any time."

"How were you able to reach Levi?" Not that the cousins are the same, but they share similar traits.

"Reach him?"

"How did he open up to you and showed you his true self?" My head hangs. "I can't even scratch the surface with Aiden no matter what I do."

She appears thoughtful for a while. "I didn't do anything special."

"N-nothing at all?"

"I only showed him my true self and in response, he showed me his. Remember the yin and yang I mentioned earlier? It's exactly like that. You take as much as you give. You can't close off and expect him to bare his soul."

"But I'm not closed off."

"Maybe not consciously, but subconsciously?" She throws her hands in the air. "I'm not that good at psychology rubbish, but all I'm saying is, if you show your genuine self, then Aiden will be compelled to show himself, too."

"What if he doesn't?"

"Then the fucker doesn't deserve you." She laughs. "But seriously. You're wrong about thinking that you can't scratch the surface with him. I believe you're already deep inside him, you just don't know it yet."

I don't think so.

"Frozen!" Levi peeks his head inside, wearing a grin that appears so much like Aiden's when he's genuine—which is rare as hell.

"Her name is Elsa," Astrid scolds.

"Frozen is a term of endearment, princess."

"Only to you."

"Morning, Levi." I wave at him.

"What's your magic trick to have that dickhead make breakfast?"

"Being herself." Astrid winks, and I can't help the smile that breaks free.

We should meet more often. She's one of the most real girls I've ever met.

Even though she's the daughter of Lord Clifford, a renowned member of the House of Lords, she's more down to earth than commoners.

"By the way," Levi shouts in a voice loud enough to reach downstairs. "He cooks like shit."

"You're only salty because you don't get to eat it." Aiden's voice comes from downstairs.

Astrid and I snort before we break into laughter.

"I'll go help." Astrid pats my arm again. "Come down when you're ready."

She stops at the doorway, stands on her tippy toes and places a kiss on Levi's mouth, then escapes before he can clutch her.

My chest warms at the sight.

They're really so compatible together. It makes me wonder about how rocky their relationship was last year.

"Are you coming?" Levi asks.

"Uh… yeah, sure."

I remove my jacket and remain in my shirt. It's too warm inside for a jacket.

Levi steps into the room as I place the jacket near the backpack.

"How is it with him?" he asks.

No idea how to answer that.

Good would be a lie. Bad would be a lie, too.

"It's complicated," I tell the truth.

"Well, he's the complicated type." Levi laughs. "You didn't listen to my warning, so you reap what you sow."

I face him. "Your warning?"

"At Ronan's party, I told you that you should stay away from Aiden for your own sake, not his."

Right. He did tell me that.

Does that mean Levi knows something about what happened to change Aiden into who he is?

Now, I have to ask without sounding too obvious.

"It's not like I had a choice." I shrug. "You know him better than anyone."

"No one actually knows Aiden. We can only try." He smiles a little. "But I'm glad you're taking a chance on getting to know him, too."

"A chance?"

"He's not conventional."

I nod once. Of course, Levi recognises Aiden's true nature. They grew up together in the same house.

"This change happened somewhere in his childhood, right?"

He nods. "He was a quiet child by nature, but that incident changed everything."

"You mean Alicia's death."

"Yes, that one was the icing on the cake, but it's not —"

"Breakfast."

Both Levi and I startle at Aiden's voice. I was so focused on what Levi was saying that I didn't notice him come in.

"How about you make a sound, you fucking creep?" Levi scoffs.

"How about you leave?" Aiden shoots back.

"Dream on." He winks at me. "Come on. Let's eat."

I start to follow him out.

A strong hand clutches me by the arm and wrenches me back. "What the fuck were you talking about with Lev?"

His eyes are darkening by the second.

It's then I notice that possessive streak. I don't know if he overhead, but he seems more concerned about Levi more than anything.

"The usual. Arsenal and football." I try to tease. "I can see who's the talker in the family."

"Elsa," he growls in my ear. "Don't push me. You know I go fucking crazy at the thought of you with another man."

"Levi included?"

"Every last fucking one of them."

He's incurable.

And because I don't want to antagonise him more, I say, "Levi might be the talker in the family, but he's not the king on my board."

A charming smile tilts his lips, and I find myself staring at it longer than needed.

He threads his fingers in mine. "Good save."

We walk down the hall when I ask, "Where did you go this morning?"

"To buy gluten-free grocery." He grunts. "Let's get this breakfast over with so they'll leave."

"Why do you not want me around them?"

"I don't want you around anyone, sweetheart." He chances a brief glance at me. "Especially my family."

But why?

What's so wrong with his family?

Levi was on the verge of saying that maybe it's not only Alicia's death that caused Aiden's change.

If it's not his mother, then what made him who he is today?

TWENTY-ONE

Elsa

Ten days pass.

Day after day, Aiden only tells me mundane things from his 'story' and never jumps to what I want to know.

Day after day, I expect him to tell me the grand finale.

I should've known better.

He's still pissed off that I put a limit on sex.

Not only is he pissed off, but he also manipulates his way into touching me every chance he gets.

The other day, he said, "Those two friends had a bet."

One sentence. That's it.

Then he fucked me against the wall in the locker room.

When I tried to argue, he said that my condition was 'If you tell me a tidbit, you get to fuck me.' I never specified how long the tidbit needs to be.

Dickhead.

Even when I thought I have any resemblance of control over the situation, he throws it out of the window. He smashes any hope I have and crushes it to bloody pieces.

But even with his mind games and tactics, I still got my say in this. If it were up to him, we'd go back to how we were before; I stay in the dark and he knows everything.

It won't be that way anymore. Even if I have to compromise with sex.

Since that night at the Meet Up, Aiden has been fucking me rough and hard as if he's teaching me a lesson.

I come every time.

Hell, sometimes, he tortures me like that night and exhausts my body until I can barely breathe anymore.

Is it a punishment if I crave it?

It's fruitless to fight him in the physical department. However, I'm not going to sit there and wait for him to feed me crumbs about hypothetical friends. He didn't even tell me their names, and while I suspect they have something to do with the mystery, I'm still not sure what is it all about.

So this time, I'm taking things into my own hands. After all, it's not a game if he's the only one who plays.

I'm in front of the King mansion's grand gate.

Clutching my umbrella tight, I stand there as the rain silently soaks the pavements.

Elites have practice and the horsemen won't be here for at least another hour. Kim has to babysit Kir so she's not coming to watch the game tonight.

Aiden told me to be at his practice and then we'll go together, but I refused, telling him I'll meet him here. That made him narrow his eyes.

He still doesn't like that I refuse to attend his games or watch him practice, but screw him.

He's refusing to give me what I want, why should I give him what he wants?

Anyway, I never told Aiden when I'll meet him at his place. I just 'happened' to come an hour earlier.

I have to investigate Aiden's 'story'. He's not the type of person who goes out of his way to learn about other people. Since he knows so much about those 'friends', then one of them has to do with him.

He mentioned the friends turned into rivals and their games

crossed the line. He mentioned that their bet shouldn't have happened.

Aiden isn't the type who uses words like limit and line. He doesn't shackle himself with boundaries. In fact, he considers them a challenge and makes it his mission to destroy them.

The fact that he used those words means that the story happened when he was younger.

Before he became a monster without limits, Aiden was a kid with limits.

This is only a theory, but I think one of the friends is Jonathan. First of all, he's a tycoon who stops at nothing to get what he wants. He didn't build King Enterprises by being a nice person. On the contrary, he took the throne by crushing everyone in his path.

Sort of like Aiden.

It makes sense that he has some fucked up rivalry with one of his friends.

The best way to check Aiden's story and my theory is to find something in the King mansion.

I never snooped before, but that's because Aiden has always been there. Even when I wake up in the middle of the night, he'll be watching me with dark, haunting eyes.

In the beginning, I thought that was because he's just Aiden. But then again, I never saw him look at anyone the way he looks at me.

Sometimes, it's filled with care. Other times, it's pure terrifying hate.

Now that I know he has insomnia, I can't begin to imagine how he spends his nights all alone in this huge place.

You can do this, Elsa.

I ring the bell and glance at the screen. The butler's face comes into view and he gives me a polite smile. "Miss Quinn, we weren't expecting you until six."

Well, shit. Of course, Aiden's butler would be expecting me. Why hadn't I thought of that?

I offer my widest smile. "Aiden is caught up at practice, so he told me to wait for him here. If it's possible, of course."

He's silent for a second, and I expect him to tell me no since Aiden didn't call him. However, the front gate buzzes open.

"Welcome, Miss Quinn."

Phew.

I give him one last smile as I clutch my backpack's strap and slip inside.

An eerie feeling creeps along my skin the more I walk through the silent garden. The rain soaks the trees, the grass, and the imposing building. Rivulets of the rain fall on the angel statue's cheeks and it appears as if he's crying.

That's not creepy at all.

I came here numerous times before, but that was before I heard Jonathan tell Silver ever so eloquently that Aiden approached me for revenge.

That was before I learnt that Aiden has been using me.

That part still bugs the hell out of me.

If he hates me, if he only approached me for revenge, then why does he fuck me like he'll die if he doesn't? Why does he soothe me after my nightmares like he doesn't like to see me hurt?

If this is all an act, then he deserves an Oscar.

Margo waits for me at the entrance of the front door. Her hands rest above each other on her stomach as she smiles.

"Hey, Margo."

"Hey, Elsa." She steps aside to give me walking room. "Come inside. It's cold, let me prepare you something to drink."

She takes my sweater, scarf, and umbrella. I try to help her, but she shoos me away.

Margo always makes me feel warm in this frigid, cold mansion.

It's like she's the only one who breathes life in here.

Aiden and his father surely don't. I doubt Levi did either when he was living here.

I follow Margo to the kitchen and she launches into a string of questions about my health and if I'm eating properly as she prepares me a hot chocolate.

I try to answer as much as I can.

In no time, I'm sitting at the kitchen counter with the steaming drink in front of me and the scent of hot chocolate wafting in the air.

Margo stands behind the counter, fussing with potatoes.

"Is that for chips?" I ask.

"Those boys will start a riot if they don't have their chips." She shakes her head. "Especially Ronan."

I smile at that. He's certainly fanatic and possessive about his chips. You can have his car, but you can't ask for his chips.

"They're lucky to have you," I tell her.

The slight wrinkles ease at the corner of her eyes. "I'm lucky to have them, especially my Aiden."

I straighten in my seat. This is my opening. "He went through a lot when he was a child." I pause, then add. "Levi told me."

Sorrow covers her features as she slows down cutting the potatoes. "He didn't talk much."

"Why not?"

"He was a lonely child. He spent his days in the library with Alicia." She scoffs. "When she was out of her room."

I lean closer, cradling the hot cup between my cold fingers. "Was he close to his mother?"

"Unfortunately, yes."

"Why unfortunately?"

"Because her madness rubbed off on him." Her lips twist. "He's never been the same since she was locking herself up with him in the library reading crazy books about crazy people."

"Crazy books?"

She throws her hand in the air. "Philosophy and psychology rubbish."

I frown. Those aren't crazy books, but I don't correct her. I can't get into an argument with her if I want to keep her talking.

"Alicia was never normal anyway." Margo watches her

surroundings before she leans in to whisper, "I heard from one of her friends that she suffered from depression after an accident. She was out with her friends and they all died except for her. She was been the same since then."

Survivor's guilt.

I heard about that. Hell, If my nightmares are of any indication, then I might even be suffering from it myself.

"Was that before she got married?" I ask.

"Yes."

Still. Alicia got married and had Aiden, so she couldn't have been that bad, right?

"There were a lot of tragic events in her life, so I tried to understand, I really did." Margo chops the potatoes harder. "But she shouldn't have brought Aiden to the world if she was going to be a zombie most of the time."

"Tragic events?" I ask.

"Yes, her father was a lord, but he was abusive. Her mother committed suicide because of that and I think, I'm not sure, he continued to beat Alicia until she got married."

My heart swells for the woman I only saw through the picture. The petite, quiet-looking woman.

So basically, Alicia was a mentally unwell person. I'm curious why Jonathan would marry her. I'm sure he knew her past. These types of families do an extensive background check about the ones they're going to marry.

Jonathan King doesn't strike me as the kind of man who'd marry Alicia. His type loves the perfect housewives with perfect everything, don't they?

"Was it an arranged marriage?" I ask Margo.

"No. Mr King chose her himself."

Oh.

Maybe he did love her. But well, I find it hard to believe that Jonathan would love anyone. He doesn't even seem like he loves his own son.

This needs more digging.

I just hope I don't end up regretting it.

"Can I see the library?" I wrap my fingers around the hot chocolate. "I have some homework."

"It's down the hall to the left." She motions at the potatoes. "Sorry I can't show you."

"It's okay." I gather my backpack and take the drink. "Thanks for this."

"Let me know if you need anything to eat."

"Will do."

At first, I attempt going to the upper floor where I think Jonathan's office is, but then as I walk down the hall, I notice the small blinking cameras.

Shit.

How come I never noticed them before? And who the hell keeps cameras inside his house?

Defeated, I head to the library. The space is so vast, it nearly swallows the entire ground floor. It's even bigger than the theatre room—and that says something.

Rows and rows of books extend as far as the vision can go.

Old books. Big books. Hardcovers. Paperbacks.

Hell, there are even a few first editions here.

I wonder if they have some Sun Tzu in this place.

Three dark wooden tables with cushioned seats are arranged neatly in the middle of the room. It smells of old paper, and I can't help but inhale the scent.

I place my backpack and drink on a table and walk to the wooden rows. run my fingers along some books written in Russian and in French.

Someone is a polyglot.

Keeping my head down, I check the corner in case there are cameras lurking in here.

I don't notice any blinking, but that doesn't put me at ease.

The King's mansion has this eerie quality to it. I'm on high alert the entire time.

I only let go when Aiden is around, but maybe that's a mistake, too.

A few psychology books grab my attention. Margo mentioned that Alicia read those to Aiden.

The other day, Cole also mentioned that Nausea, a philosophy book, belongs to Aiden.

I pull a paperback about the light in the mind or something. It's the first time I hear about it. It's written by J.E. Hampton. Never heard of him—or her.

There's dust on the book, so it hasn't been touched in years.

I open the book.

The dedication says,

To unknown. You should've killed me.

The 'You should've killed me' part is underlined with a red pencil.

I open the first pages and read. It talks about someone who's trying to find his way after chronic depression. I read a few pages and I notice some words underlined in red like in the dedication page.

Lost.

Help.

Live.

Alive.

Dead.

It goes on until the end of the book.

I retrieve another one. Nothing is underlined in the dedication, but inside the book, similar words are underlined.

Save.

Kill.

Love.

I pull another book then another and another. It's almost the same in all books. Then I find something different.

The dedication in another book says,

To J, Thank you for saving my life.

It's crossed in red and under it is written in elegant writing.

'You shouldn't have saved my life.'

My breathing catches. Is this Alicia?

I retrieve about ten books and sit on the table, going through them.

I find a dedication that says,

To the fighters. Stay alive.

Under it, there's that same elegant handwriting.

'The worst thing you can tell a person who wants to die is to stay alive.'

I gulp.

So she was suicidal.

Did Aiden know that?

My heart squeezes at the thought of a little boy witnessing his mother's suicidal tendencies. Did she do something traumatising in front of him?

A wave of nausea hits me at the thought.

I go through the pages some more.

I find another dedication.

To my son, you gave purpose to my life.

There's a line under it and then a smiling face. My heart warms until I read the writing beneath it.

'But I wish you were never born.'

I blink, reading it again.

Did she say that about her own son? What the hell?

The book is old and dusty and doesn't seem like it's been touched since Alicia's death. With one last look to my surroundings, I stuff the book in my backpack.

Aiden might be a bastard and I hate him sometimes, but I would never want to scar him this way. He shouldn't see what Alicia wrote about him.

I know she must've had deep-rooted mental issues, but that doesn't give her the right to wish that her son was never born. She read all these psychological books, how come she didn't know words like that from his own mother could scar him for life?

I check my watch. Shit. It's almost time for the horsemen to return. I easily wasted an entire hour digging through the pieces Alicia left behind, but I need to go.

I don't want Aiden to catch me in his library.

I put the books where they belong, take my backpack, and go back to Margo.

The moment I sit on the stool, sipping the cold hot chocolate, Ronan comes breezing through the door.

"I'm here, bitches!" He yells in his signature enthusiastic tone. When he meets my eyes, his grin widens. "Oh. Hey there, Ellie."

I smile as Xander and a solemn-looking Cole follow him inside. They're all wearing Elites' jackets which means they came straight from practice.

Xander searches beside me and all around me, for Kim, I assume.

"Kim has to babysit Kir so she won't be coming over," I tell him.

"I didn't ask." He flops on a stool and steals one of Margo's chips.

Yeah, right. Sure thing, Xander.

I seriously don't know what the hell is going on between him and Kim. Or if there's even anything going on.

"Where's Aiden?" I ask when he doesn't follow.

"Oh, that…" Ronan rubs the back of his head.

"He'll be here." Xander smiles forcing the dimples out as he snatches another chip.

I stare between them and a needle-like sensation prickles at the back of my head.

Something doesn't seem right.

"Where did he go?" I ask.

"Come on, Ellie." Ronan places an arm around my shoulder. "Let's stuff ourselves with chips."

"He's outside with Silver," Cole says with a complete poker face.

"Fuck, Captain!" Ronan all but shouts.

Xander pokes Cole in the ribs. "You better be ready for King's wrath, dickhead."

I stare between the three of them. "He's really outside with Silver?"

"You see, Ellie." Ronan offers an awkward smile—which isn't like him at all. "She invited herself over. It's not that King wanted her here. Not at all."

"He didn't stop her either." Cole appears eerily calm, it's kind of scary. "You should see for yourself."

Xander kicks him. "Do you have a fucking death wish, Captain?"

I'm not listening to them.

I'm storming down the hall, muscles tense and nostrils flaring.

He brought her here.

Silver is *here*.

I told her to stay away from what's mine, didn't I?

It's time she pays the fucking price.

TWENTY-TWO

Aiden

Queens wouldn't go home.

Nash has been acting like a little bitch and refused to deal with her.

His exact words were 'Clean your own mess, King.'

So here I am standing with Queens in front of her car.

The rain soaks us both.

So be it, because there's no way she's going inside.

Elsa has already been distrustful of me without adding Queens into the mix.

Since the pool incident, I've been slowly building back her trust, but everything will be destroyed if Queens is involved.

I can handle it when Elsa lies to herself. I can handle it when she tries to be politically correct, but I can't have any of that if she completely pulls the fuck away from me.

"You said you'll fix it." Queens stomps her feet. "You promised, King."

"I promised you fuck."

"But you said —"

"I said nothing. You assumed everything yourself." I stare down at her. "The game was fun while it lasted, but I'm not playing anymore."

"You're not playing?" She huffs. "So when it's to your benefit, you're all in, but when it's not, you just drop it?"

"Exactly. Smarten up, Queens. All what you're doing is a temporary solution."

"That's none of your fucking business." She grinds her teeth. "I knew you'd change your mind because of that little bitch."

I push into her and she flinches against the side of her car.

"Watch it. If you call her that one more time, I won't let you be, Queens."

"You can do fuck to me, King," she snarls even though her eyes are glimmering. "You know why? Because Uncle Jonathan is on my side."

My left eye twitches. I resist the urge to bang her head against the hood of the car.

It's because of her that Elsa has changed. If she wasn't being a nosy busy-body, Elsa wouldn't have slipped from between my fingers the way she did.

Queens should be fucking thankful I value Nash enough not to destroy her.

However, my patience has limits.

Queens is playing a bigger game than her. Yes, I entertained her idea. Yes, I liked the challenge while it lasted, but not anymore.

It's time she knows her fucking place.

"How about Nash, then?" I ask in a neutral voice.

Her face contorts. I smirk.

People with fucking weaknesses shouldn't be going into battle.

"Whose side do you think he's on?" I ask. "If he finds out your little games, who do you think he'll lash out on? Spoiler alert. It won't be me."

"Don't you dare, King."

"Then fucking disappear, Queens." I loom over her, squaring my shoulders. "This is your final warning. If you threaten what's mine, I'll destroy you until there's nothing left for Nash to pick up."

Despite the rain, I can see the tears shining in her eyes.

Since she doesn't cry, this should mean that my message got through.

I'm about to pull back when a small hand pushes me away. I didn't hear her approach—and it's not because of the rain.

Elsa's blue eyes are glassed over.

They're blackening and darkening on Queens.

Like the other time, she's quiet.

So fucking quiet.

Since I was a child, I was attuned to small noises. I couldn't sleep all night because of the small sounds coming from the trees' leaves.

It should be impossible that I didn't hear her approach.

For the second time.

I'm still studying Elsa and her stiffened body language when she slams her fist into Queens' face.

The latter clutches her cheek, mouth hanging open when Elsa punches her in the chest. Queens shrieks and wraps both her arms around her midsection.

Elsa grips her by the collar of her shirt. "I told you to stay the fuck away from what's mine!"

And then she goes to punch her again.

Queens tries to fight her off, but she's like a helpless toddler in front of Elsa's strength.

Elsa's brute, subconscious strength.

My body tightens as I watch her closely.

That posture. That same fucking posture.

A black halo surrounds my head, and I can't see anything past it.

No. That's a lie.

I can see a little boy.

The welts on his skin.

The darkness in his surroundings.

The fear in his eyes.

The same fear that's now on Queens' face as she bends over in front of Elsa's assault.

I grab her by the arm and pull her back so harshly, she slams straight into my chest.

She tries to fight me off, her hands still pointing in Queens' direction. The latter is crouched on the wet ground, coughing and trembling under the rain.

Elsa isn't seeing that. She's not seeing anything except for the black rage covering her vision.

Just like them.

She's just like them.

No. She's not.

This is Elsa. My Elsa.

And no fucking one will take her away from me. Not even herself.

I wrap my hand around her neck and squeeze.

Her arms stop flailing about. She blinks a few times. When she finally looks at me—like *really* looks at me—her gaze fills with horror as if she's just realising what she has done.

"Don't go there again," I whisper.

If she does, I'll have no choice but to follow her. She'll hate what I become like when I do.

She nods once even though her eyes are lost, I pull her into me and wrap my arms around her back as she hides her head in my chest.

For a few seconds, we stand there as the rain beats down on us.

"Make her go," Elsa murmurs in my chest. "Make her go away."

"Leave," I order Queens.

She stands and opens her mouth to say something, but then her gaze strays behind me and her mouth falls open.

Her bright blue eyes widen with fear.

Pure, unhinged fear.

Still staring behind me, she opens her car door with trembling hands and slips inside. And then, she's speeding out of the driveway.

Still cradling Elsa close to my chest, I glance behind me.

Nash stands at the entrance with both hands in his pockets.

A rare cruel smirk lifts his lips.

TWENTY-THREE

Elsa

My teeth clatter together.

I'm trembling and choking on air.

My heart slams against my chest so hard, I'm surprised it doesn't rip its way out.

My shirt sticks to my skin all soaked from the rain.

I don't even know how I ended up in Aiden's room, sitting in the corner, and pulling my knees to my chest.

The last thing I remember is Aiden squeezing my throat and bringing me back from whatever haze I was in.

I remember red.

Dots of blood spilt in my head like the pool from the nightmare. The next thing I know, I was hitting Silver.

I wanted to push her inside that red pool.

I wanted her gone.

If Aiden didn't stop me, what would I have done?

Tears fill my eyes, and I tighten my arms around my legs as I rock back and forth against the wall.

Something is wrong with me.

When did I become this person? When did I start fantasising about hurting people?

"Elsa."

A larger than life presence crouches in front of me. Just like Uncle Reg in that nightmare.

Will it be a red pool now?

Am I trapped in my endless nightmares?

I stare up with wild eyes.

Aiden's shirt is also soaked and is now transparent, outlining his hard muscles. He must've lost the jacket somewhere because his shirt's cuffs are rolled to his elbows. The arrow tattoos point straight at his heart.

He holds a towel in his hand and watches me intently.

My breathing slows down a little, but it's not enough to purge the disturbing images in my head.

It's not enough to make me stop thinking about what I would've done to Silver if he weren't there to stop me.

"W-what's wrong with me?" A sob tears from my throat. "She didn't even attack me, and I was about to kill her."

He slowly places the towel on my head as if not wanting to startle me. With meticulous hands, he dries off the wet strands. "She did attack you."

"No, she didn't. She just stood there defenceless."

"She provoked you."

"Provoked me?"

He continues his strokes on my hair. "It's been accumulating for a while. Not only does Queens threaten you, but she's also been provoking you."

"You think I hit her because of that?"

"Yes. You don't attack people without any reason. You only go after those who provoke or pose a threat to you."

"How do you know that?"

He clutches my arm and pulls me closer to him. I stop rocking as he manoeuvres me to straddle his lap. "It's a theory."

I peek at him through my blurry vision. "Have you been psychoanalysing me or something?"

"Maybe." He continues drying my hair. "You don't need to worry

about Queens anymore. She knows her place now and won't provoke you again."

"Why?"

"I made her."

"You made her how?"

"By less violent methods?" He grins, and I wince.

He places a finger under my chin and lifts so I'm facing him.
"You don't have to be ashamed of who you are with me, Elsa. You
can be a fucking lunatic, and I still won't let you go."

Wow. That's surprisingly sweet coming from him.

It's almost like he accepts me whole. Aiden isn't interested in
mere parts of me, he wants the whole thing.

And my heart nearly bursts open at his acceptance.

It's like I've been waiting my entire life for someone to take me
as I am and I finally found him.

He *sees* me.

And he's not scared of what he sees.

Hell, I'm more terrified than him.

My teary eyes search his cloudy ones for any sign of manipulation, but all I find is acceptance.

Unconditional acceptance.

He shouldn't accept this part of me. I don't accept it myself.

"You shouldn't joke about that," I whisper.

"It wasn't a joke. I don't care who or what you are as long as
you're mine."

My lower lip trembles and the hysterics' wave from earlier threatens to hit me all over again. "What if... what if I hurt someone?"

"Why would you think that?"

"I keep having these nightmares about pools of blood. A normal person wouldn't have those nightmares. I m-must've hurt someone before... right?"

"It could be that you were the one who got hurt."

I pull back. He pauses drying my hair.

"You know, don't you?" I choke on the words.

There's a slight shift in his features before that infuriating poker face slips back on. "I know what?"

"Tell me, Aiden, please." I grind against his erection, rubbing my arse cheeks all over him. "I'll do anything."

"Stop." He grips my arm hard, causing me to whimper. "I won't fuck you when you're like this."

"When I'm like what?" Frustration and the fear of the unknown claw at my chest and I just snap. "A mess? A fucking maniac? I hurt my aunt in the hospital, Aiden! The wound I left in her wrist is so deep, I can't look her in the eyes without feeling like a monster. I scratched you the other time and I almost bashed Silver's head to the pavement just now. I keep escalating with no way to stop it and you're refusing to fucking tell me what happened!"

Harsh breaths heave out of me after my outburst. I try to push off him, but he grips me by the shoulder and keeps me pinned to his lap.

"Do you think you'll feel better if you know the truth?" He grinds out every word.

"Of course!"

"Believe me, sweetheart, it'll be a lot fucking worse."

"Let me be the judge of that. It's my life, Aiden. Mine! I'm tired of people making the decision for me. Let me screw up on my own! I'll take responsibility for it all."

He throws the towel away, wraps a tight arm around my waist, and stands up.

I'm thrown over the bed before I can think about what's happening. Aiden lunges at me and rips my shirt open. I gasp as buttons fly everywhere. The sound dies in my throat when I stare at his crazed expression.

He's about to snap.

And I'm the one who drove him to the edge.

"You want to know, huh?" He grips the middle of the bra and yanks it open.

I cry out, but it's not only out of surprise. No. His brute strength always got me in a knot whether I like to admit it or not.

He hovers over me, straddling my stomach with his knees, and grabs a breast in his harsh hand. His fingers dig into the flesh, and my limbs shake.

As if possible, his eyes darken more.

It's like he's not with me.

I'm losing him to his demons.

"A-Aiden?"

His free hand squeezes my throat, killing my words and my air. When I try to speak again, he tightens his grip. Barely a few breaths reach my lungs.

"Let's start with this scar." His voice is calm. The frightening type of calm. "Do you know the story behind this fucking scar, hmm?"

I squirm, clawing at his hands.

He squeezes harder, cutting off the small air supply I have left. "Stay. Fucking. Still."

If I continue fighting, it'll be a war of physical strength and I won't win in that.

Smarter, not stronger.

I let my arms fall on either side of me.

Just like that, Aiden slowly eases his clutch on my neck, but he doesn't completely release it.

I gulp in sharp intakes of air and watch him closely.

Aiden massages my throat and the pulse point with an obsessive interest before his metal eyes slide down to my breast.

No. Not my breast.

My scar.

He leans over and nibbles on the flesh then sucks it into his mouth.

Shock reverberates through my entire body.

Stop it.

He flicks his tongue over the skin, licking before he bites down ever so gently.

Stop.

His assault goes on and on until I'm whimpering.

Although soft, his touch hurts.

It cuts me open like a sharp object.

I'm bleeding out.

It *hurts.*

Somewhere in my mind, it fucking hurts.

His teeth and stubble graze my scar as he speaks against it. "This scar is a sign of your weakness. Just like my scar. And guess what, sweetheart? We're not allowed to be fucking weak."

I'm breathing harshly as I stare at him. He finally lifts his head and meets my gaze with his dark one and that twitchy left eye.

He's pissed off.

No. He's enraged.

But it doesn't appear directed at me.

At least, I hope not.

Because right now, I feel closer to Aiden than I've ever felt before.

His scar and my scar.

His heartbeat and mine.

"Are our scars connected?" I ask in a small voice, afraid that a higher one will ruin the moment.

Silence.

I wrap my hand around his and slowly peel it from around my throat. I'm surprised that he lets me. He doesn't even stop me when I sit up, forcing him to sit, too.

My fingers tremble as I undo the buttons of his wet shirt. I can feel his eyes watching me, nearly drawing a hole at the top of my head, but he doesn't stop me.

I peel the shirt off his shoulders and let it drop to the floor. I try to make him turn, but he shakes his head.

So I do the one thing I can.

I flatten my breasts against his hard chest and wrap my arms around his back. My fingertips glide along the slash marks.

He stiffens.

It's just a tiny reaction, but from Aiden, it's everything that he doesn't—and wouldn't—say.

It's proof that he's scarred not only on the outside but also on the inside.

Just like me.

"I'm sorry," I whisper, inhaling his scent mixed with the rain.

"Why are you sorry for something you didn't do?"

"I'm sorry that you went through that pain."

"What makes you think I did?" His voice is quiet, too quiet, I barely hear him.

My eyes fill with tears. "My scar hurt like a bitch when I got it, and I'm sure these must've hurt you a lot, too."

He remains silent.

For a moment, I continue holding him even when he doesn't wrap his arms around me.

He just sits in the middle of the bed like a statue and lets me hug him.

I don't mind.

He's been there for me during my nightmares, this is the least I could do.

I want to support him silently as he did to me.

"Those friends were bored," he says in a neutral voice. "The mind makes you do a lot of fucked-up shit when you're bored. But they weren't normal bored people. They were sadistic bored people."

He stops talking, and I inch back to study him. There's a glint in his dark eyes. That usually means he's letting his devil come out and play.

It'd be a lie if I said I'm not scared, but this time, I won't run away.

I'm staying right here. His demons can show me their worst.

"Due to their games, they lost both their children."

My lips part. "Lost?"

"They died." He smiles. "That finally managed to stop them. Actually, no. Something else stopped them. Or someone."

"Someone stopped them?"

He nods.

"Who?"

"I can't remember." He grips me by both my hips and flips me underneath him.

I squeal.

He yanks my skirt up and buries his hand under my underwear.

A moan rips from my throat when he thrusts his middle finger deep inside me.

"Maybe I'll remember after I fuck you."

"Aiden!" I hit his chest.

He twists his finger so close to that sensitive spot.

My back arches off the bed, inviting him in.

"I miss fucking you," he whispers against my mouth. "I miss having you writhe against me while I pound inside you."

"That was only yesterday," I pant, chasing the feeling of the wicked things his finger does.

His erection nuzzles against my clit, and I subconsciously open my legs.

"It can be two minutes ago and I'd still want you, sweetheart."

He removes his finger, but before I can protest, he glides the tip of his cock over my entrance.

I roll my hips, pushing into him.

"Hmm. Someone is impatient."

I rub against him again. Why the hell isn't he inside me yet?

"You like how I tease you before driving you to the edge, don't you, sweetheart?"

I bite my lower lip as a rush of desire claws its way through me.

"Answer. Me."

I nod.

His lips hover an inch away from mine. "Then how about you lift that limit and let me fuck you any time I please?"

I shake my head.

"No, huh?" He slams balls deep inside me.

I cry out, my eyes rolling to the back of my head.

"Even if my stories will only hurt you?"

"Yes." I stare him in the eyes even as I struggle for words. "There's nothing scarier than the unknown."

"Believe me, sweetheart, there is."

And then he claims my mouth and fucks me until I think he'll never stop.

TWENTY-FOUR

Elsa

Aiden wanted me to stay the night, but I already promised Aunt and Uncle that I'd be home.

We're having a rare family dinner, and I wouldn't miss it for the world.

Besides, I need distance from Aiden tonight. He got too close and touched me so deep, I'm scared there will be no coming out from under his clutches.

We watched the second half of the game with the guys—or more like with Xander and Ronan. Cole wasn't there when Aiden and I joined them.

After the game ended, I asked Aiden to drop me off at home.

Which brings us to the now.

I slide in the passenger seat of the Ferrari as Aiden snaps his seatbelt in place.

Someone is pissed off.

"You know how rare it is to get dinner with Aunt and Uncle."

He revs the engine to life. "Did I say anything?"

He doesn't have to. I recognise the displeased energy surrounding him.

For some reason, I don't want him to be angry after he offered me one of the most unforgettable nights of my life.

The car launches in the streets. It's dark, but it's stopped raining.

I turn to place my backpack in the backseat. Something makes a noise underneath it.

Frowning, I pull the object and find… a pack of condoms?

What in the actual…?

I thrust the pack in front of Aiden's face. "What is this?"

He barely glances at it. "Condoms."

"I know what they are, Mr Obvious. I'm asking what the hell are they doing here." My breathing hitches. "Are they for Silver when you —"

"Stop." He fixates me with a glare before focusing back on the road. "I told you that I didn't fuck Queens, and I don't lie to you. Is that clear?"

"Then what are they for? It sure as shit isn't for me."

"Astor leaves them around me all the time, usually in my bag." He rolls his eyes. "Flip it and you'll find some cheesy note."

I do as he said and find a scribble in Ronan's signature messy handwriting.

Wrap it before you tap it, mate. I don't want kids running around at my parties. Mmmkay?

A smile breaks on my lips. That's so Ronan.

"Happy now?" Aiden asks.

I bite my inner cheek. "Sorry."

"You need to learn how to trust me." He glances at me. "It won't work if I'm the only one who trusts you."

I suck more on my inner cheek.

He trusts me.

But then again, I never gave him a reason not to trust me.

Unlike him.

I opt to change the subject instead of going on a fruitless argument.

I shake the pack. "Why do you never use condoms with me?"

He narrows his eyes—probably because of the change of

subject—and I expect him to refuse, but he focuses back on the road and says, "They're a barrier. I hate having barriers between us."

I don't know if he says these types of things on purpose or if he really means them. Either way, it's working.

My face heats and my toes curl.

"You should be thankful I'm on the shot. You didn't even ask if I were on birth control the first time…" I trail off, my eyes widening. "How did you know I was on birth control?"

"I didn't."

"You… didn't? What if I wasn't on anything?"

"So what?"

Oh, God. I want to bash his poker face against the window.

"So what? So freaking what? I could've gotten pregnant!"

He tilts his head to the side. "You're not."

"What if I were, huh?"

"I don't consider hypothetical situations."

"Well, consider them now. You want me to trust you, right? Then be honest with me. What would you have done if I were on nothing and fell pregnant?"

He sighs, keeping his attention on the road. "I would've taken care of it and you. I'm not irresponsible."

"Have you ever thought about my opinion? What if I don't want kids this young?"

"I didn't plan on impregnating you, but if it happens, it happens, Elsa."

"Yeah, right. You totally didn't plan on it and the proof is not using a condom. Did you do that with all your previous sexual partners?"

We stop at a red light and Aiden's icy stare bores into me. "You're the only one I haven't used a condom with. Do you think I was in my right mind the first time I fucked you? Or every time after for that matter? The moment I knew you were a virgin and that you were offering your virginity to me, I lost it. Do you think I had the

STEEL PRINCESS | 171

time to think about a fucking condom when your tight pussy was clenching my dick that hard?"

"No?"

"Fuck no." He takes my hand in his and places it on the swell of his jeans. "I'm hard just thinking about that night, sweetheart."

"Perv." I yank my hand, but my cheeks flame. "Do you have some virgin blood kink?"

"Only yours, sweetheart." His left eye twitches. "I was pissed off at the thought that someone else touched you and has been inside you, so imagine my surprise when you gave it to me."

My knee-jerk reaction is to tell him that it isn't a big deal.

But that would be a lie, wouldn't it?

I gave him that part of me, and I don't regret that he's the first one who knows me intimately.

"How was it like when you lost your virginity?" I ask, my curiosity getting the better of me.

The green light goes on and he kicks the car into gear. "Boring."

"Can you give more details?" I ask.

"I was fifteen and I was sick of Knight and Astor urging me to shag and sending me gay porn sites in case I was interested in the other sex. In comes my father's secretary. She was the only female he allowed close after Alicia's death and I didn't like it. One night, said secretary was flirting with me in the kitchen. I pushed her against the counter and fucked her from behind. Unlike what the guys warned, I didn't come pre-maturely. I had to ram inside her for fifteen minutes before I found release. Now that I think about it, the second-rate porn noises she made must've been the turn-off."

"Wow." My mouth hangs open. "I... have no words for that."

He lifts a shoulder. "You asked for the details."

Yeah, but I didn't mean so many details.

"So you fucked the woman your father was fucking?"

"Nah. Turns out Jonathan never fucked her. He doesn't screw around with work."

"What happened to her?" Please tell me she doesn't work for

Jonathan anymore. I don't like that he's still in contact with the woman he lost his virginity to.

"Jonathan walked in on us while she was sucking my dick and fired her. That's when I knew he never fucked her."

"Did you keep in touch with her?"

"Why would I?"

"You know, for sex."

"She wasn't a good fuck."

"Hey! That's rude. Do you even remember her name?"

"I don't remember names of people who aren't a part of my life. Ms Secretary gave good head, but she wasn't a good fuck."

"Does that mean you had good fucks after her?" I try not to sound jealous, but I'm not sure if I succeeded.

"Sure did."

We approach my house, and I'm so ready to leave him and his 'good fucks'.

The thought of him driving another woman as crazy as he does me makes me sick to my stomach.

"Good for you," I huff throwing the pack of condoms where I found it. "Maybe I should've had some experience of my own, too."

He slams on the breaks, I nearly topple over from my seat.

"Don't you ever fucking repeat that." He releases his seatbelt and faces me. "I'm the only experience you'll ever have. Is that clear?"

"Why can't I have memorable fucks like you did?"

"None of them were memorable. I quickly lost interest." He reaches a finger and traces it along my lower lip. "Until you."

I swear my heart jumped out of its cavities at Aiden's husky, low words.

"What if you lose interest in me, too?"

"Never." He flattens his thumb on my lower lip. "I've been addicted to you since I touched you. I can't stay away from you even if I wanted to, sweetheart. So don't ask me to. Don't even suggest it."

My breathing deepens as I stare at him with parted lips.

Because I don't think I can stay away from him either.

Not anymore.

He leans over and presses his lips to mine. I open up with a moan. With every stroke of his tongue against mine, my walls crumble all around me and I have no way to stop them.

All I can do is watch as he invades my life and flips it upside down.

And the problem is? I want him to.

No. I need him to.

I wrap my arms around his neck and run my fingers in the small hairs at the back of his head.

He pulls back way too soon, his eyes shining bright. "Go."

I frown. What?

Why is he stopping?

"If you don't leave now, I'm fucking you right here where your guardians will see us."

Oh.

I forgot that we're in front of my house.

"I'll count to three." He tilts his head. "One… three."

I snatch my backpack and open the door with flustered fingers.

A heartfelt chuckle follows me as I jump to the pavement in front of my house.

Aiden rolls down the window of his car.

I freeze.

He's smiling.

Aiden has a wide, heart-stopping smile on his lips. It takes everything in me not to go back in there and watch it up close.

Kiss it.

Memorise it.

"Night, sweetheart. I miss you already."

And then his car disappears down the road.

I stand rooted there, gaping after him like an idiot.

I'm so fucking screwed over Aiden King.

TWENTY-FIVE

Elsa

"You like literally kicked her arse!" Kim jumps up and down, punching the air. "Damn. I wish I was there to see the bitch queen having her arse kicked!"

I groan. She wouldn't let me live it down since I told her what happened yesterday—without the sex part or the part about how sore I am this morning.

"It's not something I'm proud of." I hold the math book close to my chest. "I mean, I don't want to apologise to her, but I feel like I owe her something."

"You owe her fuck." Kim jumps in front of me, stopping me in my tracks. "Did she apologise to you for all the bullying? Or for having her minions make your life hell? No, and hell to the no. Besides, she had it coming. Gosh. I wish I saw the look on her face when you went berserk on her."

"Kim!"

"She's a bitch, okay? You don't feel sorry for bitches."

She's right. Silver has always made our lives hell.

But Kim has no idea what went on in my head at that moment. Hitting Silver wasn't some vigilante shit.

I legit wanted to kill her.

The thought sends a tendril of fear down my spine.

Why the hell do I keep having these murderous thoughts? I'm not the type who's capable of hurting a fly.

Images of injuring Aunt, scratching Aiden, and punching Silver hit my memory like razor-sharp knives.

Maybe I am capable of hurting more than a fly.

Maybe I wasn't aware of it yet.

"Come on. Class is about to start." Kim drags me by the arm.

I walk with her, but my mind is elsewhere.

When and where did I pick up those murderous thoughts?

I'm almost sure it comes from my childhood, but I still can't figure out how and why.

If only I could remember.

But then again, I did everything in my might to block those memories for ten years, I can't just remember on demand.

Kim's hand in mine stiffens, bringing me back to the present. She stops in front of our class just as Xander goes inside laughing with a bombshell from the gymnasium team.

My brows furrow as I focus back on Kim. "Are you okay?"

She laughs, but it's high-pitched and unreal. Kim can't fake a laugh to save her life. "Why wouldn't I be?"

"You and Xander are enemies, right?"

She crosses her chest, nodding. "Total enemies."

I don't think so.

She's been stealing peeks at him with a strange gleam when she thinks no one is looking. I don't know if she wants to punch him or kiss him or both.

"He's a player, Kim." *And he bullied you for years.*

But I can't tell her the last part. Not when I'm all tangled up with my own bully.

"Screw him and everyone he screws." She scrunches her nose. "I just want him out of mine and Kir's life."

"One year and he'll piss off to Harvard or something, right?" I ask.

"Yeah." A sheen of sadness covers her features before she smiles. "I'll be free."

I interlace my arm with hers when movement catches my attention.

Silver walks down the hall with a scarf wrapped tightly around her face and hiding her hair. I recognise her from the hint of her piercing aqua blue eyes.

Her attention is zoned in on her phone with a glittery case. There's also her signature dainty ring with more glitter on it.

I wouldn't have known it's her if it weren't for those obvious tells.

Her gaze collides with mine. Her pace slows down for a second before she lowers her head and hurries into class.

"Did you just see that?" Kim whisper-yells. "Silver Queens just lowered her head! Man, I really should've seen the beating that turned her into this."

My stomach twists. The more enthusiastic Kim is, the deeper and the more nauseous I feel.

This isn't me.

I don't take pleasure in hurting others.

Yes, Silver can be a bitch, but she did nothing yesterday. She just stood there and I attacked her out of nowhere.

When we step into class, my gaze immediately searches Silver.

She sits at the last table and scrolls through her phone, still wearing the scarf.

Two sets of eyes aside from mine bore into her.

The first is Adam, the rugby team's captain. His thick brows draw over troubled eyes as he glimpses back at her. His bulging arms tighten against the uniform's jacket with tension.

It's like he can feel her pain.

The second is Cole. He stares back at her with a harsh gaze that makes me flinch—even though it's not directed at me.

Ronan hops on his desk like a monkey, breaking his attention.

Kim leans in like she's about to announce a conspiracy and nods in Silver's direction. "Who is she and what have you done to our own bitch queen?"

I nudge her away. She giggles and flops down in her seat.

Ronan leaves Cole and hops on her desk. "Kimmy! I missed you last night. It's no fun without you."

"Sorry. I was babysitting my little brother."

Ronan snatches a mint-coloured strand of her hair and plays with it. "Bring him over next time."

"Fuck no," Xander snaps at him.

I didn't even realise he was in hearing distance. Wasn't he chatting with that gymnasium girl just now?

"That's none of your business," Kim huffs at him and faces Ronan with a smile.

He goes on an endless monologue about last night's game.

I'm about to take a seat beside Kim when the hairs on the back of my neck stand on end.

A strong hand strokes my stomach and a hard chest glues to my back.

My heart flutters as his clean intoxicating scent fills my senses.

I wonder if there will ever be a day where I don't have this baffling level of awareness of him.

"Morning, sweetheart. Did you dream of me?"

I glance back at him so I'm half facing him. I place a hand on his chest in a fruitless attempt to push him away.

Aiden doesn't give a fuck that he's so close to me in front of the entire class. Hell. Sometimes, I think he's doing it on purpose.

I'm not him. I care.

What would it feel like if I were as free as he is?

Today, he's dashing in his uniform. He even has his hair half-slicked back as if he wants to be presentable. For what, I don't know.

Usually, Aiden would put in the effort to look presentable if he has some manipulation plot. Like the first time he barged into my house and introduced himself to Aunt and Uncle as my boyfriend.

"I told you I don't remember my dreams." *I only remember my nightmares.*

"Hmm." He pinches my cheek. "One day you'll dream of me as I dream of you."

My lips part.

Damn him and these things he keeps telling me out of nowhere.

The harder I try to pull away from him, the more he lures me back in.

It's like I don't have a choice anymore.

Who am I kidding? I never had a choice when it comes to Aiden King.

Aiden crushes the distance between us as his lips hover an inch away from the shell of my ear. He whispers in a low seductive drawl, "You're blushing, sweetheart."

"No, I'm not."

He laughs, and just like yesterday, I stare incredulously at how gorgeous he is. The low chilling range of his laughter hits my heartstrings.

It aches.

It burns.

Damn.

I'm all covered in goosebumps—and something else between my legs.

He drops his hand from my face to grip me by the waist. It's like he can't keep his hands off me.

I can't stop touching you, so don't ask me to.

His words from yesterday hit my heartstrings harder.

"What have you been dreaming about?" I ask in an attempt to dissipate the tension.

"I dreamt about…" His free hand swipes over my bottom lip. I don't know why he does that. It's like he's wiping something off it. "These lips wrapped around my cock."

My face heats as I search my surroundings with frantic eyes in case someone else has heard. "Aiden!"

"What?" He feigns innocence. "You asked what I've been dreaming about."

"You didn't have to go into details."

"You think those were details?" His lips quirk into a smirk. "Here are the actual details: You kneeled in front of me and opened your mouth like the other night. You were looking up at me with these blue eyes and begged me to fuck your mouth. Being a gentleman, I did just that. I thrust in and out of your little mouth as you begged for more." He lowers his head to whisper in my ear. "This time, you swallowed like a good girl."

My thighs clench together and tingles erupt all over my skin.

God.

His dirty talk will never grow old. It'll never stop getting to me, and making me wish the images he paints are true.

"You liked it by the way." He pulls back with a smirk as if knowing that he got me.

I scowl. "You're a dickhead."

"I'll let you give my dick head, sweetheart." He winks.

Ugh. I can never win with him.

"Are you done making babies over there?" Ronan calls. "Because the math teacher is coming."

I blush and push away from Aiden to sit next to Kim. Aiden strides to his seat, too, flipping Ronan off on the way.

"Yo, King. I'm hurt." Ronan launches into his usual dramatic monologue about abandonment issues.

I'm really starting to wonder if they're a joke or real.

While Ronan goes on and on, Aiden doesn't even acknowledge him. He glares down his nose at Cole. Elites' captain spares him a glance over his psychology book and smiles.

There's been this weird tension between the two of them lately. From the outside looking in, Xander might appear like Aiden's best friend, but since I got into their circle, it seems that Aiden is closest to Cole.

I heard that Aiden's best assists came from Cole during their football games. They're also silent and mysterious in their own ways.

Besides, aside from Levi, Cole is the only one I've witnessed Aiden play chess against.

That can only mean that Aiden recognises Cole as a worthy opponent, and Aiden doesn't recognise a lot of people as worthy opponents.

Their friendship made sense. They're both highly intelligent and move in unpredictable ways.

It doesn't sit right to witness the tension between them.

"Morning," Knox taps at my desk.

I smile up at him. "Morning."

Mr Huntington, the math teacher, comes inside next.

I feel a glare directed at me. Aiden tilts his head to the side, his left eye twitching.

"What?" I mouth.

He focuses ahead.

"Miss Queens."

"Yes," Silver answers with a small voice.

It should make me feel victorious, but it doesn't.

If anything, it brings a taste of nausea to my mouth.

"Remove the scarf, please," Mr Huntington continues. "No extra wear is allowed in class."

"I would rather not, Mr Huntington."

"Remove the scarf or I'll have to ask you to leave."

I glance behind me at the same time as she reluctantly pulls down her scarf.

Gasps erupt in the class.

Faint bruises on the side of her mouth and cheek glare back at me. And they're only faint because she must've done her best to hide them with makeup.

I feel sick to my stomach at the thought of their actual appearance.

"Are you okay, Miss Queens?" The teacher asks. "We can call the principal and —"

"I tripped and fell. I'm fine," she says, shutting everyone out.

Kim nudges me with a huge grin. "You did that."

I scold her with my eyes, chest squeezing.

I didn't want to do that.

I only wanted her away from Aiden. That's all.

And then I wanted to kill her.

Fuck me.

The teacher talks about returning our tests, pulling the class's attention from Silver.

Adam is the only one who doesn't glance away from her. Not even when the teacher starts handing out tests.

I reluctantly turn away, unable to look at her anymore.

It's like she was attacked by a monster.

And I'm that monster.

On my test, I got a 97. Knox waves his test at me, he got a 98.

Shit. I lost.

I hate losing.

As soon as the class ends, he jumps in front of my desk. "You owe me."

"She owes you fuck." Aiden appears at my side in a beat.

I swallow at the steel look in his metal eyes.

"We had a bet." Knox's smile doesn't falter. "Elsa promised to do something for me if I have a better grade and vice versa."

"And I'm telling you she'll do fuck for you. Now, piss off."

"Aiden," I hiss, standing up. "Knox is a friend, okay? Besides, a bet is a bet."

Aiden pulls out his test and slams it on the table. He got a 100.

A fucking perfect score.

Of course.

I don't know why it surprises me that he's this smart at academics, too.

He's aiming for Oxford after all.

"I had more than both of you," Aiden deadpans. "So maybe you both owe me."

"Sorry, mate." Knox smiles. "You weren't a part of the bet."

Aiden's left eye twitches.

Oh, shit.

Oh, fuck.

Knox needs to leave. Like right now.

"We'll do something, okay?" I tell Knox with a dismissive tone. "Call me."

"Sure thing, Ellie. I'll call you later."

Knox is the last one who leaves class. I stand in an empty classroom with a pissed off Aiden.

I'm about to say something.

The words disappear.

Aiden grabs me by the arm and slams me against the wall, placing his hand on the side of my face. "Call you? He has your fucking number?"

This side of Aiden is fearsome as shit, and I can't help the tremors of both fear and excitement tingling down my spine.

However, I won't let him dictate my life.

Not more than he's already doing.

"Knox is a friend. You won't take me away from my friends."

"Watch me."

"Aiden!" I clutch his biceps. "Stop it, okay? It's just a bet."

"And I'm telling you." He wraps his hand around my throat, soothingly massaging my pulse point, but there's nothing soothing about his deranged eyes. "I want the bet called off, sweetheart."

I can give in to him.

It's not a big deal, anyway. I'm sure Knox will understand.

But if I continue giving in to Aiden's tyrannical ways, then there will be nothing left of me and my free will.

I refuse to be that girl.

I'm not Aiden's toy. I'm his fucking equal.

I jut my chin out. "No."

His left eye twitches. "No?"

"Yes, Aiden. No. You don't get to tell me what to do and who to befriend."

The poker face straps around his features so tight, it's alarming.

I expect him to retaliate, but he releases my throat and steps back. "As you wish."

And then he's out of the door.

TWENTY-SIX

Elsa

The football team has practice today. We don't. Coach Nessrine is giving us recuperating time before an upcoming competition.

I love how she takes care of us, but I wish she wouldn't give us the time off. I need to run like I need air.

Or maybe I just need to keep my mind off things.

Aiden hasn't spoken to me since he took off from the first class in the morning. He didn't bug me about sitting with his team at lunch, and he didn't tell me to watch him practice.

I could've gone to him first, but that's like I admitting I did something wrong.

Which isn't the case. He's the one who's making a mountain out of a molehill.

It doesn't mean I feel less bad that he's not talking to me.

Damn him.

I've been feeling shitty since the first class.

On my way to the car park, the back of my neck prickles with chilling awareness. I stop at the threshold and spot a black car with tinted windows parked near the exit.

My shoulder blades snap into a rigid line.

It's the same Mercedes that once followed me home. It's not a coincidence that it's now at my school.

The urge to run grips me by the gut.

I need to save myself. I need to —

The car's engine revs to life and the vehicle slips out of the car park.

I heave out a harsh breath, but the feeling of contempt won't go away.

One step after the other, I walk into the car park and watch my surroundings.

What if that car returns? Should I report it to the police or something?

My feet stop of their own volition when I meet malicious eyes.

Adam Herran.

He leans against the wall separating the 8th tower from the car park, glaring at me. No. Not glaring. He seems as if he's barely stopping himself from attacking me.

Adam Herran is the biggest bully in RES.

He made mine and Kim's life hell these past two years by using every trick in the bullying book. The one who locked me in the showers for five hours? Adam. The one who tripped me on my first day in the cafeteria? Adam.

Last year, Kim received an anonymous love letter. She was over the moon at the thought of someone having a crush on her. Said someone asked her to wait near the 6th tower after school, and she did.

After one hour of waiting, Adam and his goons poured paint and water all over her and laughed in her face.

Who in their right mind would love a fat pig like you? Are you on delusional pills?

Kim ran home crying and after that, she came up with her transformation plan.

Silver, the bitch queen herself, witnessed the event and didn't appear amused at all.

I was so livid, so humiliated on Kim's behalf that I went to the principal. And surprise, surprise, Silver was already in the office. She witnessed against Adam along with me.

That got him suspended, but it didn't stop him.

Now that I think about it, that was practically the only time Silver did a decent thing.

She even told me something once we were out of the principal's office.

'You need to pick your battles, Frozen.' Then she rolled her eyes and buggered off before I could ask her what the hell she meant by that.

Bottom line is, Adam is bad. However, he's backed off since Aiden stepped up for both of us.

Whoa.

Now that I think about it, Aiden stopped the bullying for Kim and me.

Adam is the captain of the rugby team and somewhat popular. He also has some aristocratic title behind him, but his power doesn't compare to Aiden or any of the horsemen.

He's been smart enough to not antagonise Aiden or get on his radar, but his glares chill me out of my skin.

"What are you looking at?" I jut my chin.

"Nothing," he says with nonchalance, pushing off the wall. "Just waiting to see the clusterfuck you'll be in."

And then he's heading inside the tower.

I want to follow and ask him what the hell he means by that. However, that could be exactly what he wants and I don't give bullies what they want.

Well, except for Aiden. But that dickhead takes without asking for permission anyway.

Ugh. I really hate that he's not speaking to me.

Maybe I should text him or —

No. Nope. I won't cower away.

Kim texts me that she's waiting for me by the car. I text back that I'm almost there.

When I round the corner, I find her blocking Silver's way to her car. From the expression on my friend's face, it seems like she's taunting her.

I like Kim's confident change. I really do. But I don't want her to turn into the bullies who ruined our lives.

We're bigger than them.

We're bigger than Adam Herran and Silver Queens.

Hell. We're even bigger than Aiden King and Xander Knight.

I hurry to them and grip Kim by the arm. "Let's go. We won't lower ourselves to their level."

Silver has the scarf wrapped tightly around her face. She stares at me, but it's neither of maliciousness or fear. It's more like with calculation.

I narrow my eyes. Is she trying to challenge me again right now?

"You ruined everything, do you know that?" she asks me.

"What are you talking about?"

"This is a bigger game than you and I, Elsa."

I pause for a second. That's the first time she calls me by my actual name. Usually, it's Frozen this and Frozen that.

Huh. Did it take a beating for her to finally respect me?

"I have one piece of advice for you."

"We don't need your advice," Kim snaps at her.

Silver doesn't pay her attention and continues in a calm tone. "If you still want King, then stay away from Cole."

She sidesteps us, then stops. "And oh. You watched me fall. One day, I'll return the favour and watch you fall, too."

She storms to her car with fast steps.

"Bitch," Kim hisses. "You should've let me tell her a piece of my mind."

"We're not Silver, Kim. We were bullied all our lives, we won't be those type of people, okay?"

"Whatever." She throws her hands in the air and stalks to her car.

Great.

Inside, I receive a text.

Knox: Are you free tonight?

I check my texts from Aiden just in case. He'd usually send me his plans. The last few days, his texts were along the line:

Aiden: Today, I'll fuck you harder than usual because I'm pissed off about the limit.

Aiden: P.S I'm still pissed off.

Aiden: See you at the Meet Up. Don't wear anything under that skirt or I'll rip it off.

Aiden: Hmm. I can't taste you from last night. I'm taking my refill tonight.

There are none of those texts today.

Screw him for ignoring me.

I pull back Knox's text and type.

Elsa: Sure. What did you have in mind?

Knox: How about I pick you up and then we decide?

I bite my lower lip and scroll back to Aiden and type.

Elsa: Are you going to stop being a dickhead?

He sees it immediately. Isn't he supposed to be in practice?

Aiden: Are you going to do as I asked?

Elsa: No. I told you that you don't control my life. I've given you enough leverage already.

He sees it, but he doesn't reply.

You know what? Damn him. I'm not going to play this game.

I pull Knox again and type.

Elsa: Sure!

After we agree on the time, I pocket my phone in my backpack with a smile.

Aiden can go suck it.

"You're planning trouble, aren't you?" Kim asks from beside me.

"Why would you say that?"

"You have this almost sadistic look in your eyes and a smirk when you do."

"Really?"

"Uh-huh." She laughs. "I'm teensy bit starting to regret asking you to live an adventure."

"Did I always have this expression?" I frown.

How come I never knew about it?

"Sometimes." She glances at me. "Are you okay?"

It's the usual question she, Aunt, and Uncle ask.

As usual, I smile. "Why wouldn't I be?"

"Just checking." She grins. "You want to join me and Kir for mac and cheese?"

"I'd love to, but I'm going out with Knox."

"You're kidding, right?"

"No, why would I?"

"Eh, I don't know, Ellie. Because of King? He'll flip his shit if he hears you're going out with Knox."

"Knox is a friend who saved my life. Aiden should get used to it."

She taps her fingers on the steering wheel. "You're right. I know that, but King has no filter whatsoever. He treats you like I've never seen him treat anyone else."

"And how is that?"

"Like he wants to shield you from the world. I don't think you even notice it, but sometimes, he looks at you like he can't breathe without you. And believe me, that's not the King everyone knows."

I tighten my hold on the backpack. "What are you saying, Kim?"

"All I'm saying is; if he feels this intensely towards you, he'll react tenfold worse if you threaten him."

"You're my friend. You're supposed to be on my side."

"I am, Ellie." She sighs. "That's why I'm telling you not to stir King's ugly side."

Aunt and Uncle come home early. It's so rare that I can't help hugging them more than needed.

Then I find out they're only coming to check on me before going back to work.

I contemplate cancelling with Knox just so I can get some alone time with them and maybe have dinner together.

"No, hon." Aunt ruffles my hair. "Go and have fun. Don't let us keep you here."

"I'm sure Knox will understand," I argue.

"Go on. Don't keep him waiting. He seems like a nice boy."

"We're just friends, Aunt." I take a carrot and munch on it. I need to keep my stomach full in case Knox takes me to dinner in a place where they don't serve my special food.

She grins. "Sure thing, Elsie."

"Stop it, Blair." Uncle comes behind me and massages my shoulder. "You go and have fun, pumpkin."

I nod, glancing back at him.

Since the pool accident, I can't help noticing the change in Uncle's demeanour or at least the way he looks at me. It's like he's torn inside and doesn't know how to communicate it.

He releases me and heads upstairs, probably to freshen up before they're out again.

"I'm going to change," I tell Aunt and she beams at me.

I take the steps two at a time so I can follow Uncle. I freeze at the top of the stairs when I find him standing in front of my room.

He's clutching his briefcase with the jacket on top. His shoulders are drooped and he gazes at my room with utter sorrow as if he's about to cry.

My own eyes fill with tears at the sight.

What is it, Uncle? What is it that you're not telling me?

He shakes his head and continues to his room.

"Uncle..."

He stops and turns around with a smile plastered on his face. The smile falls when he meets my gaze. A tear must've fallen on my cheek because I taste salt.

I don't even know why I called him or why I'm crying, I just know that I need something.

Uncle lets the briefcase and the jacket fall to the ground and hurries towards me.

"What is it, pumpkin? Are you okay?"

I nod, but more tears stream down my cheeks and my lips wouldn't stop trembling. I don't want to worry him.

What the hell is wrong with me and these tears coming out of nowhere?

"I'm sorry." I wipe at my eyes with the back of my hand. "I don't know where these tears are coming from."

"It's okay. Come here, pumpkin." He wraps his arms around me and I'm a goner.

A complete utter goner.

I couldn't stop the tears even if I wanted to.

My nails dig into his shirt and I inhale his aftershave with the scent of cinnamon and citrus.

A scent from my childhood.

It's like I'm that little girl again. That seven-year-old girl who slept in Uncle's embrace for weeks because I couldn't fight off the nightmares.

Back then, Aunt would sleep on a chair because I didn't want her with us. I couldn't sleep if she touched me.

"It's okay," he soothes, caressing my back. "I'm here for you, pumpkin. No matter what happens, you know that I love you, right? You're the only child I ever had and ever will."

I nod in his chest, gripping his shirt tighter.

"What's going on?"

At Aunt's voice, I break away from Uncle wiping my eyes, but I keep my back to her.

Damn it.

I don't want Aunt to see me this way either.

"Elsa was just having a bit of exam stress, right, pumpkin?"

I nod, not turning around.

"Go on and change." Uncle smiles down at me. "Your friend will be waiting."

I run to my room.

"Elsa," Aunt calls, her footsteps sounding behind me. "What's going on?"

"Let her go, Blair."

I'm glad Uncle stops her as I go into my room. I barge into the bathroom and wash the itch beneath my hands. That stupid itch that wants to break free.

After freshening up, I change into simple skinny jeans and a tank top.

It's going to be okay.

I think.

My phone vibrates.

My heart flips at the thought that it's Aiden. I need him so much right now. I wish he'd just text me something.

Anything.

If he tells me it's okay to have a life and my own decisions, I'll cancel with Knox.

I'll go to him instead.

Knox isn't the one I want to see right now. It's strange that when I'm a mess and need comfort, Aiden is the first one who comes to mind.

The text is from Knox, telling me he'll be here in a few minutes.

Disappointment tugs at my stomach.

Of course, Aiden wouldn't forfeit. It's always his way or the highway.

Screw him.

I turn off my phone.

After pulling my hair into a ponytail, I exit my room. I'm about to go downstairs when I hear hushed yells coming from Aunt and Uncle's bedroom.

The door is closed, but I do something I never did before.

I tiptoe closer. No sound comes out. Was I always able to move this silently?

I glue my ear to the door and listen in on their conversation.

"Enough is enough, Blair!" Uncle hisses. "Can't you see that she's stressed?"

"She'll get better with Dr Khan," Aunt replies with that air of confidence.

"She can't get better from a disease she doesn't know about. You can pretend all you want, but she's remembering, Blair. She's smart to know those recurring nightmares mean something."

"She's not remembering," there's a note of panic in Aunt's voice.

"Even if she isn't, she will soon. Or those people will come for her."

People? What people?

"She'll choose us." Aunt's tone hardens. "Elsa will choose us."

"Even if she does, you can't pretend that all of this is okay just to protect yourself."

"Protect myself?" I can almost imagine Aunt scoffing. "I did everything to protect *her*. I don't want her to go back to that phase of her life, I want her to start anew. I thought you want that for her, too."

"I do, but as Dr Khan said, she can never really move on if she hasn't dealt with the trauma."

"She's dealt with it by forgetting all about it."

"She was a seven-year-old child, Blair! That was her only defence mechanism. It doesn't mean she dealt with it. She didn't know how to deal with it at that age."

"And you think she does now?"

"She needs to know." His voice softens and my heart breaks. "Are you blind to the lost look and the tears in her eyes? Are you blind to her screams after the nightmares? Because it cuts me open every time."

"She'll be fine. She will."

"Fuck this, Blair!" He yells. "I won't let her suffer just so you won't feel guilty."

"Keep your voice down," she whisper-yells.

I glue myself further into the door, my heart almost beating out of my chest.

"I'm done, Blair. Okay? I'm done keeping her in the dark just because you don't want her to hate you. If you don't tell her, I will."

"You don't know the whole story."

"I'll tell her what I know."

"Shut up, Jaxon."

"I won't shut up. You need to face that you abandoned her and her mother when they needed you the most."

"I did *not* and you know that."

"You ran away and never looked back. Elsa lost her mother and family because of it."

My knees shake and I can't remain standing. No other sounds come out, and I quietly leave from their door.

My heart slams in my chest.

Thump.

Thump.

Thump.

Aunt abandoned us?

What is that supposed to mean?

Aunt didn't abandon us. She saved me. She couldn't have saved me if she abandoned me. Uncle must be wrong.

He has to be.

TWENTY-SEVEN

Elsa

I'm distracted out of my mind during the dinner with Knox.

He brought me to the coffee shop where Aiden and I usually have our meals. I'm surprised he knows such a place exists.

Even with the familiar setting and Knox cracking jokes, I can't concentrate.

I've been picking at my salad, but I barely took a bite.

My legs bounce under the table. I emptied the hand sanitiser, but the itch under my skin wouldn't go away.

The conversation between Aunt and Uncle keeps playing at the back of my mind on an endless loop.

He said she abandoned us. *Abandoned* us.

And I lost Ma because of that? How so? How the hell did that happen?

"Elsa?"

My head snaps up at Knox's voice. I'm gripping the fork so tight, my knuckles are white. I think my face is the same, too.

"Sorry." I force out an awkward smile. "I'm a bit distracted tonight."

"It's okay. We can do this another time if you like."

"Absolutely." I glide my fork in the salad. "I'm really sorry, Knox. I love your company. I'm just not in my right state of mind."

"Family problems?"

I wince. "Sort of."

"I completely understand. I also have an overbearing father."

"You do?"

"He's a control freak and is hardly satisfied with anything. I think he rubbed off on me."

I smile despite myself. "You're not a control freak, Knox."

"I can be." He grins. "Anyway, all I'm trying to say is that parents are like that. I try to be a good son and give him what he wants even if it can be nearly impossible."

I clutch his arm briefly. "I'm sure he's proud of you."

"That's what I hope." His eyes appear lost for a second. "I want to be his favourite son."

"I'm sure you are."

He shrugs. "Not yet, but I found an opening to snatch the position. Anyway, I understand how it feels to have parents expect a lot from you."

If only it were about that.

Aunt and Uncle's expectations are Cambridge, and I'm already sold on that. But this is bigger and more dangerous.

How am I supposed to deal with secrets from the past?

On our way outside, I catch sight of the middle-aged man sitting at a back table.

He's the same man who usually sits upstairs.

It's a weird, out-of-body experience to see him change the setting. He was a part of the decor upstairs when Aiden and I are together.

That makes me miss Aiden.

Damn him.

He couldn't be there for me when I need him the most.

Knox has to go pick up his father, but he offers to drop me off first. I decline and take a taxi. I already burdened him enough for the night.

The traffic is suffocating, it takes me about an hour to get home.

I'm physically and mentally exhausted as I punch in the code and go inside.

I stand in the darkness of the entrance, arms falling on either side of me.

Tears fill my eyes and I fight the need to collapse in the entryway.

It's absolutely terrifying to stand here at the place I've called home for the past ten years and feel like a stranger.

Like I don't belong.

The walls. The darkness. All of it seems wrong.

I'm not supposed to be here.

My home is in Birmingham.

I close my eyes at the random thought. I have nothing in Birmingham and certainly no one.

London is my home. This is my home.

So what if Aunt abandoned us? She came back for me and raised me like her own daughter. She once told me that she and Uncle Jaxon decided early on in their relationship to not have children because their life goals would clash with the care they need to provide for a child.

But after they got me, they decided that I'm the only child they would ever have.

They sacrificed a lot for me by taking loans out for my heart surgery. I can't be an ungrateful brat just because of what I heard earlier.

Even if it still hurts to know that Aunt abandoned her sister and only sibling once upon a time.

I guess I'll have to wait until she tells me the reasons herself.

I hit the light switch and hang my coat.

My feet stop of their own volition at the lounge's area entryway. I gasp, the bag falling from my hand to the floor with a thud.

Aiden sits in the chair opposite the entrance. His elbows rest on his thighs and his fingers interlace under his chin.

His metallic eyes appear glassed over as he watches me with a chilling, haunting interest.

"You scared the shit out of me." I search around him, expecting to find Aunt or Uncle.

But they should be at work, pulling another all-nighter.

"What are you doing here?" I remain rooted in place, not daring to get close.

He looks on the verge of combusting if someone touches him.

"I told your Uncle I forgot my textbook and he gave me the code."

Of course, he did. Uncle likes Aiden more than he cares to admit.

"We both know that's a lie," I say.

He motions at the table where a textbook lies. "I did leave it, but I did it on purpose in case something like this comes up."

"Something like this?"

"The whole masquerade you're doing."

I hate the neutral way he speaks with. It's like he's preparing for the punch. I'm nearly fidgeting, waiting for the other shoe to drop.

Aiden is never good when he's pissed off. He's never good when he's calm either.

I watch him closely, he's still in RES's uniform, minus the jacket. That means he didn't go home.

My eyes widen when I notice the red marks in his knuckles. I run towards him and sure enough, his knuckles are bruised and the skin is reddening and cracked in some places.

"W-what happened?" I search his face for a sign that he's hurt. There's a small bruise at the side of his eye, near the mole. Other than that, he appears fine.

Aiden isn't the violent type. He'd rather manipulate his way out of any situation. After all, he lives by being smarter, not stronger.

"Aiden?"

He remains silent, staring ahead.

I lower myself to his level so I can watch him properly. "What is it?"

He grabs my wrist and I cry out as he yanks me down. I fall on his lap, sitting sideways on his hard thighs.

"I sent you a text to meet, but you ignored me and went out with the new boy."

He sent me a text? Does that mean he was willing to compromise? I don't know why that makes me happy.

I place a hand on his shoulder. "I turned off my phone and forgot —"

"In our coffee shop." His hand wraps around my waist so tight, it's like he's gripping my bones. "You took him to the place that should be ours. Why did you do that, hmm?"

Shit. I didn't think about it that way. Besides, how would I know Aiden would be watching? Now, he'll think I did it to spite him which was absolutely not the case.

"I didn't take him there," I soften my tone. "He's the one —"

"How would it feel if I took Queens there, hmm?" He's still talking in the frightening calm voice.

My temper flares at the mere mention of her name. "Don't threaten me with Silver."

"Do you realise what a fucking double standard that is?"

"It's not a double standard because Knox is just a friend. Silver is your ex or fuck buddy or whatever. It's different."

"Nothing is different." His free hand reaches to my throat and he strokes the pulse point. "You know I hate feeling threatened, but you went ahead and did it. You went ahead and fucking pushed me."

I try to get off him, but he grips my thigh sitting me back down. "I warned you. I'm fucking crazy when it comes to you."

He's mad. I can see it in his metallic gaze. The busted knuckles aren't helping either.

This is the volatile side of Aiden that I should be wary of.

The monstrous side that grandmothers warn their grandkids about.

Still, I keep my chin high. "You took Silver to our pool, too, remember? To spite me."

"I didn't take her. She went there herself."

"Oh, yeah. You just sat with her then. I saw the picture on her IG."

"That wasn't me."

"Then who was it?"

"No one you should worry about, and don't change the subject. This is about you, sweetheart."

He flips me around and I cry out as my knees hit the floor. I end up half-lying against the sofa.

"I guess I have to remind who you belong to, huh?" He yanks down my jeans and cold air hits my backside. "I'll fuck you until you can't move let alone think about anyone else."

A tendril of excitement and fear shoot through me. As much as I crave Aiden's intensity, he's volatile right now.

Besides, I told him he won't touch me without telling me a tidbit of his story.

He's off guard and blinded by anger, so it might be my perfect chance to get something out of him.

You're playing with fire, Elsa. You'll burn.

I would rather burn than lose to him all the time.

He yanks the tank top over my head leaving me in only my underwear.

"You'll pay for every second you spent with him." He grabs my arse cheeks harshly. "A friend? Fuck that and fuck him for making you think that."

"What are you talking about?"

"He doesn't look at you as if you're a friend. He looks at you like he wants to threaten what's fucking mine." The sound of a zipper comes from behind me. "We'll fix that. You'll let me fuck you until you can't move, and then you'll beg for more, hmm, sweetheart?"

I suppress a moan trying to claw its way out. If I show that I like this, Aiden will take full advantage and consume me until there'll be nothing left.

"Tell me something." I grip the sofa's edge.

He tsks. "You lost the right to negotiate when you fucked up and broke my rules, sweetheart."

"You don't have rules."

He yanks my bra open, letting it fall to the ground. My breasts bounce free and my fully erect nipples throb as they brush against the sofa's edge.

"I do now." He reaches a hand and pinches my nipple so hard, I gasp. "You don't go out with other guys. You don't look at them. You don't fucking breathe near them. Is that clear?"

I purse my lips shut, refusing to let him have the satisfaction of seeing me agree.

He rips my underwear down and I jolt at the friction. My eyes flutter closed for the briefest bit.

Oh, God.

If he keeps touching me this unapologetically, there's no way I'll be able to resist him even if he tells me nothing.

His hard cock nuzzles between my thighs, threatening at my entrance. "I didn't hear your answer. Is that fucking clear?"

When I say nothing, he pulls my arse cheeks apart with rough hands and glides his cock to my other hole.

My eyes widen and I fist the sofa harder. "A-Aiden? What the hell are you doing?"

"Waiting for your answer," he sounds casual, but I recognise the darkness in his tone. "And contemplating fucking you here. Hmm. It's the only hole I haven't claimed yet."

His cock pushes more into me, slightly stretching from behind.

My shoulder blades tighten with fear. He wouldn't do it, right? I heard anal takes a lot of preparation and shit.

"Just so you know." He leans in to whisper in hot sultry words. "It'll fucking hurt."

I gulp, but that doesn't stop the tiny bursts of pleasure clenching my core.

There's really something wrong with me.

He's threatening to fuck my arse for the first time and I'm freaking turned on.

It takes me a second to get my bearings together.

"Tell me something, Aiden. Anything."

"Why should I? I can just take from you. Hmm." He trails a finger from my pussy to my arse, smearing my wetness around his cock that's still at my back entrance. "You're so fucking wet already."

"A deal is a deal, Aiden." I clamp my lips around the moan trying to clamp its way out. "You're breaking it right now."

"And I'm supposed to care about that?"

"Yes, you are! Because it's hurting me inside."

He stops for a beat. I think he'll withdraw or something but he only slides his cock to my entrance, the tip settling there.

"Not like you did."

"Stop saying vague things like that." My eyes rim with tears. I don't know if it's because what I overhead from Aunt and Uncle or the way Aiden is mad at me or my nightmares.

Or all the above.

But right now, I want him to hold me. I want him to lower himself once.

Just once.

I want him to be there for me.

I try to turn around, but he grips my head and slams my face down against the sofa.

"I want to look at you," I murmur.

"And I don't."

"Aiden, please."

"I might not seem like it but I'm so fucking mad at you right now."

"I might not seem like it, but I need you so fucking bad right now."

A beat of silence goes. Two.

Three —

Aiden slowly peels his hand from my hair and pulls back enough to turn me around.

I glance up at him through blurry eyes. I feel like a mess.

All of it is a freaking mess.

He pulls me in his arms and lies me on the sofa and then he's hovering over me, pulling himself on his elbows to not crush me.

The look in his eyes is like nothing I've seen before. It's full of hate, but at the same time, there's that *thing*.

Something I've seen before. Something like… affection?

But Aiden doesn't do affection, right?

I reach a hand and run my fingertips over the side of his eye and that mole I fell in love with the first time I met him.

His face tenses and his shoulders stiffen the more I touch him. He grabs my hand and slams it on the sofa above my head.

He seems on the verge of something. What, I don't know.

"Aiden."

"Stop."

"Stop what?"

"Stop calling my name with that tone. Stop looking at me with those damn eyes and engraving yourself under my fucking skin."

My heart beats faster. This means I'm affecting him, right?

"You want me to tell you something, sweetheart? *Anything?*" He grits out.

I nod once, unsure where he's going with this. He thrusts deep inside me. I arch off the sofa with the force of it.

Holy shit.

I think I'm going to come right here right now.

"You're lucky, Elsa. You're so *damn* lucky I like you enough to fuck up everything for you."

And then he claims my mouth in a passionate, rough kiss.

TWENTY-EIGHT

Elsa

I wake up with a moan.

My legs are open wide and I'm tingling with ecstasy.

Holy shit.

My eyes snap open to find myself in pleasure land.

Literally.

Aiden has his face buried between my thighs as my ankles dangle over his broad shoulders.

The only thing I see is a dark, tousled hair as he laps at my sensitive core.

"Oh…" My back arches off the bed as his wicked tongue glides up and down and thrust inside me.

He certainly knows how to drive me wild with that tongue.

As if that isn't enough, he adds a finger to the mix. I grip his hair, my fingertips digging into his skull.

Oh, God.

I can't last when he does that double thing with his fingers and his tongue.

"Aiden…"

"Hmm, sweetheart?" The rumble of his husky voice against my most intimate part nearly throws me over the edge.

"Oh, God, don't —" My voice catches in my throat when he nibbles on the sensitive skin.

He tugs at it with his teeth.

Soothes it with his lips.

Sucks it into his mouth.

I'm a goner.

An absolute goner for the orgasm he's wrenching out of me.

I couldn't speak even if I wanted to.

Aiden breaks the spell and lifts his head. A wicked grin animates his devilishly handsome face. He licks his glistening lips.

My breathing crackles.

"Don't?" He wraps both hands on my legs over his shoulders.

"Don't stop..." I pant as if I'm coming down from a marathon. "Don't you dare fucking stop."

"I love it when you demand your pleasure, sweetheart." He smirks before he's back to devouring me.

My eyes roll to the back of my head.

My whole body tingles, aching—no, *begging*—for that release.

Hell. He fucked me until I couldn't move and he had to carry me to my room last night.

I'm also sore as shit, but I can't resist his tongue, teeth, lips, and fingers.

The devil gives it all when he goes down on me.

I can't get enough of him touching me hard enough or burying himself deep enough.

It's not the sex that blows me apart, it's his raw intensity.

The glint in his eyes, the tick in his jaw, and the diligence of his touch.

My heavy breathing fills the room. All I can smell is us.

Both of us.

I can't sleep anymore without smelling him on the bed and amongst my sheets.

"You want me to make you come, sweetheart?" he speaks against my clit.

I nod, arching my back.

"With my tongue or with my cock?"

Can't I have both?

When I say nothing, I can feel his smirk against me. "You want me to take that decision, sweetheart?"

I answer with a moan when he slowly works his finger inside me.

"You don't want to let me have the decision because I'm tempted to give you neither."

Wait. What?

"B-but why?" My voice is so breathy I can barely recognise it.

"I'm still pissed off about yesterday."

"Aiden! Didn't you take it out on my body all night long?"

"Not enough."

He pounds his finger into me and hits that spot. Stars form behind my eyelids as they flutter closed.

I scream and muffle the sound into the pillow.

My entire body shivers with overwhelming bolts of pleasure.

And I know, I just know that it's not a matter of physical connection anymore.

I wish it was.

I wish he was only owning my body.

When I orgasm, my entire being is tuned to him.

Every fibre of my body and soul are drawn to him in ways I can't stop even if I wanted to.

It's scary as hell.

It's dangerous as hell.

But it's impossible to end.

When I come down from my orgasm halo, Aiden is already wrapping his arms around me.

It doesn't help that he's hugging me a lot lately.

Like he needs me close, and not only for sex.

"Morning, sleepyhead," he rasps in that sexy as hell tone.

"Morning." I bite my lower lip before I tell him to wake me up this way every day.

Best wake up call ever.

He stands up and carries me to the bathroom and runs the bath for me.

"Why do you always run me baths?" I ask as he sits me inside the bathtub and pours in my coconut bath bubble. He smells like it sometimes from the number of times he sits with me.

"I told you. Warm baths help when you're sore."

I raise an eyebrow. "How do you know I'm sore?"

He stops to stare down at me. There's that strange gleam in his eyes again. I would call it care if I didn't know that Aiden doesn't do that.

"I know I don't take it easy on you. I'd say I'm sorry, but I'm not. I can't control myself with you, Elsa. I tried and it's impossible." He grins. "I can, however, run you baths and give you massages."

"That's so fucked up."

"I was always the fucked up type, but you already know that."

Yeah, I do.

I guess I'm fucked up, too, if I can't escape his orbit.

Souls are attracted to each other.

Kim's words hit me like an arrow to the chest.

Aiden steps behind me and wraps his legs around me so I'm nuzzled against his semi-hard cock. I swear the thing is never soft.

At least not around me.

The scent of coconut lingers in the air as Aiden lathers my skin. He draws those usual circles on my back.

It's like he's scribbling something.

Warm water and his soothing touch cover me in a halo. I let my head drop back against his chest.

His fingers stroke my hair, then the pulse point in my throat, then my scar.

The three parts he's so obsessed with.

Then he goes back to holding me against him.

I close my eyes wanting to continue sleeping. Can we skip school today?

We have about an hour before we need to go, but I'm too comfortable to move.

"Did you sleep last night?" I ask, still closing my eyes.

"No."

"What did you do all night long?"

"Watched you, sweetheart."

I bite on my inner cheek. I'll never get used to that no matter how many times he says it.

"That's stalkerish, you know."

He says nothing, and I can almost imagine him shrugging his shoulders. Aiden would never be apologetic about this part of him.

"So I know you like chess, football, swimming and working out," I say. "Is there anything else you like doing?"

"Fucking you, sweetheart."

My eyes fly open as my cheeks heat. I elbow him without looking back. "Something else."

"Sucking on your little pussy. Fingering you to orgasm. Teasing your tits. Take your pick."

"Aiden!"

"What? You asked what I like doing. You're my favourite thing to do."

You're my favourite thing to do, too.

I pause at my sudden thought. I didn't mean that.

I *can't* mean that. Aiden isn't my favourite thing to do. That'd mean he's my favourite person and that's not true.

…right?

"Something that doesn't involve me," I nudge.

"Hmm. There aren't many of those."

"How about your hobbies? Your favourite music? Your favourite film? Your favourite book?"

"You know about chess, football, and swimming. Those are hobbies, I guess." He pauses. "I don't listen to music. As for films, it's probably Twelve Angry Men. It was the last film I watched with Alicia and Jonathan. Books. Hmm. I have no favourites, but the ones

I remember the most were written by the renaissance era's French philosophers."

"Because Alicia read them?"

I feel his nod.

"If you didn't watch that film with Alicia or read the books with her, would you still have favourites?"

"Probably not."

"Why not?"

"I don't understand why people obsess about favourites. It's a matter of preference and shouldn't be given so much weight."

That's his lack of empathy speaking. I honestly think he doesn't know why people are emotional about things he considers trivial.

But he based his favourites—or what he thinks are his favourites—on his mother.

There's something there.

Something deep and raw that I wish to uncover. If I figure out Alicia's exact relationship with Aiden, I might figure out why he's become the way he is after her death.

"How did you spend time with Alicia?" I ask.

"How did you spend time with your mother?"

His question catches me off guard.

"You know I don't remember that."

"Then maybe I don't remember either." The closed-off tone means that he's done opening up.

I remain quiet despite the frustration rising inside me.

My eyes get lost in his arms surrounding me and his arrow tattoos covering the scar.

"Tell me something," I murmur.

"Tell you what?"

"You went down on me. That counts as oral sex and you have to tell me something in return."

The silence stretches for longer than comfortable.

I slowly turn around and find him peering down at me with narrowed eyes.

"That doesn't count, sweetheart. It's a continuation of last night."

"Nope, Aiden. You're not manipulating me on this. New day, new story."

"Hmm. Still doesn't count. You asked me not to stop. Demanded it even."

"My reaction doesn't matter. Our deal does."

He watches me with that cold calculative streak and I know he'll manipulate himself out of it like usual.

I place a hand against his mouth before he can speak. "Don't even think about it. That deal means a lot to me. If you don't keep it, I won't keep any of your rules."

He wraps a hand around my throat. "Careful, sweetheart. You know I don't like being threatened."

"Then keep your word," I'm glad my voice comes unnegotiable.

He lets his hand flop in the water. "Only this time."

I bite my lip against a grin. I got him in one of his games. That makes me so proud.

"Turn around," he tells me.

I noticed this the other time and it solidified yesterday. Aiden doesn't face me whenever he tells me these stories.

Yesterday, he said that he doesn't want to look at my face because he's pissed off. Is that what he feels whenever he tells me these tidbits?

Angry?

I face ahead, but I let my hand fall under the water. I wrap it around his hand that's holding me by the stomach.

"Those two friends always had women at their disposal, but they got bored of easy women. So they had a bet to marry a mentally unstable woman and make her fall in love with them."

"That's an odd bet. Did it work?"

"It did. Until they got bored and moved on to their next bet."

"And what was it?"

"That, sweetheart, is for another day."

"Ugh. Aiden." I face him. "You can't keep throwing me crumbs like this."

He smirks. "Sure can."

"You're such a sociopath."

"Hmm. Are sociopaths born or made, sweetheart?"

I crane my head against his shoulder. "Why are you asking me?"

"You're smart and you psychoanalyse me a lot in that head of yours."

"I do not."

"Sure do, or you wouldn't have been able to thwart my plans."

I thwarted his plans? When the hell did I do that? I need to commemorate the moment on my wall.

"Sociopaths are made," I say. "It's the circumstances and the upbringing that makes them what they are."

"So a good upbringing can kill their sociopathic tendencies?"

"Sometimes, yes."

"Only sometimes?"

"Well, yeah. Some people remain sociopaths no matter what type of upbringing they have."

"Hmm. Interesting."

"What are your thoughts about it?" I ask.

He lifts his hand, strokes my hair back and swipes his thumb along my lower lip.

"Monsters are born." He leans over to bite my lower lip then whispers in dark words. "As they grow up, they either deny it or fully embrace it, but it doesn't change what they are."

TWENTY-NINE

Elsa

Despite the bubble bath, I'm still walking a little funny at school.

Aiden has me glued to his side with his arm wrapped around my shoulder.

It appears casual, but there's nothing casual about Aiden. He just uses casualty to appear normal.

My gaze strays to his bandaged hand dangling off my shoulder. I asked him about it when he was bandaging it earlier, but he just deflected his way out of it.

Aiden isn't an open book, but he's not completely closed off either. He has multiple layers that he carefully chooses which to hide and which to show.

His methodical thinking is maddening sometimes.

Okay, most of the time.

That doesn't mean I'll stop probing him.

We're walking through the long hallway when I ask. "Were you a quiet kid?"

He narrows his eyes. "Have you been talking to Lev?"

That means Levi knows more about him than he's letting on.

I lift an eyebrow. "Maybe."

He grips me by the shoulder and pushes me to the side of the ninth tower.

My back hits the stone and he sandwiches me between the wall and his hard body.

"Don't talk to Lev."

"Why? Are you afraid I'll figure everything out and you won't be able to blackmail me with sex anymore?"

He lifts my chin with his thumb and forefinger. "You can lie to yourself and think that I'm blackmailing you with sex any day, sweetheart."

The amusement in his tone pisses me off.

"Isn't that the truth? If it were up to me, I'd vote for the story without the sex part of the deal."

"Hmm. Is that why your tight pussy begs for my cock the minute I'm out of you? Or is that why you demanded, and I quote, *Don't you dare fucking stop?*"

I block his mouth with a hand and search my surroundings with my cheeks in flames.

Damn him and his dirty mouth.

I'm almost sure he's doing it on purpose to make me squirm at school.

He removes my hand to reveal a sly smile. His fingers thread in my hair, tugging the band free. And just like that, his poker face returns. "Don't talk to Lev. I mean it."

"If you have nothing to hide, why shouldn't I?"

"It's not about that. He won't tell you anything."

"Then what is it about?"

He scoffs and resumes walking. Aiden just freaking *scoffed* at the mention of his cousin.

I keep up with him, tying my hair back, and watching his body language intently. There's something about his reaction that I can't put my finger on.

"By the way," I probe. "Isn't Levi your cousin? Why did he specifically choose Cole for the captain position and not you?"

"Because Nash appears normal and he's all about compromises and team spirit."

Appears normal? As in he isn't?

"Wow. Levi must take football more seriously than you. I guess that's why he went professional and you won't."

He stabs me with a glare. "Are you done?"

"Done with what?"

"Idolising Lev."

It hits me then. I suppress a smile. "You're jealous of him."

He remains silent, but I know I'm on point.

"You are." I laugh. "Why? Because he was so popular? He had all the girls and the attention? Even Jonathan came to RES so many times because of him, and not you."

"I don't give a fuck about any of that." He wraps a hand around my arm. "I told you not to idolise other men in front of me."

"Does that mean I can idolise them behind your back?" I taunt.

He gives me the stink eye.

I laugh. "Is that a yes?"

"That's cheating." His expression darkens. "And you know my rules and my reaction to that."

Geez. Only the level of Aiden's possessiveness would consider idolising other men cheating.

Now that I think about it, if Aiden idolises any other woman in front of me, I might flip.

Hell. I dislike the woman he lost his virginity to and he didn't even speak that highly of her.

I poke him as we continue walking towards our class. "Don't worry, King. You're popular, too. Levi is just more approachable."

He continues glaring at me as I laugh. It's fun to get on his nerves. It's almost as if our roles are switching.

Maybe I really need to have a talk with Levi and see if he would tell me anything. I'll have Astrid there to loosen him up.

God. I'm starting to think with a manipulative mind like Aiden's.

Down the hall, Silver and Adam walk to class together. She

doesn't have the scarf or the bruise today. She must've done a killer makeup job to make it disappear.

Wait. Silver and Adam?

Now that I look closer, they're not walking together or even talking.

However, their steps are almost in sync.

Wait.

It's Adam.

He's a few steps behind her, keeping his footsteps in sync with hers.

It stands out because he's tall and buff and his steps are usually wide. He wouldn't walk in moderate, elegant steps like Silver.

The latter is scrolling through her phone, appearing oblivious to her surroundings.

But is she oblivious to Adam's existence, too?

Although they're both bullies—Adam more so than Silver— they never struck me as being close. She wouldn't have testified against him last year if they were.

But maybe I was wrong.

Silver slips inside the class. Adam pauses and meets my gaze.

It's brief, barely a second, but it's enough to send chills down my spine.

Stay the fuck away.

I can read it in his eyes even if he says nothing.

Stay away from what? From whom?

He couldn't have known I noticed the creepy way he hangs around Silver.

The moment ends when he quickly breaks eye contact and strides into class.

"Hmm. Interesting."

I jolt at Aiden's contemplative voice. For a second, I forgot he's there.

"What do you mean?"

"Nothing you need to worry about, sweetheart." He watches the place where Adam just stood. "It'll be taken care of."

I gulp. He couldn't be meaning what I think he's meaning, right?

Adam is a fucking bastard, but no one deserves Aiden's wrath.

But then again, maybe the bastard shouldn't have glared at me.

Or bullied me and Kim.

Or had creepy vibes around Silver.

He had it coming.

"Ellie!" Kim runs towards me and interlaces my free hand with hers. "Morning, King. Stop taking my best friend away from me."

"Morning, Reed." His poker face is on. "And no, I don't share."

I suppress a smile as Kim laughs.

It makes me fuzzy inside to see her happy. She deals with lots of demons and even though she doesn't tell me, it breaks my heart to see her being an adult to her baby brother when she wants the whole teenage life.

In class, Aiden finally lets me go. That's only because Ronan pulled him to the side to tell him about his last night bang—in all explicit details.

Aiden listens with a poker face.

I wonder if he ever tells his friends about our sex life or the way he fucks me. I mean, he always talks dirty and he's not the type to be embarrassed.

For some reason, I don't think he does. Even though he doesn't seem like it, Aiden is a private person. I never heard him brag about anything—unless he uses it to put someone in their place.

Oh, and he's possessive to a fault. He definitely would never let others think of me in a sexual way.

I smile at that.

"So?" Kim turns in her seat to face me. Her elbows are on the desk as she cradles her face with both hands. A stupid joyful gleam shines in her green eyes.

"So what?"

"I thought you were going out with Knox."

"I did."

"Then you texted me that King is giving you a ride this morning. Did he spend the night?"

I bite my lower lip.

She squeals, but she's careful enough to keep her voice down. "It was a wild night yesterday. I can tell."

Wild is the understatement of the century. First Aunt and Uncle and then Aiden.

Now that I think about it, the whole time I've been with him, I haven't thought about the chaos with Aunt and Uncle.

That's... strange.

"You have a hickey." She points at my neck.

I slap a hand on the spot. "What? Where?"

He only left hickeys on my breasts, around my scar, and down my stomach. I made sure nothing was visible on my neck.

Kim laughs and lowers my ponytail so it covers the back of my neck. "There. It's all hidden."

I glare at Aiden. The arsehole must've left it when I was asleep and in a place I can't see. That must be why he's been releasing my hair.

He only grins at me before Ronan steals his attention again.

Dickhead.

"I want details." Kim hisses, still grinning like an idiot.

"It was... well," I lean in to whisper. "I can't walk properly."

Her eyes bulge and she comes even closer. "I knew King was the rough type."

"You can say that again. Wait." I narrow my eyes jokingly. "How did you deduce that?"

"He has that vibe." She steals a glance at Cole and Xander who are tossing a ball at one another. "Cole, too. Those silent types are usually the wildest. I heard he's into kink."

She's talking about Cole, but the only one she has eyes for is the golden boy and his dimples.

"How about Xander?"

She clicks her tongue and faces me again. "That one doesn't matter."

"If you say so."

"I mean so." She narrows her eyes then clears her throat. "Can I ask you something?"

"Anything."

"How do you know if you like it rough?"

"You just do, I guess. It can be overwhelming, but you feel like every part of your body comes alive to the point that even pain is pleasurable." I pause, realising what I just said. "Please don't think I'm weird."

Kim watches me for a few seconds, her lips parting before she grins. "I'll never judge you, Ellie. Besides, remember what I said about the silent types being the wildest? You're one of them."

I swat her hand playfully. "Stop it."

"How about Knox then?" Her nose scrunches. "King wasn't mad about that?"

"He's still mad."

But I can take care of him.

He needs to learn that he won't control my life.

It's curious that he's only this way about Knox. When his horsemen touch me or talk to me, he becomes a dick, but he doesn't act as intensely as he does with Knox.

Maybe it's because he trusts them? The level of trust Aiden could give, anyway.

I fail to think that Aiden would feel threatened by someone as easy going as Knox.

Hell. He should be thankful to him for saving my life in the pool.

"Oh, here he is," Kim says then gasps.

I follow her field of vision and my mouth hangs open. Knox walks into class with a busted lip, bluish bruises around his left eye, and pinkish ones near his temple.

"Oh, my Gosh, Knox." Kim jumps from her seat. "What happened?"

The entire class falls silent.

Except for Ronan.

He loses the sense of space and time when he's engaged in his animated speeches. Cole continues half-listening to Ronan and half-reading from his book. At least he has the decency to stare over his book at the scene.

Xander cuts a glare at Knox and Aiden leans back in his seat... smirking.

He's fucking smirking.

My eyes widen, bouncing between his bandaged knuckles and Knox's face.

No.

No, no, no...

"I was attacked out of nowhere yesterday," Knox winces.

I stagger on unsteady feet and approach him. "W-Where?"

"Right after you got into the taxi. It looks worse than it actually is. I was able to get help and..."

I'm not listening to him anymore as thousands of scenarios flash into my head.

Aiden admitted to watching us in the coffee shop. Yes, he was at my house when I got in there, but he has a faster car.

I feel sick to my stomach.

Aiden fucked me after he brutalised Knox. I let him touch me with those hands that made Knox's face almost unrecognisable.

"Are you okay?" I ask Knox in a small voice.

He nods. "It's nothing compared to the shit I was into in my old school."

"Did you..." I swallow. "Did you see who did this to you?"

"Yes, Van Doren. Have you?" Aiden stands, shoulders squaring as he strides towards us.

Xander follows, his tone mocking, "Tough shit."

Knox stares between the two of them.

I watch intently for any secret message.

Aiden has a poker face and Xander becomes unreadable all of a sudden.

Kim jerks back. Like she literally glues herself to the table behind her, slowly shrinking away from the circle.

Knox lifts a shoulder. "It was some gangster who wanted money. I already reported him to the police."

"Wait. What?" I gawk at him. "Did you see his face?"

It couldn't have been a gangster. It was Aiden, right?

"I gave the description to the police."

"I'm sure they'll catch him," Aiden says.

"I'm sure they will," Xander adds with mock sarcasm.

Mrs Stone comes into class and stops at the scene.

"Is everything all right, Mr Van Doren?"

"I was assaulted and reported it to the police." He shows his non-injured knuckles. "It was one way, I promise."

"Please let the principal know. Now, Mr King, Mr Knight, and Ms Quinn. Please take a seat so we can start."

We all do.

I inch closer to Knox. "I'm so sorry."

"Why should you be? I'm glad it happened after you left." He smiles then winces.

I wince, too.

No way in hell will anyone convince me that Aiden isn't behind this.

But Knox saw his attacker.

Also, if it wasn't from assaulting Knox, where did Aiden get those bloodied knuckles?

I spend the entire day with Kim whether in class or in hiding at her old secret spots in the back garden. I tell her it's because I'm tired, but the truth of the matter is; I don't want to see Aiden.

Every time I look at Knox's brutalised state, I can't help thinking that Aiden is the reason behind it.

It brings a taste of nausea to my mouth.

I'm happy when the whole day is over so I can finally go home and recuperate.

"Let's go watch the football team's practice," Kim begs.

"Pass."

"Come on, Ellie. You'll get to see Aiden being a football sex God."

That's the last thing I need right now.

"Let's just go home, Kim. I'll watch any soap opera you like."

"Fine." She puckers her lips. "Mood killer."

Kim and I are walking to the car park when a large presence cuts in front of us.

Aiden.

Shit.

"King," Kim sounds as astounded as I feel. "I thought there was practice today?"

"My ankle hurts so I'm getting a pass."

"Oh. I hope it's nothing serious."

"Not at all." He's speaking to her, but his metal eyes darken on me. It's like he's ripping my face open and dipping his fingers into my brain.

"Reed?"

"Yes?"

"How about you go watch practice?" He smiles at her. "The guys will be happy to have you cheer for them."

She bites her lower lip. "You think?"

"I'm sure."

"Deal! Take care of Ellie."

She slips from under my arm, slaps a noisy kiss on my cheek and is off in the school's direction before I can stop her.

I swallow as I meet Aiden's metallic gaze. The smile he offered Kim vanishes in thin air and the loathsome poker face takes reign.

"Stop manipulating her like that." I cross my arms over my chest.

"I only encouraged her to do what she already craved."

Which is another form of manipulation that works in his favour.

Dickhead.

"You've been avoiding me today," he says.

"I just wanted to spend time with Kim."

"You know I can tell when you lie and you still lie anyway. It's curious."

I fixate him with a glare. "I know you did that to Knox, okay? I can't just act all normal."

"I did that, hmm?"

"Then where did you get the bruises from? They sure as hell didn't come from punching a wall."

"Maybe they did."

"Aiden! What the hell is wrong with you? How could you do that to him?"

"Do what?" He advances towards me and I have no choice but to step back so he doesn't slam into me. "You heard him. He said he saw his attacker's face and reported him to the police."

My back hits the side of his car. I startle as an electric shock snaps through me.

I place both hands on his chest. "Please tell me the truth. Tell me you didn't do it."

He slaps my thighs apart. I cry out as he thrusts his knee between my legs. The material of his trousers rubs against my boy shorts.

My frantic gaze searches our surroundings. "Aiden, stop it."

"You stop it, Elsa. Stop trying to paint me as this politically correct person you want me to be. I'm not and I'll never fucking be."

"That's not what I'm talking about. All I want to know is that you didn't brutalise Knox just because you saw him with me in the coffee shop."

"Then maybe he shouldn't have been there, huh?"

My lips part. "You did it, didn't you?"

"Who cares who did it? He had it coming."

"Aiden!" Harsh breaths heave out of me. It takes all my cool head to speak in a level tone. "Please don't make me hate you."

"Don't you hate me already?" He raises an eyebrow. "You said it the other day."

I wish I meant it.

True, I hate his character sometimes.

I hate that I can never win with him.

I hate how he makes me gravitate towards him.

I hate that I can't kill my interest in him.

But the truth is? That hate is growing and intensifying into something I can't recognise anymore.

Something potent and scary.

"If you beat people up just because you're a possessive freak, I'll end up hating you."

He's silent for a while. "I'm not violent. You know that."

"Your busted knuckles say otherwise."

"I'm not violent," he repeats slowly this time as if he's making me understand the meaning behind his words. "Smarter, not stronger, remember?"

Does that mean he didn't hit Knox? He didn't completely deny it, but he's not owning up to it either and Aiden always owns up to his actions.

"I might not look like it, but I'm still pissed off about yesterday." His voice turns chilling. "And yet, you stand here talking nonstop about the reason why I'm pissed off. What are you trying to do, sweetheart, hmm? Provoke me? Push me? Congrats. It worked."

That strange awareness from the first day I saw him slashes at the bottom of my stomach and straight to my chest.

Maybe it's not awareness after all. Maybe like the hate, it's morphing into something entirely different. Something like excitement and thrill and belonging.

He wraps a hand around my throat and glides the pad of his thumb over my bottom lip. "This is mine." He cups my core harshly through my skirt. "This is also mine. Everything about you is fucking mine so don't push me into marking my territory in front of everyone."

"Aiden!" I search the car park in a frenzy.

It's empty—thankfully, but anyone could come through the door. Anyone could walk in and see Aiden gripping me by my throat and my pussy.

"We're in public," I murmur.

"Hmm. A good place to mark my territory."

He starts to lift my skirt.

Oh, God.

I want to think he's only threatening, but there's no doubt he'd do it.

He'd take me right here right now, and it'd get us into huge trouble with the school.

And knowing Aiden, he couldn't care less about anyone when he's in this possessive zone.

Judging from the twitch in his eyes, he's royally pissed off, too.

I have one chance to stop him and cool him down.

Only one.

And I need to act fast.

Searching around us, I inch to the side so I'm hidden by the car opposite us.

I wrap my hand around his.

"Don't even think about it," he grits out. "I warned you against provoking me."

"Let me."

He narrows his eyes. "Let you what?"

I coax him into releasing my throat.

Before he can make his next move, I drop to my knees in front of him.

THIRTY

Elsa

I'm on my knees in the car park in front of Aiden.

Before I start analysing the situation, I unbuckle his belt with trembling fingers.

I wish it's only due to the fear of getting caught, but it's also due to the sick kind of desire shooting down my spine.

This is the first time I've initiated anything sexual with Aiden. He's usually the one who's hunting me down and manipulating his way into my body.

Maybe he's made me crave him. Maybe I can't get enough of him.

Or maybe, just maybe, I'm as attuned to this type of sexual gratification as he is.

"What are you doing, sweetheart?" His voice is rougher than usual.

I bask in the feeling that I have this effect on him.

That feeling becomes tenfold deeper when I free his cock. It's rock hard and pointing in my direction.

I glance up at him as I fist his dick with both hands.

His eyes are droopy as he groans deep in his throat, but he's watching me with furrowed brows as if he can't figure out my angle.

In the beginning, all I wanted was to stop him from fucking me in public.

I thought it'd work if I turn all the attention to him. He's a bit easier to handle when I snatch some of the control.

I thought wrong.

Right now, as I take him in my hand, slowly stroking the skin, all I want to do is keep going.

There's this need to engrave myself inside him deeper.

Stronger.

Harder.

So if, one day, he wants to get rid of me, he wouldn't be able to.

Just like I'm unable to erase him from my mind, heart, and soul.

"Are you going to open that mouth for me, sweetheart?" he asks with a spark in his eyes.

I nod once.

"You're going to take me deep in your throat like never before?"

I swallow and nod again.

"You'll make me come, hmm?"

His dirty talk draws tingles at the base of my stomach. It's about him, but it doesn't make much difference.

Instead of answering him with words, I open my mouth.

Still clutching the base with my hands, I take him as far as I can and suck hard like he always told me to.

Aiden likes everything hard and rough, even a blowjob.

His fingers thread into my hair and he pulls the band free, letting the blonde strands cascade on my shoulders.

A groan rips from his throat, the masculine sound echoing all around us.

My heartbeat escalates at the thought that someone will hear or see us.

I fasten my pace, my movements frantic and somewhat all over the place.

"Fuck, sweetheart." He grunts. "That mouth of yours is mine. Only mine."

I nod, licking and sucking him in. My jaw hurts and so do my knees from kneeling on the hard asphalt, but I don't stop.

I can't even if I wanted to.

Aiden is letting me control the rhythm for the first time in... ever.

He rocks his hips and clutches me by the hair, but he's not thrusting to the back of my throat or fucking my mouth.

He's letting me please him as I see best.

"You're getting good at that, sweetheart." He grunts with an appreciative sound.

I continue with fast strokes.

He's close.

I can feel it in the hard way he fists my hair.

In the stiffness of his muscles.

He thrusts in my mouth a few times, but they're not brutalising. It's more like he's chasing his orgasm.

A taste of precum drips on my tongue.

Aiden stops moving.

I glance up at him with questions written all over my face.

He pulls out.

My back goes rigid with panic. Shit. Is he going to fuck me anyway?

Right here?

He wraps a hand around his still-hard cock, but he doesn't pull me up.

He reaches his free hand out and squeezes my cheeks. "Open your mouth."

I stare at him, incredulous.

"Open that fucking mouth, sweetheart."

I do, not sure where he's going with this.

He pumps his cock in his fist and for a second, I'm too mesmerised by the raw masculinity to focus on anything else.

He looks like a god. A sex god.

He directs his cock at my mouth and comes all over my tongue and lips.

"Hmm." He groans as I glance up at him with what must seem like a stunned expression.

He watches me, too, but it's more with a sadistic type of possessiveness. His metallic eyes continue boring into mine even after he's done coming down my throat and on my face.

"Swallow."

I close my mouth and do.

I just… do.

There's something about the way he orders me to do things that makes me all hot and tingly.

If we weren't in public, I might've even wanted him to fuck me.

Shit. Even in public, I still want him to fuck me.

I can almost imagine him slamming my back against the car and taking me hard and fast until I orgasm.

There's seriously something utterly wrong with me.

Aiden touches his thumb to my mouth which is still covered with his cum. He smears it all over my lips then presses his thumb at the opening of my mouth.

"Now, suck."

I take him inside, twirl my tongue around his thumb, and suck as I did with his cock.

All without breaking eye contact.

For some reason, staring at his stormy eyes adds more intimacy to the moment.

More connection.

More… belonging.

"Hmm. Good girl."

That makes me suck harder.

It's sick how much I love the havoc he wreaks in my body or that euphoric, pleased look in his eyes.

I love that look. I want to see it for the rest of my life.

Whoa.

That's a scary thought.

I don't want Aiden for the rest of my life.

Why the hell would I think that?

The sound of an engine cuts through the car park.

I let Aiden's thumb pop free and scramble to my feet. I snatch my band from the floor and pull my hair into a ponytail while smoothing my clothes.

Aiden doesn't seem the least bit fazed. He tucks himself in with ease and that's it. In a second, he appears all too normal while my cheeks are on the verge of exploding.

I reach for a napkin in my jacket and wipe my mouth. The fact that I still taste him shoots tingles between my thighs.

I'm trying to school my expression when Aiden pushes into me.

His chest flattens mine as he smirks down on me. "Are you wet, sweetheart?"

I clamp my lips together.

"I can do interesting things with your clothes on."

I should be mortified but the only question in my mind is: interesting things like what?

"There you are."

Both our attention snap towards the very familiar, older voice. Jonathan King.

He steps out of his Mercedes, wearing a three-piece dark brown suit and black leather shoes.

His jet black hair is slicked back and he appears completely relaxed.

I instinctively jerk away from Aiden. It feels wrong to be near him after I heard Jonathan's conversation with Silver.

It feels like I'm not allowed near Aiden.

Jonathan's face brings back that itch.

It's like I'm still floating in the pool and having my lungs filled with water.

So much fucking water.

He approaches us and I have the urge to shrink behind Aiden. I don't know why I'd think that Aiden is a better demon than his father.

They're both demons, aren't they?

Before I can cower behind Aiden, he clutches me by the arm and keeps me firmly by his side.

Aiden's face is stone cold. The playful expression from earlier completely disappears. I would've called it a poker face if it weren't for the slight twitch in his left eye.

"Elsa." Jonathan smiles at me as if we're old friends. "Have you been well?"

"What are you doing here?" Aiden asks before I can answer.

"You and I are going somewhere." Jonathan smiles. "If it's okay with you, of course, Elsa."

I nod once unsure what to say.

"I'll meet you back home," Aiden speaks in a calm, almost nonchalant tone, but I can feel the tension radiating off him in waves.

"You'll come with me," Jonathan says in a non-negotiable tone. "Keep your car here. Someone will drive it home for you."

You'll come with me.

It's a flat out order.

Since Aiden doesn't like to be told what to do, I expect him to fight.

Instead, he releases me.

A strange gust of cold seeps under my skin at the loss of contact.

Aiden doesn't let go of me.

He never lets go of me.

It feels empty now that he did.

"I'll text," he says without any emotions and strides to his father's car.

After Aiden slides inside the Mercedes, Jonathan offers me another smile.

The welcoming expression instantly drops as soon as he gets into the backseat beside Aiden.

Something clenches in my chest as the car leaves the school grounds.

I have a bad feeling about this.

Super bad.

THIRTY-ONE

Aiden

Silence is the only language in the car.

Jonathan is on his phone, probably finishing up business. I'm surprised he even showed up in the human world around this time.

In the afternoons, he's usually speaking Chinese with other tycoons from the other part of the ocean.

Or Japanese.

I retrieve my phone and find a text.

Elsa: Text me when you're done?

A smile tugs on my lips. I can almost hear her tentative voice if she were to say that.

I didn't miss the worried note in her eyes or the fear she tried to hide when I left.

Jonathan scares her and for that alone, I want him the fuck away from her. That's why I chose to go with him willingly.

I type.

Aiden: I'll be doing a lot more than texting you back when I'm done.

The reply is immediate.

Elsa: Like what?

Aiden: Like finish what I started. You owe me a fuck, sweetheart. I need to pound in you so deep, you won't be able to walk tomorrow.

Aiden: Also, I need to come down your throat again just to engrave the image from earlier to memory.

Only it's already engraved in memory.

The way she looked up at me with her mouth filled with my cum will stay with me until the day I die.

My dick strains against my trousers just thinking about it.

Now that I've had that visual, I need to do it over and over again because I don't get enough.

Not when it comes to her.

Elsa is an addiction that first got under my skin, but is now flowing through my veins and into my bloodstream.

I need to bleed out to get her out.

And even then, I doubt she'd leave.

She sees my texts. The dots appear and disappear as if she's thinking about what to reply.

Elsa: I'll let you do that.

I raise an eyebrow.

Aiden: Is that so?

Elsa: After you tell me a story. You'll owe me two after a fuck and a blowjob *winking emoji*

Hmm. She's being manipulative more than usual lately.

It makes me so fucking proud.

Aiden: Pass.

Elsa: But I was looking forward to repeating today.

Little fucking tease.

Oh, she's good. She's getting so good at playing my game.

Aiden: Kinda want to fuck the shit out of you right now, sweetheart.

Elsa: I'm good with that, too.

Fuck me and this girl who's toying with my damn mind.

Aiden: You'll let me do anything?

Elsa: Maybe.

I smile.

"Is that Steel?" Jonathan's voice wipes the smile off my face.

Fuck.

I forgot that he was just here—and probably watching me the entire time.

I tuck my phone in my pocket and face him with my neutral expression. "Why did you pick me up from school?"

He narrows his eyes because he doesn't like to be ignored. "We're here."

The car comes to a stop and the driver nods at us from the mirror.

I stare through the window and tighten my grip on my phone.

Fucking Jonathan.

Pine trees stand tall in the distance like stones of memories.

Jonathan opens his door. "Come out."

I close my eyes and take a long breath before I follow him.

He faces a tree with his hands in front of him like he's a soldier.

The cliff beyond the huge tree appears like a giant mouth, ready to be fed.

The area is desolate with no people or animals in sight. Jonathan made sure to buy it so no trespassers would come near this road.

He even has his top-notch security company guard this place. Two agents dressed like MI6 spies nod at us. They stand in front of their black cars a short distance away—but not within hearing range.

Jonathan doesn't nod back or acknowledge them.

His entire attention remains on the tree.

This tree stood tall for the past ten years despite the scratches at its trunk.

It's funny how some things never change.

I stand beside Jonathan and shove both my hands in my trousers.

"Do you know what today is?" he asks without sparing me a glance.

"Alicia's birthday."

"Happy birthday." His tone is emotionless, cold even. "You would've been forty today."

I grind my jaw but say nothing.

"Alicia died here," he repeats the piece of information as if I don't know it.

His voice is still detached, but his eyes say something entirely different.

There's a softening in there.

Something I never see him offer anyone. Not even Lev and I whom he considers his legacy.

I face the tree again, not wanting to see that expression.

Jonathan is probably playing one of his tricks and I won't fall for it.

"She died trying to find you," he continues, plunging the knife deeper. "She died without seeing your face. Four hours, Aiden. She remained in pain for four fucking hours."

"Are you getting to a point any time soon?"

He rips his gaze from the tree as if it pains him. "Have some fucking respect to your mother and quit playing house with Steel."

"I'm not playing house. I'm —"

"Enough." His voice is cold and unnegotiable. "End it. I want it to be humiliating and painful so she'll come into her power as a shell."

My left eye twitches, but I ask in a calm tone. "What if she never becomes a shell?"

He's a fool if he thinks he'll be able to break Elsa.

She's the strongest person I know.

But just because he can't break her, doesn't mean he can't hurt her.

"Let me worry about that. You only need to do your part of the deal, Aiden."

Silence falls down between us as we stare at each other with identical eyes. "Or what?"

He approaches me so he's looking down on me. "When I say end it. You fucking end it, do you hear me?"

I meet his harshness with mine. "Or what, Jonathan?"

"Or I'll end it myself." He throws one last glance at the tree as if he can see Alicia's ghost and heads to the car. "You have until tomorrow."

Fuck him and his tactics.

As long as I'm around, no one will hurt Elsa.

Jonathan included.

As soon as the car door slams shut, I briefly close my eyes and face the tree.

"Maybe you're right, Alicia. Maybe I shouldn't have been born, huh?"

THIRTY-TWO

Elsa

Aiden doesn't text me back.

I stay up all night, trying to finish homework, but all I do is watch my phone like a maniac.

Chaotic thoughts barge into my mind all at once, and none of them are good.

I hated that he went with his father. However, when he texted me in his usual crude way as soon as he got into the car, I thought things were okay.

Maybe they're not.

Earlier, Uncle came to check on me before he went to bed. I didn't miss how he barely made eye contact. His dark circles were more prominent like he hasn't slept in days.

The possibility of being the reason behind that crushes me.

I haven't seen Aunt since overhearing that conversation, and it's for the best.

I still don't know how to act around them just yet.

With a groan, I push off the desk and throw my body on the bed. It's useless to study when I've been reading the same paragraph for hours.

I pull up Aiden's number.

Elsa: Are you okay?

I bite my lip, waiting for him to see it.

Nothing.

Damn it.

I throw the phone under the pillow and close my eyes.

Everything will be fine in the morning.

A small hand surrounds my smaller one.

The one who shall not be named?

I glimpse up at him, his pretty trousers and shoes. His tousled black hair that falls on his forehead like silk.

He smiles down at me with a twinkle in his dark eyes.

His smile is like the sun.

Rare, but blinding.

I love his smile. It makes me feel safe.

Why am I not as pretty as he is?

I'm the girl, right? I should be prettier than the one who shall not be named.

"Can I say your name now?"

He places a forefinger in front of his mouth. "Shh."

"Shh," I repeat, tears filling my eyes. "Ma doesn't like it."

He grips my hand harder and leads me to the back garden. Bushes grow on either side of us like walls.

Dad doesn't like it when I come here.

"Them monsters are here," I tell the one who shall not be named.

"Shh," he motions at the house.

Ma stands near the window, doing her red lipstick.

"Dad doesn't like it," I say, shrinking behind him.

The one who shall not be named fastens his pace. I jog along, watching his hand around mine.

It's familiar.

It's safe.

It's… happy.

"I miss you." My voice trembles. "It's lonely without you. Ma goes to them monsters sometimes."

"Shh." He points ahead.

He's tall so I lean aside to see past him.

I come to a screeching halt, feet gluing to the grass.

The lake.

The murky, black lake.

"No, no…"

"Shh!"

"No! I won't go in there. I don't want to go there!" I shriek, my voice crackling with sobs.

My heartbeat skyrockets and everything in my chest aches. I try to pull away from the one who shall not be named, but his grip tightens.

It's like he can't let me go even if he wanted to.

No, please.

The murky lake appears almost black under the gloomy weather.

That lake took everything from me.

Everything.

"Eli, please. It's scary."

He stops and his face turns into a blur. "You shouldn't have said my name."

His hand slips from mine.

My fingers fist around the air as I try to grab him.

No.

No.

His back is the only thing I see as he strides with purpose towards the lake.

"E-Eli?"

He doesn't turn around.

Black smoke swallows him until I can barely see him.

I run after him with shaky little feet. I trip and nearly fall.

"Eli, C-Come back… Don't go, please… I'm s-so sorry… d-don't… go."

Something warm touches my toes.

I stop at the shore of the lake.

Black water covers my feet and my limbs start shaking.

Eli walks deep into the lake. Only his head is visible.

"Eli!" I call.

I want to go save him. I want to bring him back, but if I do, them monsters in the water will take me.

Them monsters are taking Eli.

"Eli, c-come back! Come back!"

His head disappears underwater and doesn't surface.

"ELI!!!"

I wake up with a start, tears streaming down my cheeks.

Eli.

Eli...

No. No. No.

That's not true.

Eli didn't go.

He couldn't have been gone.

A taste of nausea hits the back of my throat and I run to the bathroom. I fall to my knees against the hard tiles and empty my stomach in the toilet.

I remain there even after I'm finished, catching my breath.

Tears fall down my cheeks and to my hands.

"Eli..." I sob. "Eli is the one who shall not be named."

Why can't he be named and why isn't he in my life anymore?

I clutch my head between my hands and hit it with a fist over and over again.

Why can't I remember? Why the hell can't I remember?

My heart nearly bursts open with a crushing wave of grief.

It's like having my chest ripped open and slashed apart and all I can do is watch.

Just like I watched when Eli went into that lake and I couldn't follow.

Eli.

Who the hell is Eli and why do I suddenly feel like I'm missing a big chunk of myself?

"Eli…" His name comes in a strangled sob.

The itch beneath my skin digs into my arms and hands like needles. I stagger to my feet and wash my hands over and over again.

I don't stop even after my skin becomes red and stingy. I want to use bleach on my hands.

But even that won't make them clean, will it?

I stare at my dishevelled picture in the mirror. My hair points in all directions and my eyes are bloodshot. The tears leave streaks over my pale cheeks.

This isn't just any ache.

It's chronic pain.

Eli was someone important from my past that I erased him just like I erased Ma and Dad.

Just like I erased everything.

"What's wrong with you?" I whisper to my reflection. "Why can't you be normal?"

You know what?

Enough.

I've had enough of putting everyone else's wellbeing before my own. I'll confront Uncle and demand he tells me everything he knows.

I'll demand he takes me back to Birmingham.

For ten years, I thought I could survive without knowing my past.

But there's no future without roots. I'll always be stuck in this whirlwind of emotions and frightening nightmares.

And grief.

Crushing grief.

I can barely breathe as I think about Eli. Uncle needs to tell me who the hell Eli is.

After washing my face and freshening up, I put on my uniform. On my way out of my room, I check my phone, but there's still no text from Aiden.

My heart smashes further into its cavity, but I swallow the pain down. I exit my room with determination bubbling in my veins.

Today, I'll face my fears.

Today, I'll know everything Aunt and Uncle have been hiding for years.

It's no longer an option. It's a need now.

I take the steps down, breathing deep and summoning all the courage I have in my bones.

This is the first time I'll demand to know something about my past.

I'm counting on Uncle's understanding. Here's to hoping he didn't change his mind.

"She's right upstairs," Aunt says with a strained tone. "Let's talk someplace else."

I stop at the base of the stairs at the corner of the lounge area from where her voice comes through.

So she returned home last night.

"This is as good of a place as any."

My muscles tighten at that voice.

The voice I never wanted to hear in my house.

Ever.

Could it be that I'm hearing things?

Leaning sideways, I peek slightly inside.

I wrap a hand over my mouth to smother the gasp.

It's him.

Jonathan King.

Jonathan fucking King is sitting on the chair at the head of the lounge area. He's wearing a black suit that seems straight out of an Armani fashion show.

Aunt and Uncle sit on the sofa opposite him.

I have a side view, but I can make out the horrified expression on Aunt's face and the blackening of Uncle's features.

What the hell is going on?

"Mr King," Uncle speaks in a respectful calm tone. "Please let's do this outside."

"I would rather do this right here." He appears completely relaxed like he owns the place and everyone in it.

It's clear from whom Aiden got his infuriating confidence.

"We're thankful for your help ten years ago," Aunt says. "But we already paid you back."

"Paid me back?" Jonathan deadpans. "Nothing can pay back saving a person's life, Mrs Quinn. If I hadn't paid for Elsa's heart surgery, do you think she would've been alive?"

My heartbeat skyrockets, slamming against my ribcage and buzzing in my ears.

Jonathan paid for my surgery? Why the hell would he do that?

"You're right," Aunt rushes. "We didn't have the finances and if you didn't offer a generous hand, we wouldn't have Elsa with us."

"I'm no generous man, Mrs Quinn." Jonathan plants his elbow on the armrest and leans against his hand. "I'm a businessman. I only made an investment for the future. After all, she's the heiress to Steel's fortune."

"There's no fortune!" Aunt jumps to her feet. "She'll go nowhere near that filthy empire built by blood."

Steel's heiress. Empire?

I'm reeling from so much information thrown in my face. I feel like I'm going to throw up again.

Jonathan smiles. "The fact that it's built on blood makes it even more desirable. Don't you think?"

"My Elsa will go nowhere near that money or that name. She's Elsa Quinn," Aunt snaps.

Uncle sits her down and places a hand on her thigh as if to keep her from standing up again. He faces Jonathan with a much more rational expression than Aunt's. "You said no conditions back then."

"I said no conditions, but I said I'll return when she's eighteen."

Aunt's lower lip twists.

"And what do you want, Mr King?" Uncle's voice hardens. "Because you won't meet Elsa. You'll have to get through me first."

"With all due respect, getting through you won't be so hard, Mr Quinn."

"What do you want from her?" Uncle grits out, his entire demeanour radiating tension.

"I let Elsa live ten years ago and I'm letting her live now, but the moment I decide to burn Steel's blood running in her veins, no one will stop me." He pauses. "I'll finish the life I saved in a heartbeat."

My back snaps and my fingers tremble.

I'll finish the life I saved in a heartbeat.

What the hell does he mean by that?

"She has nothing to do with her father!" Aunt yells. "She's *not* him."

"Are you certain about that?" Jonathan's eyes darken. "After all, she's Steel's little princess for whom he sacrificed everything."

"Leave Elsa alone, or I won't stay still," Uncle speaks low but threateningly.

"I appreciate the courage, but you can't do fuck to me, Mr Quinn." Jonathan stands and buttons his jacket. "Now, if you'll excuse me, I have a board of directors meeting to attend."

He suddenly lifts his eyes and meets mine as if he knew I was listening all along.

I freeze as a cruel smirk tilts his lips before he turns and walks out the door.

Neither Aunt nor Uncle sees him out. Aunt's face reddens and Uncle holds her by the shoulders as if he's keeping her from falling apart.

I stand behind the wall, my insides breaking into a million pieces.

Everything Jonathan said whirls in my head like a hurricane with no ending in sight.

I'm too shocked to process everything, but I know, I just know that whatever happened in my past isn't something pretty.

Pretty or not, this is my only chance to know the truth.

I inhale deep, shaky breaths and stride into the lounge area.

Uncle glances up first as I stand in front of them. Alarm tightens his features.

Before they can say anything, I speak in a calm voice I don't feel. "I heard everything. Now, I want you to tell me about my past."

THIRTY-THREE

Elsa

Uncle stands up, forcing a smile. "Pumpkin, what you heard just now is —"

"The truth." I cut him off. I never cut Uncle or Aunt off, but today is different. "And I want to know the rest of it."

"H-hon," Aunt stammers. "It was a long time ago."

"Abandoning me and Mum was also a long time ago, Aunt?"

She gasps, her hands covering her mouth.

"I heard you the other day." My voice is neutral, almost too detached.

I don't know how to speak in any other tone without breaking down.

"You owe me an explanation," I tell them.

A deep sigh rips from Uncle's chest as he staggers backwards and falls beside Aunt. "Tell her."

Aunt touches her temple with trembling fingers. "N-No."

"We knew this day would come, Blair." Uncle's jaw clenches. "Just tell her already. She deserves to know."

"I said no, Jaxon!"

I rip my gaze from her and focus on Uncle. "Who's Eli?"

His eyes widen like I've never seen them before.

Like he's having a heart attack.

"Oh, God," Aunt's voice catches on a sob.

Usually, I would do anything not to see them like this, but not today.

Today, I need answers even if I have to hurt them in the process.

"I had a dream—no, a nightmare—about clutching his hand before he disappeared into the lake." The itch starts under my skin. "Who is he?"

"It was just a nightmare, hon," Aunt doesn't even sound convincing anymore.

"They were never nightmares, Aunt. The ache and the pain and the tears were never nightmares. The blood, the screaming, and the whimpering were never freaking nightmares!"

"What on earth have you been through, pumpkin?" Uncle sounds defeated, completely and utterly worn out.

What have I been through?

They're the ones who are supposed to tell me that.

"I'm asking for the last time, Aunt. Who the hell is Eli?"

"He was your brother," Uncle says in a low voice.

I grip my backpack's strap so tight, I'm surprised it doesn't snap. "W-Was?"

"He died in that lake you always have nightmares about."

It's as if someone took a knife and jammed it straight into my defective heart.

I'm bleeding and no one can stop it.

"H-how?"

Uncle's eyes fill with sympathy. "He drowned, pumpkin. He was just seven at the time, a year older than you."

No.

Eli can't be dead. Eli has to be alive.

"You're lying," I shriek.

Uncle starts to stand up, about to comfort me no doubt, but I hold up a hand.

"No. Don't even come close. I need to know why that happened."

I glare at Aunt who's been watching her shoes and rocking back and forth. "Tell me, Aunt."

Uncle nudges her. She flinches, but she doesn't lift her head.

"I loved Abby. I really, really loved her. She was a shy girl who always took the shit our Da threw our way. He was a fucking lunatic when on the liquor, but he became worse after Mum's death." She continues rocking back and forth, appearing like a lost puppy instead of the alpha women I always knew her to be.

"Mum went to pick up Abby from her music class and they had an accident in which our mum died. Da took all his anger on us, especially Abby since she looked so much like Mum. He told her, a twelve-year-old at the time, that he wished she died instead of Mum." Aunt meets my gaze with tears in her eyes. "Da was a cruel man, Elsie. He was vicious and unapproachable when he was drunk. I always spent most of my time outside, but Abby was there. She refused to leave his side even when he beat her, when he beat us. After I got my scholarship for Cambridge, I begged her to come with me, but she refused. I told her I'm never returning to Birmingham, to a place that killed me slowly and to a father who suffocated me. I told her that I might not see her again, but she didn't change her mind."

She swallows audibly as if summoning the courage to say the next words. "Then, a year later, she sent me wedding pictures with your father. She told me she was happy and she wanted me to be happy. Then..." She clears her throat. "She sent me pictures of her firstborn, Eli, then... of you."

"And you still never came," I ask.

"I had a trauma in Birmingham, Elsie. The moment I step into it, all I recall is Dad throwing an ashtray at my head because I hid his liquor." She pulls the side of her ginger hair up to show me a faded scar. "I bled until I thought I was going to die. After I was discharged from the hospital, I packed my things and promised to never return to Birmingham again."

"What do you know about my parents' marriage?" I ask.

"Elsie..."

"Tell me, Aunt."

"Abby was mentally unwell." Aunt sighs, appearing lost in her own thoughts. "She suffered from depression and some manic episodes since our mother's death. It became worse with Dad's treatment of her. When she got married, she seemed like she was getting better. She smiled more and was slowly healing from Dad's abuse. Ethan looked like he took care of her. He was the richest freaking tycoon in Birmingham at the time. He owned coal and steel factories and everyone feared him—Dad included. I was happy that he couldn't hurt her anymore."

"Wait." I hold up a hand. "Ethan? I thought my dad's name was John."

"We wanted to hide you from your father's people," Uncle says.

My father's people? What is that supposed to mean? "Why would you want to hide me from them?"

"Because they want to take you away from us," Aunt snarls.

"Blair," Uncle soothes her.

"Tell me more," I say.

"More what?" Aunt frowns.

"You said Ma was healing, but something wrong happened, didn't it?"

"I told you, pumpkin." Uncle appears pained. "Eli drowned."

A sob catches in Aunt's throat. "I don't think Abby has ever been the same after that. You were six and he was seven. You were playing by the lake when he went in and never resurfaced again. Abby wrote me letters telling me that she holds you to sleep. She called Eli the one who shall not be named because now, she'd only focus on raising you."

My heart beats so fast as if it'll come out of my chest.

It all makes sense now.

The way I remember she held me like she wanted to squeeze the life out of me. The way she'd sing me that song in that haunting voice.

Why couldn't I remember what happened with Eli?

How come he only visited me once in my dreams?

"What about my dad?" I ask. "Where was he?"

"He helped her." Aunt sniffles and wipes her tears. "Or tried to, anyway. Now that I think about it, Eli's death destroyed her just like Mum's death destroyed my dad."

Silence falls in the room short of my harsh breathing.

I should stop, process all the information I just gathered and then return with questions.

But now that I started, I can't just stop.

I'm like an insatiable monster.

"How did I survive the fire, Aunt?"

"I really don't know, Elsie." She glimpses at Uncle and he takes her hand in his. "We were called for being your next of kin that day. We found you in the hospital, injured, and screaming. Sometimes, you'd hit me. Dr Khan said it's because I remind you of your mother."

"Injured?" I stare at them, incredulous. "I thought I needed the surgery because of my heart condition."

"There was never a heart condition," Uncle says.

"Jaxon!" Aunt shrieks.

"She needs to know everything we do, Blair."

"W-what do you mean there was never a heart condition, Uncle?" My breathing deepens as if I'm an injured animal. "Then what about the scar? The doctor? The appointments?"

"Those are true, pumpkin. You did have heart surgery, but it's not because of a heart condition."

"Then because of what?"

"You were shot," he says the word with pain. "It damaged your internal tissues and you developed a heart condition because of that."

My feet falter and it takes all my strength to remain standing. "Who... who shot me?"

"We don't know, Elsie." Aunt sobs. "Even the police didn't know. We were just happy you remained alive."

"And how did Jonathan King come in the picture?"

Aunt wipes her cheeks. "He just showed up and told us he'd pay for your surgery and that we can pay him back later."

"He never said why?"

Both of them shake their heads.

"We were desperate, pumpkin," Uncle says. "We didn't have that much money for the surgery, and we couldn't process your father's will when he just deceased."

"My father's will?"

"Your father, Ethan Steel, was a tycoon." Uncle rubs the back of his head. "He has people running his fortune until you come of age to inherit it. You're Steel's heiress."

"No, she's not," Aunt snaps then her eyes soften when they meet mine. "Steel empire was built as ruthlessly as Jonathan King built his. You don't want that, right? You're Elsa Quinn, not Elsa Steel."

My gaze strays from Uncle to her. They're watching me expectantly as if I'm about to drop a bomb.

I couldn't care less about the Steel money or the last name.

The only image that keeps playing in my head is Ma singing me that haunting lullaby before someone drowned me in the water.

Ma was lonely.

She was mentally ill.

She needed help and no one gave it to her.

"You abandoned her," I tell Aunt with a chilling calmness. "You abandoned your only sister when she needed you the most."

"Elsie, I…"

"Am I your way of redemption. Is that it?"

"No, Elsa. I love you. You're my daughter."

"I only became your daughter at the expense of losing my real mother, Aunt."

Before she can say anything, I drop my backpack on the chair and walk out of the door.

Then I start running.

THIRTY-FOUR

Elsa

I run.

I go at it for hours or a day, I'm not sure.

I run until no breaths remain in my lungs.

I run until everything blurs.

The rain pounds down on me, soaking my clothes and my hair. My fingers become stiff with the cold and my shoes slouch with water.

My heart's palpitations become scarier by the minute, but I don't stop.

I *can't* stop.

No tears come out no matter how much I want to cry. Droplets of rain stream down my head and my cheeks as if rinsing me.

But there's no rinsing me from the past.

Everything will come back.

Everything will hit me again.

I gulp air, but barely anything reaches my lungs.

There's a monster in my chest, a dark ugly monster who claws at my walls.

The monster wants to be set free.

It's one of the monsters from the nightmares. A monster that will eat me alive.

The same monster who took Eli.

My heart thuds at the thought.

Eli.

My brother Eli. My mother Abigail. My father Ethan.

My family.

How can I not even remember their faces properly?

They're a blur. A shadow. Black fucking smoke.

Is that what's been wrong with me all this time? The itch, the nightmares, all the triggers have been a way to make me remember, weren't they?

So why the hell can't I remember them?

I come to a screeching halt, catching my breaths. My heart thunders in my chest in that irregular, frightening rhythm.

The heart that Jonathan saved just so he can destroy me when I'm older.

The heart that was shot at.

Who shot me? Who the hell would shoot a seven years old girl?

The rain blurs my vision. The buildings surrounding me start to double then to triple.

I lean against a wall, breathing harshly.

I don't feel so good.

My heart beats so fast. I take deep inhales and release long exhales.

It's not working.

I reach for my phone, then stop. I left the backpack with my phone in it at home.

With trembling hands, I push my hair back and try to walk. I stumble and nearly fall. I clutch the wall with stiff, wet fingers.

I search around me, but it's deserted, probably because of the rain.

A buzz goes off in my ears and my eyes flutter closed. I lean against the wall, inhaling heavy choked breaths.

"Crybaby." Eli's voice rings in my head. "Come with me."

My heartbeat slows down until it's no longer scary but it's also not there either.

"Why did you go, Eli?" I whisper and I feel like that six-year-old girl whom he released her hand. "Why did you leave me alone?"

"I didn't leave you alone, crybaby. Another Eli came."

"Another Eli?"

"Shh."

His voice drifts and so does his image. I try to catch him, but he turns into smoke.

Eli...

Tears rim my eyes and I fall.

Or I think I do. Someone clutches me before I hit the ground.

Strong arms surround me, lifting me off the ground.

It smells good.

It smells safe.

"I got you," that voice whispers.

My eyes flutter closed and I let go.

I got you.

A headache hits my temple.

I groan while sitting up.

For a second, I'm too disoriented to figure out where I am.

The bedroom's dark decor with the large bed prickles my memory.

The Meet Up.

My eyes open wide and I push my hair back.

Aiden.

My heart beats then sinks into itself at the thought of him.

How did he find me? Also, why the hell would he even find me after the show Jonathan pulled at our house this morning?

Only a bathrobe and a sheet cover my nakedness.

The room's temperature is warm. It almost feels like a cosy morning.

Almost.

The door opens without a sound. My shoulders strain with tension at the thought of seeing him.

I can't even pretend that his presence doesn't wreak havoc in my heart and mind.

Hot chocolate scent wafts in the air from the steaming cup he's carrying.

His tousled hair seems damp. He's wearing dark jeans and Elites' royal blue jacket.

No uniform. That means he didn't even consider going to RES.

He appears his usual self, calm and composed as if nothing is wrong.

As if my life hasn't been crashing down all around me today.

No. Not today.

My life has been crashing down since Eli's death. I just spent the last ten years pretending like it's not.

"The doctor came to see you." Aiden takes my hand in his and places the steaming hot cup between my fingers. "He said it's not alarming, but you should have tests done with your supervising heart physician."

"The doctor?" I ask.

"Our family doctor."

Of course, they have a family doctor who does home visits.

Then, at the thought of his family, a bitter taste fills my mouth.

"Jonathan came over today," I murmur. "He made it clear that he paid for my heart surgery when I was a kid just so he can destroy me whenever he wished. And oh, by the way, I just learnt it was never a heart condition. I was shot."

Aiden takes two steps back and sits on a chair opposite the bed. It's the first time he intentionally puts distance between us.

If it were the old Aiden, he'd invade my space and make me accept him even if I didn't want to.

Being close is one of the intimidation methods he uses so well.

Not today, apparently.

Maybe I shocked him. But then again, Aiden is a mastermind, and usually a few steps ahead. Is it even possible to shock him?

His poker face doesn't help.

"Drink. I made it the way you like, more chocolate, less milk." He motions at the hot chocolate. "You need internal heat."

"You knew about Jonathan's plans, didn't you?" My clutch stiffens against the cup. "Hell, you've been an accomplice all this time."

"Drink your hot chocolate," he repeats as if I didn't hear him the first time.

"I won't drink the damn thing!" I slam it not so gently on the nightstand. A few hot droplets burn my skin, but I don't pay them attention.

What stings the most is the boy sitting across from me.

My heart bleeds at the thought that Aiden has only been with me according to Jonathan's plan.

For some reason, I need to hear it from his mouth.

If I do, I'll be able to hate him properly.

"Say it. You're so almighty and don't lie, right? So fucking say it, Aiden! Say that all of this has been a game."

He remains in his chair but he glares at me down his nose as if he wants to strangle me.

Then his left eye twitches.

I should've run. I should've cowered away, but I didn't.

Or more like I don't get the chance.

Aiden stands and before I know it, he's pinning me to the bed. His hand wraps around both my wrists and he slams them on the headboard above my head as he straddles my lap.

"A game." He seethes. "Yes, Elsa, it was a game, but you refused to play by the fucking rules."

"What rules?"

"My rules."

I laugh, the sound humourless and a bit hysterical. "Your rules? Do those include destroying me like you said that first day we met?"

He says nothing and just continues looming over me like a grim reaper all complete with dark eyes and jet black hair.

"Were they your rules or Jonathan's rules?" I mock. "Because he seems like the one who controls the game."

"Jonathan doesn't scare me, sweetheart." He tightens his hold around my wrists. "And he shouldn't scare you either."

I scoff even though my heart bleeds open. "Are you starting another game, Aiden? Are you going to make me trust you again just so I'll fall harder? That's what Jonathan told Silver the other day, you know. He said that the prey ought to fall harder if she knows there's no danger."

"Don't let them get between us. Forget about them."

"Forget about them?" I shriek, angry tears rimming my eyes. "I already forgot many things, Aiden. I forgot about my parents and my brother. I forgot who I am for ten fucking years, so don't you go telling me to forget about anything! Actually, no. There's an exception. I'll forget everything about you."

"You'll forget everything about me, huh?" His tone is calm but chilling.

"I will." My heartbeat throbs with every word I say. "You used me and ridiculed me. I'm already a wreck. Are you happy now?"

His lips crush to mine. He kisses me with tenderness and passion that leaves me breathless.

A sob catches at the back of my throat. The tears I held onto for the whole day spill free.

He licks my bottom lip, coaxing me to open up.

Open up and do what? Be the same fool that I've been since the beginning of the year?

Fall for him all over again just to be hurt?

I bite his lower lip, but that only turns his kiss more savage.

He tugs my hair free and fists it in his hand. His tongue thrusts inside and claims mine. He kisses me until there's no breath left in my lungs.

He finally pulls back and growls against my mouth, "There's no forgetting about me, sweetheart. Is that fucking clear?"

"Then tell me the truth, Aiden! If you don't, I swear to God, I'll hate you."

"You'll hate me," he repeats the words with menace, gripping my hair tighter.

Aiden doesn't like to be threatened but screw him. He's threatened me enough. It's time he takes a taste of his own medicine.

"I'll hate you," I repeat with conviction. "I don't care if it takes me a month, a year, or a decade, but I will forget about you."

His left eye twitches and he glares at me as if he's challenging me to do just that.

To test him and bear the consequences.

I glare back at him, not cowering away.

The air ripples with tension as neither of us break eye contact.

After what seems like forever of staring at each other, he releases me.

My hands fall on either side of me, but he doesn't get off me. It's as if he needs the closeness.

And maybe. Just maybe, I need it, too.

I don't know when Aiden became the only person I always need close.

He just is.

Since he remains silent, I decide to take it into my hands. "The friends you told me about are Jonathan and my father, right?"

It makes sense with all the tycoon part and how they both married mentally ill women. Alicia and my mum were just a part of the King and Steel bet.

He nods.

"You said there was a bet that ruined everything?"

"A business deal," he says and for the first time, Aiden doesn't meet my eyes.

He's staring at my scar through the small opening in my bathrobe. I'm tempted to hide it, but I don't want to stop the flow.

"What type of business deal?" I ask.

"They often had a bet on who makes more money through gross production during that month."

"That seems normal."

His eyes draw a hole through my surgery scar as he speaks. "Jonathan had inside info that Ethan's gross production would surpass his, and Jonathan doesn't lose. He had an insider at Steel Factories disrupt production. It was supposed to be a fire in the middle of the night, but the insider messed up. Steel's coal factory caught fire during the day when many workers were there. There were many human casualties and catastrophic damage to the factory."

"That sounds familiar…" I gasp. "The great Birmingham fire."

He nods.

"But, when I read about it in the article, no one mentioned that the factory belonged to Steel. Even the article about the domestic fire made it seem like my parents were unimportant. They didn't mention that my father owned factories. Granted, I didn't read the entire article, but still."

"That would be Jonathan. He controls media in any way he wants to. Besides, Ethan Steel was a very private man. He didn't get off on attention like Jonathan."

"Why would your father bury my parents' death like it was nothing? Wait…" I watch him with wide eyes. "D-did he have anything to do with it?"

He remains calm as he shakes his head. "Jonathan is many things, but he's not a murderer."

"Then why did he bury the fire?"

"Because it relates directly to the great Birmingham fire. He didn't want his name mentioned in a nation-scale tragedy." He releases a long breath. "Since Steel's productions were handicapped, Jonathan won that month, but he lost more than money."

"Like what?"

Aiden's eyes finally meet mine and they appear glassed over like something is completely dead inside.

"Like Alicia."

My heart aches at the mention of her name. She was just another pawn in Jonathan and Ethan's game.

Just like Ma.

Just like Aiden.

Just like me.

I raise a hand and stroke his cheek right beneath the mole. "Do you miss her?"

"No." His facial expression doesn't change. "What's the point of missing someone who'll never return?"

Ouch.

As much as mentally unwell Alicia was, something tells me Aiden looked up to her. She was the break of pattern between him and Jonathan.

Since her death, Aiden took after his father's steps.

"She used to sit me beside her as she read her philosophy and psychology books," he says in a distant voice. "I was her only audience."

"Aiden..."

"She should've died." His jaw tightens. "She was too fragile and wouldn't have survived in a world filled by the likes of Jonathan King and Ethan Steel."

"Is that why you became like Jonathan?"

"I didn't become like Jonathan, I chose to be like him. People like Alicia are insignificant. One has to be the king to survive."

For some reason, it doesn't feel like he's ridiculing his mother. If anything, he sounds sad when he says her name.

I cradle his cheeks with both my palms and give him a tentative smile. "It's okay if you miss her."

"I don't."

"I miss my mum, my dad, and Eli. I don't even remember them, but I miss them. I think I've always missed them, that's why I was having those nightmares. It's like a punishment for forgetting about them."

He watches me intently as if I'm about to grow a head. Or two.

Tears fill my eyes as that grief hits me out of nowhere.

I can't fight it even if I want to.

"It's weird, right?"

He remains poker-faced, but his hand reaches out to stroke a stray strand of hair off my face.

"It's not weird to miss people." He twirls a strand between his fingers. "I think I missed you, too, sometimes."

Before I can make out the meaning behind his words, his lips press to mine with a tenderness that startles the shit out of me.

Aiden doesn't do soft. He's all rugged and rough.

He wraps a hand around my nape and pulls me closer. I willingly open when he probes my lips. He kisses me slowly, too slowly, as if he's re-learning me.

As if he lost me and finally found me.

I moan in his mouth as he cups my breast through the bathrobe. My nipples harden and strain against the cloth.

He traces a finger up and down my scar as if he's engraving it to memory.

I close my eyes and surrender to his onslaught. There's nothing more crushing and levitating as being kissed by Aiden.

No. I'm not only being kissed by Aiden.

I'm being worshipped.

He's taking my world and reshaping it without my permission.

He doesn't break the kiss as he reaches between us and unbuckles his belt.

In no time, he's nudging at my entrance, and slowly, too slowly thrusts inside me.

I'm too wet, but he still finds resistance because of his size.

His groan matches my own as he pulls the slightest bit from my mouth to stare at my face.

Thump, thump, thump.

I place my hand against his heart. My lips fall open at the maddening heartbeat under my fingertips.

His thrusts are slow and almost gentle, like that first time when he waited for me to get used to him.

Is he also waiting for me to get used to him now?

"I missed you, sweetheart," he rasps against my lips.

My heart beats so loud, I'm surprised I'm able to hear him.

"Say you missed me, too." He continues caressing my scar as he thrusts deeper, hitting that spot inside me.

I open my mouth to say the words, but his thrusts render me speechless.

This intimacy will kill me.

"Say it," he grunts and pulls one of my legs up to get more depth.

"I missed you," I breathe as the wave hits me deep inside.

I don't get a choice as I unravel all around him. My eyes roll to the back of my head as I nibble on my lower lip.

Aiden kisses me again, replacing my teeth with his. His pace grows faster and rougher, filling me to the rim.

My nails dig into his back as if I'm holding on for dear life.

He grunts, and I watch his handsome face turning rigid as warmth coats my insides.

When he pulls out of me, sharp emptiness slashes me.

I'm tempted to reach out and put him in me again.

Instead, I wrap my arms around his torso and snuggle to his side, both my arms and legs wrapped around him.

His fingers spread through my hair, stroking it back.

I'm in that dreamy place between wakefulness and sleep when I hear his whisper in the dark. "We'll never miss each other again, sweetheart."

THIRTY-FIVE

Elsa

Later on, I wake up to a rustle of clothes.

Blinking the sleep away, I sit up in bed.

I plop my elbow on the pillow and lean on my palm to watch Aiden dress.

There's such a masculine beauty about the way he yanks his jeans up his muscular football thighs and to the V of his hips.

No boxer briefs. Mmm.

My thighs clench at the thought.

Pity I can't see the front properly since his back faces me.

My gaze strays to the hard contours of his naked shoulders as he fetches his T-shirt. His tattoos ripple with the veins as if taunting me to watch them up close and personal.

My lusty mode comes to a screeching halt at the full view of his naked back.

It disappears all too soon when the T-shirt covers him, but the sight is engraved deep in my memories.

The slash marks on his skin.

The faded scars.

I swallow the sensation gripping me by the gut. Aiden doesn't parade his scar around.

He called it a weakness.

I never asked him again about that, but I will. Just not now.

Maybe, just maybe, I'm starting to figure out Aiden. It's not that he's closed off, it's that he dislikes being pushed. If I take my time with him and make sure he's well satiated, he'll be on my side.

He'll tell me everything I need to know.

All I have to do is be patient and stop antagonising him when he's volatile.

It'll take work, but I'll get there.

Eventually.

I also need to teach him not to antagonise me either.

"Like what you see, sweetheart?" he spins around.

The playful gleam in his dark eyes hits my heart in all the right places.

"Maybe." I smile. "Where are you going?"

The spark leaves his features just as fast to be replaced by his poker face.

"What is it?" Alarm grips me by the throat.

"I have to meet Jonathan."

I straighten. "Don't go."

"Worried about me, sweetheart?" He grins.

Yes, and I don't want Jonathan between us.

"Just don't go."

"I have to or he'll come here."

"Oh."

The resemblance of happiness from earlier withers away.

Obviously, Jonathan King holds a grudge against me—or my father. Aiden is his son. When it comes to choosing, he'll be on his father's side and I'll only get hurt.

Aiden strides to my side with purposeful, confident steps.

He places two fingers under my jaw and forces me to face him.

"I told you I'll protect you from everyone." He leans over and drops a peck on my cheek. "That includes Jonathan."

My breath hitches as he pulls away.

Did he just say what I think he said?

I think Aiden said he'll go against Jonathan for me. But that can't be true, right? Something must be wrong with my ears.

"Repeat that," I breathe.

"I'm not your enemy, sweetheart." He glides his thumb on my lower lip. "Don't make me into one."

"Don't make you into one?"

"As long as you don't put anyone before me, I won't put anyone before you."

Chaos invades my mind as I reel from the weight of his words.

He retrieves his phone. "Your uncle and aunt called me several times. I didn't pick up."

I wince, thinking about how I left the house. According to the clock, it's close to the afternoon.

They must be running a search party now.

"Can I use your —" I cut off when he hands me his phone without second thoughts.

I smile. He can be so attuned to my needs that it becomes scary sometimes.

He even has it on the chat tab with Uncle. I type.

Aiden: This is Elsa, Uncle. I'm fine. Please stop looking for me. I'll come back tomorrow.

With one last breath, I hit send.

Uncle and Aunt might have hidden the truth from me, but that doesn't erase how they raised me for the past ten years. They've been my anchors and my rocks.

I might not be ready to forgive Aunt just yet, but I won't completely cut them off from my life.

Uncle sends a text almost immediately.

Jaxon Quinn: We understand, pumpkin. Stay safe, okay?

My eyes fill with tears, but I exit the text, hitting the home screen. The wallpaper makes my mouth hang open.

Our first kiss in Ronan's party.

I stare at Aiden with bafflement. "Why do you have this as the wallpaper?"

"Because."

"I'll change it for you."

He snatches the phone from between my fingers and tucks it in his pocket with a scowl. It's as if I just offended him. "Absolutely not."

"Is it that important to you?"

"It was the day I decided you'll be mine till the day I die."

For a moment, just a second, I wonder what it would feel like to be with Aiden forever.

Forever.

That's a scary thought.

"When was the moment you decided I'm yours?" His question drags me out of my stupor.

"There was no such moment."

"Hmm. I think you're lying, sweetheart. I think your moment was when you attacked Silver in front of the doctor's office."

My face heats. "No, it wasn't."

"Your exact words were: *stay away from Aiden.* You were ready to murder her."

I purse my lips. Why does he have to remember everything?

He pulls my cheek. "You're so fucking adorable when you pout."

I push his hand away. "Aren't you supposed to go somewhere?"

He chuckles, the sound easy. "I won't be long. Knight, Astor, and Reed will come over shortly."

How does he know I don't want to be alone right now?

"How about Cole?"

"Not him."

"Why not?"

"Because." He runs his knuckles over my cheeks. "Be good."

"I'm always good."

He huffs. Aiden actually *huffs* before he turns towards the door.

"Aiden?" I call with a lump in my throat.

"Hmm, sweetheart?" He glances at me over his shoulder.

"Come back, okay?"

A genuine heart-stopping smile lifts his lips. "I'll always come back for you, sweetheart. You're a queen, not a pawn."

Then he's out of the door, leaving me to pick my heart up off the floor.

Did he just call me his queen?

I caress the place where my heart lies.

Easy there, heart. Don't go crazy just yet.

Too late.

I'm about ready to jump the bed and punch the stars.

I head to the bathroom with a huge smile plastered on my face.

After taking a shower, I find a denim dress and a sweater beside the shelves. On the clothes, there's a note in Aiden's neat handwriting.

They're Astrid's. She and Lev always leave shit around. I'm sure she wouldn't mind.

I laugh to myself as I put on the clothes. According to Aiden, no one would mind if the result plays in his favour.

Once I'm done dressing, I take the stairs to the kitchen and I'm surprised to find soup and two types of salad.

Another note from Aiden sits in between.

Eat so I can eat you later.

God. The shit Aiden says will be the death of me.

My stomach growls at the appetising scent of food. I sit down and eat the soup in record time then I pick on the salad until I'm full.

It's still raining outside. The water forms rivulets down the lounge area's windows.

Rain is beautiful.

Dad used to take me running in the rain.

Wait. How do I know that?

A knock sounds at the door, and I startle from my daydream.

I push the hazy memory away and stagger to my feet. As soon as I open the door, I'm attacked by a hug from Kim.

"Where were you today? I missed the hell out of you. I'm officially not going to college without you."

"Hey, Kim," I smile in her neck before pulling away.

"Brought chips." Ronan motions at his bag.

Xander shakes his head. "More like he stole them from Margo."

"*La ferme*, Knight. No chips for you." Ronan pushes him and Kim aside to clasp me in a bear hug. "How's my second favourite girl?"

"Second favourite?" I nudge him in the stomach.

"Sorry, Ellie. Kimmy came first in my heart."

Both Kim and I laugh as I wrap my arms around him, feeling about ready to cry again.

I didn't realise how much I needed their friendship until now.

I know the horsemen aren't the type to offer their support, so the fact that they showed up for me makes me grateful.

Ronan is known as a player, not a friend. A hug from him isn't to be taken for granted.

"King is here!" Xander shouts and Ronan jerks back from me.

Xander burst out laughing.

Ronan hits him upside the head and drags him to the lounge area with a laughing Kim following after them.

I laugh, too, closing the door. I stop when another one comes inside.

"Hey, Elsa," Cole gives me his welcoming smile.

"Oh, Cole." Didn't Aiden say he won't be coming?

"You seem surprised to see me."

"No. I'm glad you're here."

I really am. I always felt more comfortable around Cole. Even though Ronan and Xander crack me up, there's something about Cole's calm that soothes everyone in his vicinity.

It's not the threatening calm like Aiden's. It's a wise-pacifying type of calm.

We all walk to the lounge area. Ronan and Xander are fighting playfully—mostly—and Cole goes to break up the fight.

I search in the refrigerator for something to drink.

Kim joins me, propping her elbows on the counter opposite me. There's a spark in her eyes as she watches her surroundings.

"So this is the Meet Up. It's such a legend from how everyone at RES talks about it. I didn't expect it to be so... cosy."

"Yeah." I bring out bottles of juice and place them on the counter.

"What's going on, Ellie?" Kim rounds the counter and takes my hands in hers. "King said that you're not feeling well and we should visit. He scared the shit out of me. I thought something like the other time happened."

I bite my lower lip. "It's about my past."

She blinks twice. "Your past?"

"I'll tell you all about it. Just not now." I motion at the commotion in the lounge area. "Later, okay?"

She hugs me. "I love you and I'm always here for you whenever you're ready."

"Don't make me cry, Kim."

"We can cry together."

I wrap my arms around her and we stay like that for long seconds.

"Ooh, is there room for one more?" Ronan's voice cuts through the moment.

We break apart to find Xander and Ronan watching us.

Xander is glaring—at Kim, not me.

Ronan is grinning like an idiot. "By all means, don't stop on my account. Proceed, *Mesdemoiselles*."

That gets him a slap upside the head from Xander.

"Ow, what was that for, fucker?" He's about to attack Xander.

The latter ducks and heads to the refrigerator. He ignores the juice and snatches a beer.

"I knew Captain Levi keeps this place loaded."

"That would be King," Cole corrects, grabbing his own beer.

"So, Ellie," Ronan wraps an arm around my shoulder and leads me to the lounge area where everyone is headed. "Remember my suggestion about a threesome the other time?"

I laugh. "I do."

"I changed my mind about the participants and I came up with a brilliant plan. We'll put sleeping powder shit in King's water and get rid of him. Then, the threesome will be you, me, and Kimmy." He waggles his eyebrows. "Genius, right?"

"You know Aiden will wake up at some point, right?"

"It'll be worth it even if he kills me." He stops. "*Alors?*"

"I don't know."

"Pff. I guess it'll just be me and Kimmy then. Your loss, Ellie."

"In your dreams, fucker." Xander slams his shoulder into Ronan's on his way inside.

"If you want to drug Aiden, it'd be more effective if you put the powder in an alcoholic drink." When I raise my head, both Ronan and Xander watch me with curious expressions. "Just saying."

"Have you ever seen King drink?" Xander flops on the sofa right beside Kim who visibly stiffens.

Right. Aiden doesn't drink. "Why doesn't he drink?"

"He thinks it's beneath him," Cole says from beside me.

"Which is cool since he's an alien, anyway." Ronan barges between Xander and Kim and wraps an arm around her shoulder. "Isn't that right, Kimmy?"

She smiles, but it appears more from relief rather than agreement.

"How is he an alien?" I ask no one in particular, but I glance at Cole. For some reason, I want his read on Aiden.

"I thought you'd never ask!" Ronan jumps up on the coffee table. "For one, he was the last to lose his virginity amongst us. I was the first. Not to brag or anything. But he's the second oldest, come on."

"Who's the oldest?" Kim scoots away from Xander and closer to the edge.

"That'd be me," Cole says. "Then King, Knight, and Astor."

"Buuut." Ronan points a thumb at himself. "I lost my virginity first. Again, not bragging or anything, but they were all behind. I thought Aiden and Cole were gay until I saw their kinky shit."

"Shut it, Astor," Cole reprimands.

My interest peeks. "No, tell us. Why would you think they were gay?"

"First of all, they never had sex in front of us. Never tried to hook up with girls. They were sexually dead, I'm telling you. But their dicks looked good enough in the showers. Not as much as mine, but still."

"You spied on them?" I ask, incredulous.

"*Mais bien sûr.* I needed to look out for my mates. I even told King to fuck a guy or two and see how it goes. I was cool as long as he has sex."

I smile to myself. That must be why he sent him gay porn.

"Then I walked in on him in a threesome and changed my mind."

My eyes bulge. "A threesome."

"And not any threesome. It was a kinky as fuck threesome. The girl was tied, blindfolded and gagged."

Wow.

Aiden never mentioned that. Not that I asked.

That green monster rears his head, but I try to ask in my most innocent tone. "And who was she?"

"Dunno. The room was blue and dark. She had this grey hair shit. I only saw the part where King was tying her. Ask Captain, he was the third party of the threesome."

My attention snaps to Cole, not sure how to feel.

He stands beside me, his expression neutral.

Cole had a threesome with Aiden and another girl.

It eats at me not to know who she is.

"Shut up, Astor," Cole says with more resignation than anger.

"What? I'm still hurt I didn't participate."

"You were high," Xander points out.

"As if captain and King let anyone in their kinky shit." He thrusts a finger in Xander's direction. "You weren't high, why didn't you participate?"

"I wasn't interested."

"So you knew and didn't tell me? Why am I always left out?"

Xander throws a pillow at him. "You're left out because you're horrible with secrets."

"No, I'm not!" Ronan throws it back and they go on another round of bickering.

Kim sips her juice and watches them with a smile.

I'm about to join her when Cole leans in to whisper, "Can we talk?"

The request takes me by surprise, but I nod. "Sure."

He motions to a door to the right. I follow him to the back entrance. Xander and Ronan's chatter withers away as Cole slides the back door closed behind us.

The chilly air blows my hair back. I wrap my sweater around me as I step onto the wooden patio. Three chairs surround a built-in table. The rain beats in the distance, making the vision blurry.

Tall pine trees are the only things in sight. Hmm. So the back door leads to a forest.

Cole sits at one of the chairs. I drop opposite him, rubbing my arm.

"Sorry." Cole removes his jacket and offers it to me. "It's cold out here."

I accept his jacket with a smile and wrap it around my shoulders. It smells of cinnamon and expensive body wash.

It's warm.

Just like Cole.

Although, I must admit I never thought he'd be into the 'kinky shit' Ronan talked about.

The silent ones are indeed the wildest.

If it wouldn't make me appear pathetic, I'd ask him who's the mystery girl who attracted both his and Aiden's attention.

Wait. Maybe they were multiple mystery girls?

Did they make it a habit to have threesomes?

"What did you want to talk about?" I ask instead.

"I'll cut straight to the chase."

"Okay."

"Aiden, Xander, and I were kidnapped when we were children."

I gasp, my fingers strangle each other in my lap. "K-kidnapped?"

He retrieves a pack of cigarettes from his trousers and lights one. Nicotine fills the air as he blows a cloud of smoke.

I never saw Cole smoke.

This is a first.

"We were seven going on eight at the time." He takes a drag of his smoke. "We don't usually go home in the same car from our primary school, but that day, Xan and I caught a ride with Aiden. The driver was on their side. He took us to a deserted place where they ambushed us. There was a black van, three men wearing masks, and the rest is history."

"W-what do you mean the rest is history?"

He grips the cigarette with his thumb and forefinger as he meets my gaze. "We were taken to a storage house blindfolded. Then we were separated for what seemed like hours or days, I'm not sure. The next thing I know, I was thrown in a deserted place. I assumed my parents paid the ransom or something. Xander was also thrown in a similar deserted place."

"How about Aiden?"

He shakes his head slowly. "When we finally got home, we found out that Xander and I were taken for two days."

"And Aiden?"

"He disappeared for ten days."

"Why? Jonathan didn't pay the ransom?"

He couldn't have stood by when his only son was kidnapped. He couldn't be that heartless.

"That's the thing." Cole's eyes blacken to a frightening green. "The kidnappers didn't ask for ransom for any of us."

That's weird.

No. That's terrifying.

Why would they kidnap three rich kids if they didn't plan to ask for a ransom?

"D-did Aiden lose his way? Is that why he was missing for longer?"

Please tell me that's the case, please.

"I don't know." He takes another drag of his cigarette. "King doesn't talk about that time, not even between the three of us."

"How was he found?"

"Jonathan found him. I don't know how, but he did."

I watch Cole intently. "Why are you telling me this?"

"You deserve to know and King would've never told you."

"Why now? Why haven't you told me before?"

He smiles as he throws his cigarette to the ground and crushes it under his shoes. "Because King forced my hand and I dislike it when my hand is forced."

What is that supposed to mean? Is this some sort of feud between him and Aiden?

"It has nothing to do with you, Elsa. You're good." The chair scrapes against the wooden floor as he stands. "Maybe even too good for him."

I watch him for a few seconds, not sure what to say. I'm still helplessly trying to process what I just heard.

It aligns with what Levi hinted at. He said it wasn't just Alicia's death that changed Aiden, there was something else.

Like the kidnapping.

All the slash marks and scars make complete sense now.

"There's something else you need to know."

My head jerks upright at Cole's voice.

"Aiden has been hiding his —"

The door to the back entrance slides opens with a bang.

Xander stands there, watching us both with narrowed eyes. "What the fuck did you do, Nash?"

"Throwing his punch back."

"You better be ready when he fucks up your face," Xander snarls.

"King doesn't scare me, Knight." He pushes past him. "Nothing does anymore."

And then he strides inside.

Xander gives an awkward smile, and even then, the dimples make an appearance. "Is there a chance you'll forget what you just heard?"

I shake my head twice.

"Fucking Nash and his vindictive arse." He mumbles as if to himself. "I told King not to provoke that little bitch and his —"

"Hey, Xander."

"Yeah?"

"Can you give me a ride? I need to go somewhere."

THIRTY-SIX

Aiden

"Our meetings are becoming frequent." I drop my weight on the sofa in Jonathan's main office. "Twice in two days. That's almost a record."

He unbuttons his jacket and sits opposite me. A crystal chessboard rests on the coffee table between us as a witness to our upcoming war.

Jonathan's office is so big, the huge glass windows nearly show the entirety of London. His leather sofas and desk are pitch black.

I thought he'd have a triumphant look all over his face after the stunt he pulled at Elsa's house this morning, but he appears calculative.

Which means he's not done.

That head of his is concocting another plan, and this time, it'll be more brutal.

Jonathan in a nutshell; if he doesn't win, he destroys everything to get what he wants.

And he wants Elsa wiped out.

Or more like he wants her family's name erased from existence.

"You're keeping her with you." He grabs the white king piece and twirls it between his fingers.

"It's no surprise that you've been watching me." I lean my

elbows on my knees. "But have you also been watching Elsa all this time?"

He narrows one of his eyes. "She's being watched?"

Elsa always mentioned that she felt eyes on her. I confirmed it earlier when I found her about to faint. A black Mercedes followed us almost all the way to the Meet Up. They only disappeared when I changed lanes.

I was sure it was Jonathan's control freak side, but if it wasn't him, then who the fuck has been watching her?

"You did what you wanted. Now, back off."

He laughs, the sound is loud and humourless. "Who do you think you are to tell me to back off, Aiden? I'm the reason for your existence."

I knew he would say that.

I grab the black king between my fingers. "Then it'll be you against me, Jonathan."

A smirk tilts his lips. "I always win."

"Not this time, King."

I don't care if I come out of this battle dead, but I won't let Jonathan have Elsa.

Jonathan and I started on the same side. He was out to destroy everything that remained of the Steel name, which happens to be Elsa.

Jonathan wanted to weaken and break her emotionally so she becomes useless when she takes her position at the head of her father's company.

With a weak head, Jonathan can pressure her and take over Steel's empire.

Which is, in his mind, the greatest form of revenge.

Ethan took Alicia, and he'll take Elsa and the company.

I realised all of this too late.

Jonathan already set the game in motion ten years ago.

He never told me about her. He never stopped to tell me she's alive somewhere.

Instead, he kept her guardians close by offering them huge work opportunities with King Enterprises and used the chance to keep an eye on her.

Then, at the right moment, he made one of his employees recommend Royal Elite School to Elsa's Aunt, knowing exactly how much she wanted a great education for her niece.

That day I saw her again, I came home to find Jonathan smiling with triumph. He was happy that his battle had started.

He didn't ask for my permission when he brought her over. He didn't even prepare me.

But Jonathan is all about the surprise factor.

The opponent is easier to handle when he's taken off guard.

He likes to use that tactic a lot. In chess. In work. In life. Everywhere, basically.

Since the day Elsa walked into RES, Jonathan and I have been playing on the same side of the board.

Until I touched her.

Tasted her.

Became fucking lost in her.

The moment I decided that Elsa is mine and no one else's, she stopped being a pawn on Jonathan's board.

Yes, she was a pawn in mine. Yes, she didn't have a choice to be dropped on my side of the chessboard.

But what she wouldn't understand is that being my pawn is much fucking better than being Jonathan's.

I don't want to hurt her—not in that sense.

But Jonathan?

Jonathan would set her on fire and watch as she turned to ashes.

Elsa is lucky.

She's damn *lucky* that she got under my skin and became an inseparable part of my being.

If I didn't know better, I would even suspect that she had me hooked on her to save herself.

"You have one more chance to change your mind." Jonathan raises an eyebrow. "Seize it."

He doesn't offer second chances, so the fact that he's going out of his way says a lot.

Not that it matters anymore.

I already chose my side.

And it's not his.

I slam my king at the head of the board. "The game starts with two kings, Jonathan."

He hits my queen with his king. "But it ends with only one."

I stand up, but not before straightening my queen. He won't be bringing her down.

Not on my watch.

My phone dings with a text.

Knight: Nash ran his mouth about the kidnapping to Elsa. She asked me to take her to her shrink. I'm in the waiting room.

My grip tightens around the phone.

Fucking Nash.

I'm going to fuck him up.

I pull up Queens' number and type.

Aiden: Nash fucked Johansson from the track team.

The reply is immediate.

Queens: What the fuck?

Aiden: I thought you should know.

I smile on my way to the door. That will teach him to stop fucking around with me.

If he wants a war, then a war is what he'll get.

"She's Steel, Aiden. Destruction is in their blood," Jonathan calls after me.

I stop, but don't turn around. "And ours."

"Do you think she'll still love you after she remembers your monstrous past?"

My left eye twitches, but I wait for it to subside as I spin around to face him. "Alicia loved you even after knowing you're a monster."

His face falls as he drops his own queen. The sound of the chess piece hitting the board echoes in the silent office. "We both know how that ended up for her."

THIRTY-SEVEN

Elsa

Sweat covers my limbs and beads on my forehead.

My breathing comes out rugged and out of control.

The leather creaks underneath me.

It's too dark behind my closed eyes.

"Do you see the steps?" Dr Khan asks from across from me.

"It's those same dark stairs. There's an old wooden door in view. It looks like something you see in those World War Two films or something."

"Go on," he urges.

My shoulders snap upright, but I don't stop to focus on the fear.

Fear is temporary compared my thirst for the truth.

Now more than ever, I need to know what's in that basement.

I told Dr Khan that I'm not blocking myself anymore. That this time, I'll remember.

I'll remember Eli and my parents.

I'll remember *everything*.

My breathing slows as I take the steps down.

The light becomes dimmer with each step I take. The shadows darken, forming a black fog around me.

I can feel those monsters whispering on my skin and clawing at my back.

Return where you came from.

You don't belong here.

No. This is my home and exactly where I belong.

With a deep shaky breath, I keep going. All I focus on is the old basement door.

There's something important there.

Something like the truth.

Don't they say the truth sets you free?

"Slowing down and shutting down," Dr Khan's voice lowers in volume. "Slowing down and shutting down. Slowing down and shutting down... shutting down completely."

I stand in front of the door, only it's not me. I bring my hands up to my face and they're small, little hands. My feet and body are also small. The top of my head barely reaches the handle.

The seven year-old version of me.

The one who erased everything.

Keys dangle from my right hand and a small lamp from the other.

I stole them keys from Ma.

She put on red lipstick and went to bed, so she won't be coming here.

The keys jingle and my breathing trembles with it.

This is the first time I steal them keys from Ma. She'll be mad, but I'll give her a red rose so she stops being mad.

I glue my ear to the door.

It's here again. The whimpering.

Hmmm.

Hmmm...

Hmm...Hmm...

Pain slashes through my heart like them monsters are squeezing it.

Since the one who shall not be named went to heaven, I hear them voices like this in the basement.

Dad told me to never come back here again.

Uncle Reg told me it's for 'my sake'. Dunno what 'for my sake' means.

Last month, Ma found me lurking here and hit me on the back with her horsewhip.

I didn't tell Dad about it because he'll fight with Ma and I don't like it when they fight.

So I stopped coming here. I don't want Ma mad at me. I don't want Dad mad at Ma.

But today is different.

Before, them whimpers and moans only stayed for a day before they disappeared. These whimpers have been going on for three days.

Three whole days.

Them monsters must be doing something like they did to the one who shall not be named.

They're pulling someone else into the dark waters and not giving them back.

"Eli," I whisper and watch my surroundings.

Ma doesn't like me saying his name. She takes me to the lake when I do. Even after I stopped, she still takes me to the lake sometimes.

I hate that lake water and them monsters in the lake.

I miss Eli.

We used to play together but then he became the one who shall not be named.

When I'm alone at night, I murmur his name so I don't forget about him.

Dad said Eli went to heaven.

Sometimes I hate Eli. He said we'll always go to places together, but he didn't take me with him.

When I told Ma I wanted to go to heaven to Eli, she took me to the lake and made me swim.

I hate swimming.

I hate them monsters in Ma's eyes when she's all in white.

With one last glance behind me, I tiptoe and put the key into the hole then turn it.

The door squeaks and my heart stops beating.

Stop squeaking, little idiot.

I slip inside, gripping the lamp tighter.

The whimpering stops.

Everything stops.

I stay glued at the door and cover my nose with the back of my hand.

Smells like pee and throw up.

Eww. Who made a mess?

Using the lamp, I move it around the basement. I've never been in here before. All the walls are stone with no windows like a cave.

Something clinks in the far right corner.

Gasping, I direct the light in that direction.

I stop in my tracks. My hands tremble, causing the light to shake.

In the corner stands a boy as tall as Eli. He has dark hair like Eli, too. His shirt and trousers have dirty smudges. A cuff surrounds his ankle, attached to a chain that's dangling from the wall.

Silver duct tape covers his mouth so tightly, it appears painful.

He squints at the light from the lamp, then slowly, too slowly, opens his eyes.

Dark eyes.

Metal eyes.

They look like Eli's eyes.

With slow movements, I approach him. "Are you Eli?"

He doesn't say anything.

I stop a small distance away, watching him closely.

He's not Eli, but he looks so beautiful. I want to become friends with him.

His face is smudged with dirt. I reach into my dress's pocket and retrieve a napkin. It's a present from Daddy that I always keep on me, but it's okay.

I can wash it later.

I approach the boy. My heart squeezes at the red marks surrounding his ankle from the cuff.

He flinches back when I'm within arm's reach.

I wipe the side of his eyes where there's a beautiful mole.

He remains still, watching me intently as if he's about to snap any second.

"I'm Elsa. What's your name?" I frown "Wait. You have tape."

Slowly, I remove the duct tape from around his mouth.

He winces then licks his dry lips. His eyes meet mine for a second as I wipe the side of his face with the handkerchief.

He grabs my hand harshly. I gasp and the handkerchief falls to the dirty ground.

Eli's look-alike whispers in a scratchy, haunted voice, "Help me."

THIRTY-EIGHT

Aiden

When Knight sent me a text saying that he drove Elsa back to the Meet Up, I thought he was fucking with me. He's not as vindictive as Nash, but he's still holding a grudge about how I hugged Reed—and every time I used her against Elsa.

It's around five when I step into the house. It's pitch black. Everyone else left.

The rain is the only sound that can be heard inside the house.

I head upstairs with slow steps. I don't know why Elsa went to her shrink right after that fucker Nash told her something she didn't need to know yet, but my instincts tell me it's not good.

As soon as I walk into the dark room, I hear the sound of running water coming from the bathroom.

With quiet steps, I stalk to the door and push it open.

A shadow stands in front of the sink.

I hit the switch. White light bathes the bathroom.

Elsa doesn't squint or move. It's like she wasn't even aware that she was standing in a pitch-black bathroom.

She's scrubbing her hands under the water over and over again. Her expression is serene, peaceful almost.

It's so similar to *her* expression.

I hate that expression on Elsa's face. My Elsa isn't a washed-up version of someone else.

Elsa is Elsa with her infuriating stubbornness and breakable innocence.

She's *not* that woman.

Her hands have become red, which means she must've been at it for a while now.

"Elsa," I call her name.

She doesn't pay me attention as if I don't exist. She continues scrubbing and scrubbing and *scrubbing.*

At this rate, her hands will bleed.

I step to her side and clutch her arm.

She pushes me away and shoves her hands under the tap again. "They're dirty. I need to clean them."

"They're not dirty, Elsa." I try to pull her away again, but she squirms free.

I let her. Any type of force will have the exact opposite effect on her.

"I saw you," she whispers.

"You saw me," I repeat, unsure where she's going with this.

"You were chained in the basement. That's the reason for the scar on your ankle." Her lower lip trembles and her scrubbing turns more aggressive. "Was it Ma or Dad?"

My left eye twitches.

She remembers.

She *finally* fucking remembers.

"No. Don't tell me that," she blurts. "I think I know. When Jonathan burnt Ethan's factory down, Dad must've kidnapped you as a fuck you to Jonathan. Cole and Xander were taken by mistake, that's why they were returned almost immediately and the kidnappers never asked for ransom. Ethan didn't need the money. He only wanted to hit Jonathan where it hurts the most."

I remain silent. If she remembers, everything else will start making sense.

She's smart to connect all the dots.

"But it wasn't Dad who kept you, was it?" *Scrub. Scrub. Scrub.* "It was Ma. The worst part is, I don't think you were the first boy that she kept in the basement since Eli's death. But usually, they're gone after a day. You're the only one she kept that long." A tear slides down her cheek and clings to the teardrop in her upper lip. "You're the only one she hurt that much."

My face remains the same. I knew this time would come. I knew Elsa would remember, but hearing her choked tone and watching her trying so hard not to break hurts more than I thought it would.

I want to hold her.

Protect her.

But I doubt she'd let me.

"I'm a carbon copy of her." She finally stops scrubbing, but her hands remain under the water.

Her eyes meet mine.

Those electric blue, *blue* eyes.

They're rimmed with tears and red like she's been crying since I left her ten years ago.

"How can you look at my face?" Her voice is barely a whisper.

"I told you," I murmur. "You were a ghost."

"You saw my mother in me that first day at RES, didn't you?" Her voice cracks as if she doesn't want to say the words.

I did. And sometimes, I see her when she's slipping out of her element.

But not once have I mistook her for anyone else.

This is Elsa.

My Elsa.

I'll fight the fucking ghosts away from her if I have to.

"W-what did Ma do, Aiden?" Her hands and legs shake. She's all shaking as if she's coming down from an adrenaline rush.

"Don't."

"Don't what?"

"Don't ask questions. Not now." I pull her wet hands from under the water and cradle them in mine. "I want to feel you, Elsa. I want to engrave myself under your skin as deep as you engraved yourself under mine."

"How?" She sobs, gasping on the words. "H-how can you want me when I hate myself right now?"

"You can hate yourself, and I'll still want you, sweetheart." I tug her into me and grip her by the hips. "I told you I'll protect you, remember?"

She stares up at me with broken blue eyes.

That look makes me want to rip my heart out and lay it at her feet.

It's the same look she gave me when she first saw me in her parents' basement.

And the look she gave me when I last saw her in that fucking house.

It's her. Not her mother.

Elsa has always been different from the monsters who ruled her life.

She can be them sometimes, but deep down, she didn't change.

She didn't become like me.

Using her hips, I push her until her back hits the wall. "I want you. I need you. You're the only one I'll ever need."

"Aiden…" Her wet, reddened hand gets lost in my hair. "I-I'm sorry. I'm so sorry."

"So am I sweetheart." Because I put her in the middle of a war against Jonathan that we both might lose.

If I end up falling with her, then so fucking be it.

I already decided that Elsa is mine and no one fucks with what's mine.

"Make me forget," she whispers, eyes still shining with tears and legs trembling.

I don't even need an invitation. I yank her dress up and my jeans down. She wraps her legs around me as I thrust inside her.

Fuuuuck.

I can't and will never get enough of the feeling of being inside her.

It's a drug dose.

It's a sense of belonging.

It's finding a piece of yourself after years of separation.

Elsa is damnation, but she's also the only fucking thing that makes sense.

The little shaky moans she makes as I thrust into her burst straight to my heart. She's biting her lower lip like she doesn't want to let any sound escape.

"Let go," I grunt near her ear. "You never have to hold back with me."

"This is so fucked up. This is so wrong." She grips me tighter with every word.

Even if it's fucked up and wrong, she still wants me with every fibre in her.

My pace picks up and I hit her sweet spot over and over again.

She cries out, holding on to me for dear life. "Oh, my God, Aiden!"

Her God.

I always loved the sound of that. Being her God is the best gift I could ever receive.

I keep pounding into her until she can no longer breathe, let alone protest. She unravels all around me and I follow soon after.

She falls limp around me, her head hiding in my neck, breathing heavy. I like how she trusts me enough to fall asleep like this all around me.

She doesn't see me as a threat anymore.

Just like I don't.

With her still wrapped all around me, I carry her to the bedroom and lay her on the bed. When I straighten up to remove my jacket, she clutches me by the hem of my shirt.

I'm gutted.

I'm fucking gutted by the pleading in her eyes.

I throw the jacket away and slide beside her. She lays her head on my shoulder and wraps both her legs and arms around me.

My Elsa.

She's mine.

Fucking mine.

And no one will change that.

Not even her.

Her breaths even out, and I think she fell asleep, but then she murmurs, "I love you, Aiden. I think I always have."

THIRTY-NINE

Elsa

"**D**-addy?"

My little feet skid to a halt.

Blood.

A pool of blood and Daddy lies in it.

My ears ring as I approach him. "D-Daddy! You p-promised you won't leave me like Eli."

"I need you to do something for me, princess."

"Anything, Daddy."

"Run. The fastest you can."

"No," I sob. "I won't leave you."

"Run!"

"Daddy!"

"RUN!"

A bang comes from behind me and harsh hands pull me by my hair.

He's not moving.

Daddy isn't moving.

Open your eyes. Tell me you love me. Don't go to Eli. I need you more.

"Daddy!"

My eyes shoot open, chest heaving. I'm lying on my side, sweat beading on my brows.

Dad.

Oh, God. Dad.

Didn't he die from the fire? How come he was surrounded by blood?

Or was that just my imagination?

No. The grief gripping me by the throat can't be imaginary.

Tears threaten to spill free, but I hold them back when I recognise the weight spooning me from behind.

Aiden's leg is wrapped around mine and his arm is securely tightened around my stomach.

His free hand draws patterns over my back.

The same patterns he's always been drawing whenever we're in the bath or after sex.

I stare at the light coming from the window.

Shafts of the sun peek through.

Sun after the rain.

Beauty after the storm.

The more Aiden touches me, the harder I fall into his warmth.

His unspoken emotions.

His unconditional acceptance.

I don't turn around for fear that the spell may be broken. I don't turn around because I can't face him after yesterday.

For the rest of my life, I don't think I'll ever be able to fully face him.

Aiden, my bully and my tormentor, is a victim of my parents.

He was just a boy back then. A little boy with tousled black hair and innocent grey eyes.

That innocence was tortured in that basement and killed when he returned to find his mother dead.

There was something abnormal about that basement. Something that makes my skin crawl.

He lost a part of himself in there. Hell, I feel like I lost a part of myself in there, too.

I just don't remember it.

Aiden isn't like me. He didn't erase his memories. He remembers everything.

Every. Fucking. Thing.

A shudder goes through me at the thought of what could've happened to him.

Since I left Dr Khan's office, my heart has been hollow. I've been on the verge of a breakdown.

I wanted to go to Birmingham and stand on my parents' grave and shout at them.

I wanted to kick their dead bodies and tell them to give me back my life.

But that would be useless. No one will give me back what was already stolen.

Just like nothing will bring back what Aiden has already lost.

My heart aches the more he touches me, but I don't want him to stop. I never want him to stop even if I'm in pain.

Even if I bleed open.

It took me ten years to remember and I don't even remember everything.

He's been living with this pain for a decade.

He's been seeing my face for two years and recalling what Ma did to him.

No wonder he looked at me like he hated me. No wonder he wanted to destroy me.

What Jonathan said makes sense now. My parents did kill Alicia, although indirectly.

She was on her way to search for Aiden after he was kidnapped, but she had an accident and never saw him again.

Aiden lost his mother.

And it's all because of Ma and Dad.

My breathing deepens and it takes everything in me not to break down in tears.

How could I tell him I loved him yesterday? How could I say that to someone who suffered every time he saw my face?

What the hell is wrong with me?

I focus on the little drawings on my back. It's like he's repeating the same pattern over and over again.

Wait. Is that...?

Steel.

He's writing and re-writing my last name on my back. Is that what he's been writing all this time?

Tears rush to my eyes and I close them, biting my lower lip.

He releases me and I remain in place, slightly hiding my head in the sheets.

Aiden's heat leaves my back. The mattress moves as he stands.

"Come on, sweetheart. Wake up," his voice is wide awake as if he didn't sleep the entire night—and maybe he didn't.

I slowly peel my head from the sheets and turn to face him.

He's smiling down at me with a warm spark. "Happy birthday, sweetheart."

I swallow the lump in my throat. A thousand words and apologies fight to be set free, but I have nothing to say.

How could he wish me a happy birthday after everything?

Hell. Even I forgot that it's my birthday.

"Meet me downstairs."

He doesn't wait before he walks out of the door.

I watch him with a crushing ache in my chest.

It's too much.

This pain. This burn.

I place a hand over my scar and dig my nails into the flesh.

It hurts, dammit.

Why did it have to be like this?

After freshening up, I take the steps downstairs slowly as if I'm afraid something will jump me.

I find Aiden putting on his jacket. Upon seeing me, he yanks another Elites Jacket from the sofa and drapes it over my shoulders. The thing swallows me whole, but it smells like him. Clean and warm.

He pulls my band and ruffles my hair, letting it fall loose on either side of my shoulders.

"Hmm. My number looks good on you, sweetheart." He tilts his head to the side. "But you know what will be better? If you wore it to watch one of my games."

I stare at him, not knowing what to say. Is he pretending that everything is okay?

No idea how he does that. It must be because of his freedom and assertiveness.

For today, just today, I also want to be free, too. I want to pretend that everything is okay and I'm with Aiden despite the darkness from the past.

It's my birthday after all.

I grin up at him. "I'm still not persuaded."

"I'll come up with something." He interlaces his hand in mine. "Come on."

He picks up a large food container and then we're out of the house through the back door.

His hand is still wrapped around mine as we walk through the trees surrounding the house. It's a forest, basically.

The entire way, I watch my smaller hand in his bigger one and I can't help thinking how safe it feels to be with him.

Like in that basement.

Although it was dark and smelled awful, our breathing calmed down the moment we touched each other.

His face appears normal as if yesterday didn't happen.

We come to a stop in front of a lake with a deck and a few old boats in sight.

My gaze bounces between him and the lake as if he brought me here to drown me.

Wait. Is that why he brought me here?

"W-what are we doing here?"

"Eating." He tugs me down to sit at the foot of the tree and opens the food container.

I remain rooted in place, shivering. "I don't like it here."

He continues pulling toast and juice and loads of food that I have no idea when he had the time to put together.

"Let's go back," I plead, avoiding direct contact with the lake.

He motions at the food. "The faster you eat, the faster we go home and I'll give you your birthday present."

I finally rip my gaze from the lake to focus on him. "Why are you doing this?"

"This?" He passes me a toast with jam. "I only made you breakfast."

I take the toast from him and sit carefully on the ground as if expecting it to shift and I'll find myself inside the lake.

Aiden watches me as I take tentative bites from the toast. It's hard to eat when there's a demon in the form of a lake right in front of me.

Eli died in a place like this.

I lost my brother to the monster of the lake.

The need to throw up assaults me.

"Alicia used to read to me here," Aiden chews on his eggs slowly.

"She did?" I ask.

"She liked it here. It was away from people and interruptions. We spent most of our time in this place."

"Did Jonathan join you?"

"Sometimes. He doesn't like being cut off from his business world."

I swallow the bite of toast and study him closely. "What else did you do with Alicia here?"

"We had picnics and mostly read." He grins. "Then we'd go for a swim."

The toast nearly falls from between my hands when he abandons his eggs and stands to his full height.

In a few seconds, he strips, remaining in black boxer briefs.

My eyes widen, and it's not only because of his sculpted physique.

Tendrils of fear grip me by the gut as he takes a step back in the direction of the deck.

Even the sky darkens. Gone is the sun from this morning. Huge clouds fill the distance.

"W-what are you doing?" I gawk at him.

"Going for a swim."

"But it's freezing!"

He grins in that lopsided way. "Fun, huh?"

"Aiden, don't." My voice shakes at the end.

"Do you want to join?" He winks.

"No way in hell."

"Come on, you know you want to."

I shake my head violently.

"As you wish." He lifts a shoulder and before I can say anything, he turns around and takes a dive into the lake.

The toast drops from between my trembling fingers.

My muscles lock together every time he disappears under the water. I stop breathing and only take gulps of air when he resurfaces.

"Join me!" He grins, all wet and exotic and... alive.

He's alive right now.

But what if the monsters of the lake come after him as they went after Eli? What if —

I shut that voice. "Come out, Aiden."

He takes one dive after the other, swimming on his side and on his back.

The more he remains in the water, the harder I shake. Sweat covers my brows and beads on my forehead.

"Come out!" I call, the sound echoing all around us.

He's not Eli. *Not Eli.*

He can't drown when he's such a good swimmer.

"After one more!" he calls back then takes a dive.

Ten seconds pass.

Twenty.

Thirty.

Oh. God.

He's not resurfacing.

I jump on unsteady feet, the jacket falling to the ground.

"A-Aiden?" I slowly approach the edge of the deck, my heart thundering against my ribcage.

"This isn't funny, Aiden!"

No answer.

Oh, God. No.

Oh, please. Not Aiden, too.

Please. Please.

"Aiden!" I shriek. "Stop playing around!"

He's not coming out. He's drowning. Like Eli.

Just like Eli.

No.

I kick off my shoes. My movements are frantic at best, but I don't stop.

I won't let him die.

Not Aiden, too.

I don't care if I die in my quest to find him. Lake water and my phobias be damned.

A hand grips my ankle.

I shriek.

Aiden's wet face resurfaces as he uses the deck to jump beside me.

I watch him closely, my eyes filling with tears. "Y-You're here."

He comes closer, his chest glistening with water and his hair sticks to the side of his face. "What's wrong —"

I wrap my arms around his waist and hide my face in his chest. "I lost my brother that way! Eli drowned that way!"

"I didn't know that. I didn't mean to scare you."

A sob tears from my throat. "Don't ever do that again! I thought you were dying. What am I supposed to do if you die?"

His wet fingers stroke my hair and he tugs me closer to him. "That means you'll be free of me and I don't like that idea."

I snort in his chest, breathing him in. "You're incurable."

"For you?" He kisses the top of my head. "Always, sweetheart."

I pull back to look at him.

He's watching me with a strange gleam. It's like affection mixed with obsession.

I knew Aiden has been obsessed with me for a while, but now I realise just how much I'm obsessed with him, too.

There's no way in hell I'll let him be free of me. Since the moment I saw him in the basement, I always had this feeling that he's mine.

Only mine.

I reach a hand to stroke his hair back. "Are you going to hurt me, Aiden?"

"Maybe."

"Maybe?" I choke.

Aiden takes my palm in his and flattens it against his heart. "I already made my choice, Elsa. I chose you. Now, it's your turn." He lifts my hand to his face and kisses my knuckles. "Be with me, not against me. Choose me."

Oh, shit.

I think I'm going to faint.

"You *chose* me?"

He nods once.

"I meant it last night." I take a deep breath, the words burning in my throat. "I love you."

He places a finger in front of my mouth. "Don't."

My brows draw together in questioning as I remove his finger. "Don't what?"

"Don't say things you don't mean."

"I know my feelings well, thank you very much," I snap.

The dickhead manages to piss me off even when I'm confessing my feelings to him.

"Maybe you don't."

"I didn't ask you to say it in return, but you don't get to tell me how I feel, arsehole."

I shove my feet in the shoes, pick up my—his—jacket, and storm in the direction of the house.

I'm so fuming that it takes me some time to find my way through the trees.

Okay. Maybe I'm lost. So what?

Aiden catches up to me, his trousers are barely done and his hair is a wet mess. The jacket is open and his shirt is barely buttoned.

He points in the opposite direction. "The house is that way."

"I know that," I snap.

He smirks in that infuriating way. "Sure thing, sweetheart."

I start to push past him, but he grips me by the hips, his fingers teasing.

"Let me go. I'm pissed off at you right now."

He nuzzles his nose in my cheek. "I told you, we can be mad at each other while I touch you."

I melt in the way he drags his nose down my throat. My body ignites to life.

"Why do you not want me to love you?" I whisper.

"Loving me is a one-way road, sweetheart. You can never go back. You can never fall out of love or any of that shit. It's permanent and it's for life."

For some reason, those words don't scare me as they should. It's almost as if I want all that with him.

"Promise you won't go back on your word," he wraps his hand around my neck, stroking my pulse point.

"I promise."

He presses his lips to mine.

His kiss tastes of sweet, bitter surrender, of pain, and of desperation.

I want all of that. As long as he offers it, I'll take it.

Loving Aiden didn't start now. It started at that moment I found him in the basement.

It was put on pause for eight years and resumed when I first saw him at RES. He gripped me from first sight.

Although I hated him during the past two years, I was always aware of him. Of his dark gaze.

Of his silent madness.

It was only at the beginning of this year that the awareness morphed into something more.

The first droplets of rain hit my nose.

I step back, giggling. "Let's go back."

"I'm good right here." He starts to kiss me again.

I stop him with a hand to his chest. "I'll let you do anything you want inside."

He raises an eyebrow. "Anything?"

I nod.

"You shouldn't give me the *anything* option. Now, you're well and truly fucked, sweetheart."

Maybe that's exactly why I told him he can do anything.

A burst of excitement shoots through me at the thought of what he'll do.

I take his hand in mine and we run to the house. We go through the back entrance, laughing.

In fact, I'm the only one laughing. Aiden watches me with that intensity.

That intensity used to suffocate me, but it warms my heart and makes me all fuzzy inside now.

Aiden lunges at me when a rustle comes from the lounge area.

Both our attentions turn towards the sound.

Aiden and I freeze at the sight of the two people sitting on the sofa.

Jonathan and Silver.

Jonathan smiles at us, but it's downright cruel.

"Nice of you to join us. Sit down. We have news to share."

FORTY

Elsa

Jonathan and Silver are here.

I stand rooted in place, trying to wrap my head around that piece of information.

Jonathan takes the chair at the top of the room like a king in his court.

Silver sits diagonally from him, looking as if she's about to throw up. Her skin is pale as she clutches her phone with stiff fingers.

The urge to turn around and get out of this place overwhelms me.

It flows in my blood and creates an itch under my skin.

I don't give in to it.

My fear won't consume me.

To say Jonathan is intimidating would be the understatement of the century. He's not only intimidating, but he's also able to crush me with one word.

He's able to turn my life into a living hell.

I choose you.

Aiden's words explode in my chest like fireworks.

Aiden chose me. Jonathan wouldn't scare me anymore.

The other time, I shrunk behind Aiden, but today, I stand right beside him and stare at Jonathan and Silver head-on.

They don't scare me.

I might not have figured out all of my past but I will. I choose to do it with Aiden by my side.

It's not only my past.

It's *our* past.

As if in tune with my thoughts, Aiden grabs my hand and interlaces our fingers together.

I smile up at him and he gives me a small nod.

Together.

We're in this together.

"I thought Levi told you that you're not welcome in this place," Aiden deadpans at his father before he directs his attention to Silver. "You, too, Queens. Leave."

"Slow down, now." Jonathan appears calm. Too calm. It's the type of calmness Aiden shows before striking.

Maybe he learnt that tactic from his father.

He's like a predator stalking his prey; he'll stop at nothing before eating it alive.

"Let go of that hand," Jonathan tells his son.

Aiden tightens his hold in response.

Something in my chest is set free.

When I first saw Aiden in RES, there was a prisoner who tried to claw his way out.

That prisoner is now free.

Unlike that time, Aiden isn't out to destroy me.

No.

He's protecting me as he promised.

Who knew there would be a day where Aiden King would be my knight in shining armour?

Jonathan's attention slides back to me. "How about you, *Steel?*"

I don't miss the way he nearly snarls my name.

I jut my chin. "Steel or not, I wasn't born to take orders from you."

"Interesting." Jonathan's dark gaze shifts from me to Aiden and back again as if he's trying to read between the lines. Or he's search-ing for weakness like Aiden usually does.

The entire time, Silver remains slumped in her seat without even lifting her gaze. It's like she was forced to come here.

"Do you know that your parents kidnapped my son and tor-tured him for ten days?"

His casual words are like stabbing a knife straight through my heart.

"She knows," Aiden remains calm, not showing any emotion whatsoever.

"I assume she also knows that you lost your mother because she was trying to find you." Jonathan leans forward. "What type of monster are you to still hold on to my son after all that?"

My breathing turns shallow, and a part of me believes him.

That part also thinks that Aiden must only see Ma when he looks at me.

His torturer.

His hell.

His monster.

I internally shake myself.

Jonathan can try his best, but I won't fall for his games.

Aiden and I didn't start like some fairy tale, but our dark past isn't everything we are either.

No one has the right to get between us—Jonathan included.

"The past won't define us," I tell him. "We have the future ahead of us."

"Are you certain about that?" Jonathan tilts his head to the side, meeting Aiden's gaze. "Does she know why you're alive?"

"Jonathan," Aiden says with clear menace.

"Yes, that's the right look, son" Jonathan smiles. "Unfortunately, you have no chances left with me. I offered you one and you refused it. Now, it's my turn to play."

"What is he talking about?" I frown at Aiden.

"You said you have your future ahead of you, but here's the

thing, Steel, you have no future with Aiden." He stands and offers his hand to Silver who takes it reluctantly. "Because he's already engaged to Silver."

My blood pumps harder in my veins as my gaze bounces between Silver, Jonathan, then back to Aiden.

His jaw tightens, but he says nothing.

"Is that true?" I whisper.

This must be a joke.

Jonathan and Silver planned this to make me feel insignificant.

Aiden will throw the joke right in their faces.

He'll tell me it's all a ploy and that he only belongs to me.

He's mine.

I stare at him for long seconds, but he's not saying anything.

Why isn't he saying anything?

"It's a lie, right?" My voice is barely audible.

"You're the only lie in this game, Steel." Jonathan smiles. "Silver has always been the queen to the King's name."

No.

He must be joking.

He has to.

Why isn't Aiden saying anything? He doesn't lie so if he denies it, that should mean they're liars.

Unless… he's not denying it because it's the truth.

The bell rings. Silver pulls her hand from Jonathan's, "I'll get it. It must be Cole."

And then she's running towards the door.

I continue watching Aiden who still hasn't broken eye contact with his father.

"Aiden…?"

"Tell her, son." Jonathan taunts. "She deserves to know that she's been a game all along."

"What are you doing here?" Silver's voice comes from the front door.

Knox walks inside accompanied by a middle-aged tall man.

The smile drops from Jonathan's face.

"Knox, what are you…?" I trail off when I focus on the man's face.

He's dressed in a black suit that clings to his body just like in my memories.

The high cheekbones. The square jawline. The dark brown eyes. The chestnut hair.

It's him.

This isn't a dream or a nightmare.

It's really *him*.

His deep, familiar voice drifts all around me like a lullaby from my childhood. "Happy birthday, princess. It's time for us to go home."

"D-Dad?"

TO BE CONTINUED …

The story concludes in the final part, *Twisted Kingdom*.

WHAT'S NEXT?

Thank you so much for reading *Steel Princess*! If you liked it, please
leave a review.
Your support means the world to me.

If you're thirsty for more discussions with other readers
of the series, you can join the Facebook group, *Rina Kent's
Spoilers Room*.

Next up is the final part of Aiden and Elsa's story, *Twisted
Kingdom*.

The kingdom isn't supposed to fall.

The truth screws you over before it sets you free.
Masks drop.
Secrets unravel.
Elsa's race after the past blinds her from the present.
I'll fight for her.
I'll bring her back.
I'll protect her even if it's the last thing I do.
We made a promise.
She's mine.
Are you ready for one final game, sweetheart?

ALSO BY RINA KENT

For more books by the author and a reading order, please visit:
www.rinakent.com/books

ABOUT THE AUTHOR

Rina Kent is a *USA Today*, international, and #1 Amazon bestselling author of everything enemies to lovers romance.

She's known to write unapologetic anti-heroes and villains because she often fell in love with men no one roots for. Her books are sprinkled with a touch of darkness, a pinch of angst, and an unhealthy dose of intensity.

She spends her private days in London laughing like an evil mastermind about adding mayhem to her expanding universe. When she's not writing, Rina travels, hikes, and spoils cats in a pure Cat Lady fashion.

Find Rina Below:

Website: www.rinakent.com

Newsletter: www.subscribepage.com/rinakent

BookBub: www.bookbub.com/profile/rina-kent

Amazon: www.amazon.com/Rina-Kent/e/B07MM54G22

Goodreads: www.goodreads.com/author/show/18697906.Rina_

Kent

Instagram: www.instagram.com/author_rina

Facebook: www.facebook.com/rinaakent

Reader Group: www.facebook.com/groups/rinakent.club

Pinterest: www.pinterest.co.uk/AuthorRina/boards

Tiktok: www.tiktok.com/@rina.kent

Twitter: twitter.com/AuthorRina

Printed in the USA
CPSIA information can be obtained
at www.ICGtesting.com
LVHW050416220224
772513LV00002B/21